STARDUSTED

A Frankie Franklin Mystery

Deb McCaskey

This is a work of fiction. Frankie Franklin and her friends,
family, studio, colleagues, movie and song titles and content,
are all products of the author's imagination. The roles played by
historical or celebrated persons are entirely fictional, although
these imagined versions of them do agree with the generally
known facts of their lives.

ISBN: 978-1-7332589-0-6 (e-book)
ISBN: 978-1-7332589-1-3 (paperback)

Cover design by Deb McCaskey

For Rosemary

Contents

Chapter One

The first thing you should know is: I did it.

I was up to my neck in bubbles at the time, just a cowgirl relaxing at the end of a long, dusty, and profitable cattle drive, soaking my cares away in a zinc bathtub set in the middle of my hotel room, and enthusiastically singing "Sweet Betsy from Pike."

But my idyll would be short. As I got to the part where the dog wagged its tail and looked wondrously sad, there was the ominous clump of heavy boots in the hallway outside my room, and a sharp knock on the door.

As it happened, I already knew danger was coming, and when I looked up, my face showed no fear. I was ready.

So when the two men—I had known there would be two—kicked my door open and burst into the room, guns drawn, they found that I had my own six-shooter in hand, and them in my sights. I squeezed the trigger.

There was a deafening *crack!*

And the wrong man fell down.

Irritated at first, I swore. But then shock, even horror, took over as I realized what had really happened and I leaped out of the tub, and ran for the fallen man. The gun, forgotten for the moment, splashed into the water and made a dull clank on the bottom of the tub.

"Cut! Cut, for Chrissakes!"

Director Arthur Janeway had exploded from his chair like a pheasant flushed from cover. I ignored him as I hotfooted it across the hotel room set on Fortune Motion Pictures' Soundstage Three.

There were maybe forty or so other people not far away, now

making noise and stirring in confusion, but most were back in the deep shadows on the other side of the bright lights and the cameras, and I wasn't thinking of them, anyway.

All I knew then was that a promising young actor named Sam Harvey was sprawled on the floor, gasping and holding his side as a dark, wet stain bloomed under his hand, soaking his shirtfront—because someone had put a real bullet in my Colt, where there should have only been blanks. Someone either evil or careless, who was not me.

As I knelt beside Sam, he reached his hand out and grabbed mine, squeezing it hard. A quick glance at me, and then he shut his eyes tight, his breathing coming quick and ragged. Pain contorted his long, sensitive face.

As I crouched there in my flesh-colored bathing suit, Sam's bloody hand in mine, the horror remained, now joined by surprisingly fierce anger. Dammit, this was just a picture, with costumes and made-up things to say. With blood that was just glycerin and chocolate syrup. No one was supposed to really be shot. No one was supposed to be bleeding real blood. I felt ill. I wanted Sam to be unshot. And I wanted to strangle whoever was responsible.

My dresser, Alice, had thrown a robe over me, and now I bunched up a corner of it and pressed it against Sam's side where I thought the wound was. No one had come forward from the crowd to shove me aside and show off their first-aid skills; this gave me the impression that no one else knew anything better to do.

Sam opened his eyes again and fixed his gaze on me like I was his lifeline.

"Miss Franklin ... I'm ... so sorry!" he rasped. He was worried he'd spoiled the shot, and it made me want to cry. His chest rose and fell in ragged breaths. "It's ... hot. Hurts."

He closed his eyes again, and I saw him concentrating on breathing. In and out, in and out. Painfully. God, where was the nurse?

"Help's coming, Sam," I said, hoping that was true. It had to be. Everyone has a job on a movie set. It must have been

2

somebody's to call, or run, for help.

"No, I'm sorry, Sam. I'm sorry," I said. "Just hang on. You'll be all right."

He squeezed my hand again. The blood was getting sticky and smelled metallic. I fought down nausea, and more anger. What diabolical or monumentally thoughtless person could have made me shoot Sam, a good kid who had just gotten his first chance in the pictures?

About a hundred years later the studio nurse appeared and replaced me at Sam's side. She got to work, tearing his shirt open, inspecting the wound, pulling gauze and real bandages out of her bag. Her moves were practiced, professional, and comforting.

I backed away from Sam and let Arthur put an arm around me, which he did gingerly, because of the blood on me and my robe, and also because I probably had steam coming out of my ears. I was still worried for Sam, but now that the nurse was here, I could turn my attentions to the property department, which had given me a gun that had live rounds in it. I was angry and knew I looked it.

An ambulance showed up outside the big soundstage door and the attendants put Sam on a stretcher and carried him out as the crew watched, silent and shocked. Sam lifted a hand to wave weakly at them. He was a trouper.

Around us, crew members were busy turning off the huge lights, and moving them and the cameras, microphones and booms, the miles of snaking cables, the spindly tripods and stands, the wooden boxes, a giant fan, and all the other stuff needed to shoot a picture, having urgent-looking discussions as they tried to salvage the shooting schedule for Fortune's production of *Prairie Princess,* starring Frankie Franklin.

That would be the same Frankie Franklin, right there in her bloodstained robe, whom they were now looking at out of the sides of their eyes. I guess they were wondering whether I was victim or villain. I was looking, too. I was looking for someone to punch.

John, the assistant director, hovered nearby, not wanting to

3

interrupt Arthur while he was busy comforting me or keeping me from committing mayhem on the first prop man I saw; he probably couldn't tell which. Everyone who ever has worked with me knows that I don't show anger by screaming and waving my arms—unless it's called for in the script. Instead, I get deadly silent. Sometimes that scares people.

"I'm okay," I said to Arthur, grimly. "Talk to John."

I didn't need comforting, I told myself. I only needed to know Sam was going to be all right, and then I needed to know whose head would roll.

Looking about and frustrated at finding no one to berate, I finally remembered that there had been another actor in the scene, my costar, who must be at least as upset as I was, and that I should see how he was doing.

I found him near where the camera had been, sitting in a folding canvas chair with his name on the back, pensively holding a cigarette, a tendril of gray-white smoke curling up in front of his world-famous profile. It was a great image. He looked like he was posing even when he wasn't posing.

Raymond Sinclare was a former Broadway star, former matinee idol, and—until I had the good sense to divorce him two years ago—my former drunken, adulterous husband. Drink had just about ruined his career when I persuaded the studio to give him another chance in this picture; don't ask me why. On second thought, do ask me. The answer is that, when he was sober, he was a great actor. And maybe I felt sorry for him a little.

Raymond looked up as I approached, barefoot, in my bloody robe.

"Good God," he murmured faintly. "You look like Lady Macbeth."

"That isn't funny," I said. "How are you doing?"

"I need a drink," he said to the floor in front of him, then glanced up and added, "But don't worry, it'll just be orange juice."

"Come by, we can talk later," I said. "I'm not sure what's supposed to happen now."

"There are police here," he said. "Do you think they'll arrest

4

you?"

"Don't be silly," I said. "Fixx is on the job."

I had seen the head of our studio's publicity department stride onto the set and head for the uniformed officers who had shown up. He was a square-shouldered, bull-necked figure with an imposing presence, and went in for understated and very expensive suits; today's was charcoal gray. In his breast pocket was a fancy silk handkerchief, and, in his other pockets, most of the local constabulary. If he had had more notice, there would not be police here at all. Fortune Pictures didn't have its own police force; we weren't MGM. But we did have Leonard Fixx.

He was well named, Mr. Fixx. We would have probably called him that behind his back if it hadn't been his real name, because that's what he did for the studio. He fixed things. He could be jocular or serious as needed, and right now he was expertly blending the two, his whole manner signaling that he was here to take care of problems.

Fixx was talking to some Culver City cops not far from Ray and me while the set dressers rolled up the bloodstained carpet and Louie from props fished the Colt out of the bathtub. That reminded me that I had dropped the gun on my way out of the tub. I remembered the tiny hiss as the hot barrel hit the water.

I started off in Louie's direction and saw Fixx glance over at me, a quick flicker around the eyes showing his surprise. I guess he thought I would have been spirited away by now. And sure enough, here came John, the first assistant director, having finished talking to Arthur and ready to do the spiriting. A tall, skinny, anxious young guy, he was still holding his megaphone as though it was another part of him.

"John, what the hell—" I said as he took my arm and turned me away from the cops and Fixx. I looked over my shoulder to see Fixx subside and go back to entertaining the police as John hustled me out of the way.

Alice scampered over with my fur-trimmed slippers and John waited while I shuffled into them. Then he said, gently, "Let's get you to your dressing room. The limo's waiting."

"Yeah, but—"

He kept me walking. "Mr. Fixx's orders, Frankie," he said. "C'mon, you know how it goes. Let him do his job."

"But who did this, John?" I asked as he escorted me out into the late winter sunshine and bundled me into the studio limo, a boxy black Cadillac.

"Who did it?" he repeated as he got into the back seat of the big car with me. "Well, you."

I looked daggers at him. "You're not any funnier than Raymond," I said.

He darted a glance at me. The bloodstains on my robe looked like flowers, horrific flowers, and I could tell that the sight of me was getting to him. But it was his job at the moment to whisk me out of the way, and he was determined to get that done.

"Look, sorry, Frankie," he said. "I don't know any more than you do who loaded that gun with live ammo. Except it had to be someone in props."

We were quiet for the minute or so it took to get to my private dressing room, which was a neat, small cottage on the Fortune Motion Pictures lot. Whoever's star was on the rise at the time got to use it, and it had been decorated to suit my taste for a year now. It was close enough to walk from the soundstage, but this obviously wasn't the best time for me to take a stroll around the place.

I didn't respond to John's statement of the obvious. Of course it was the property department. They were in charge of every item that performers handled in a scene. But who in props? When I first saw the Colt today, it had been hanging on the chair next to the bathtub, in the holster of my character's gun belt. The last person to have touched it before me would have been— should have been—the prop master, Vernon Stone.

Yesterday, he and I had gone over how I would use it in the scene, and it hadn't been loaded then. I knew because I checked. I felt a wave of guilt now, as I realized I should have checked it again today. No one else would see it that way, but I did. The weight of this settled on me, and it would be a long time before it went away.

Vernon was a wiry, energetic guy who seemed to take his

work seriously, but other than that I couldn't say I knew him well. I had talked to him mostly about props. And sometimes jigsaw puzzles. He liked puzzles. He bought the latest ones the moment they came out.

"So it must have been Vernon," I said aloud as we pulled up in front of the cottage. John nodded. I wanted it to be mostly Vernon's fault. Not honorable of me, but there you go. It would be simpler that way. I could demand that he be fired, maybe. But I knew it wouldn't help that much. It wouldn't unshoot Sam.

A bold-lettered sign on the door of my dressing room read FRANKIE FRANKLIN. You would have seen me posing right there in the current issue of *Photoplay,* next to a story headlined, "America's Kid Sister Grows Up."

That was me: America's Kid Sister. I had not exactly been a child star—I was twenty and married when I played a teenager in my first major role—but the studio had promoted me as a spirited youngster anyway. And the people who wrote the stories liked me, so far. One had even declared that, "Frankie has earned her place in the pantheon of pert and personable blondes" like Harlow, Lombard and Davies.

So far, Mr. Fixx had managed to keep them from writing about my brief marriage to Raymond. But the fact that it might have been him that I shot today was going to be hard for them to ignore.

"I want to talk to Vernon," I said as he walked me to the door.

"I'll bring him," John said. "And thanks, Frankie."

"For what?"

"For not being an emotional dame."

"Don't worry—in here, I'm hysterical," I said, placing a hand over my heart and giving him my most winning smile.

He looked grateful as he left me. When you get to be a big deal in the movies, people think someone should always be with you. But I didn't want anyone with me right now. I wanted to get cleaned up. And then talk to Vernon. John had said he would find him and bring him to me.

Once inside my all-white dressing room, I considered my options. Undoubtedly the police would be questioning Vernon right now, and I pictured him answering in his precise, almost fussy manner. And then he would be told Miss Franklin wanted to see him. My initial fury had calmed just a bit so that I didn't think I would actually punch him. But what would I say? How would I play it? What did I want to have him tell me, or me to tell him?

Should I be imperious? "How dare you endanger my picture?" Sympathetic? "Oh, Vernon, you must be feeling terrible right now." No, I'd probably just let him have it with a direct, "How could you be so stupid? What the hell happened?" and demand to know why he thought he shouldn't be fired on the spot.

But first I needed a shower. A modern shower, no bathtub, had been one of my first requests when the dressing room was decorated for me. When I was working, I didn't want to lounge in a bath—not off-camera, anyway. I wanted to get on with the work and get home as soon as possible. I headed across the all-white carpet, and went into the all-white bathroom.

I dropped the ruined robe on the sparkling clean tile floor—I felt bad leaving it for the maid but had no idea what else to do with it—and turned on the shower.

Picking up the fresh bar of Lux soap, I stepped into the shower, glad to let the hot water and soap sluice away the blood that was on my hands and forearms, and even on my calf, and send it down the drain, I only wished I could also steam away the vision of Sam's ashen face, and the feel of his bloody hand in mine as we waited for help to arrive.

Eventually I decided I couldn't stay in the shower forever, as comforting as it was. I got out and dried off vigorously with one of the fluffy white towels from the stack that appeared daily, as if by magic, in my dressing room, no matter how many I used.

I dressed quickly in a white skirt and blue, short-sleeved cashmere sweater, a sporty ensemble that suited southern California's early March weather. Many places in the country might still be under snow, but here we shivered and complained of the cold whenever nighttime temperatures dropped below 60 degrees. With nearly three hundred days of sunshine a year, the climate was perfect for shooting pictures outdoors, and was one reason the business had planted itself here among the orange groves.

A look in the mirror reminded me that my hair was still swept up in its 19th-century hairdo, with a pouf of curls for bangs, extra hair, and about a million hairpins. It contrasted bizarrely with my modern clothes, and I felt that I couldn't give Vernon a proper talking-to looking like this. I picked up my white telephone and called hairdressing to come and fix it, and hoped they could get to me before John brought the prop master here. I hadn't done such a great job removing the on-camera makeup either, but I'd go after what remained of it with the cold cream later.

Then I reverted to the nervous habit I had of checking my handbag several times a day, just to make sure everything was still in it: paper money in the billfold, change in the change purse, driving license, a clean hankie, lipstick, and the penknife my father had given me on my fourteenth birthday.

This small artifact, from a simpler time in my life, was always with me. It had an antler handle and a blade that was good for cutting fruit, sharpening pencils, opening envelopes: all kinds of things. It was usually in my handbag or a pocket, or even in my bra, often along with my lipstick, if my outfit didn't have pockets. A couple of my custom-made brassieres even had a little pocket sewn into them. With just these two items on me, I felt like I was ready for anything.

But making sure nothing had escaped my bag when I wasn't looking only killed a couple of minutes. Seeking distraction, I found the book I had been reading during the interminable periods of inactivity on the set: Agatha Christie's novel from last year, *Murder in the Calais Coach.* I hadn't put a bookmark in where I'd left off, and I thumbed through the first few chapters absently, until Teddy from hairdressing showed up. He relieved me of the pins and the curly hairpiece, then fluffed my own short, wavy bob back into place.

"All done," he said, giving my hair one last pat. "You look ready to slay 'em. Oh—I mean—"

"It's OK, Teddy," I said. "Let's hope I didn't."

Teddy left and I went to an armchair and sat with my book for a few more minutes, still not able to concentrate on the doings of a bunch of passengers stuck on a train in the mountains of Yugoslavia, or on the detective's methodical search for who killed the obnoxious Ratchett. I had questions of my own to ask our property master, and patience is not my strong suit.

Maybe John had gotten interrupted while looking for Vernon. Maybe he had forgotten he'd promised to bring Vernon to me.

"Maybe a lot of things," I muttered under my breath, and left the dressing room.

Chapter
Two

You could get lost in the prop department, which was like a library of things instead of books. Rows of shelves held all the items we handled for our grown-up version of make-believe: hammers and wrenches, baseball bats and gloves, dolls, baby carriages, gardening tools, paintbrushes, puppets, books, baskets—you get the idea. Framed paintings hung from the rafters like heraldic banners.

The weapons had their own room, and that's where I went now.

The door, though closed, was not locked, and it opened when I tried the handle.

"Vern?" I called. "Are you around? Louie?"

I waited a moment, breathing in the smell of oil and solvents, hearing nothing. The walls bristled silently with firearms of all sorts, as well as swords, rapiers, cutlasses, bows, Bowie knives, daggers, and even some elegantly, wickedly curved scimitars. Many of the blades and spear points were made of rubber, especially if they were going to be issued to hundreds of extras, like the ones currently working on a picture that Fortune was making, based on a Kipling story. But others could, like my Colt, inflict serious harm on man and beast. There were shelves with rifles and handguns from various eras, all capable of firing live ammunition. There was even a Gatling gun on its wheeled carriage, sitting on the floor nearby.

In the corner of this big room was a smaller one, which was Vern's office. The door was standing open, which was not unusual, I knew from my occasional visits here. When I stuck my head into the office, it looked much as it always had: a

11

wooden chair pushed up to a desk completely bare of random papers, a cup holding pencils that looked just sharpened, a couple of file cabinets, and a sofa. One of the sofa throw pillows, in a fabric featuring various fish species, had fallen to the floor. It was the only slightly askew element in the room.

But no Vern. In fact, no one at all was visible, though the place was so big and mazelike, there were probably people working off in corners I couldn't see. On a worktable just outside the office lay a handgun in pieces: not the Colt Single Action Army revolver I had used and fired, but a modern revolver that a policeman might carry.

The sun was slanting in through a high window, making a bright shaft of light populated with millions of dust motes doing their strange little dances. Now I noticed it was lighting up something near the leg of the table outside Vernon's office: something metal. I bent to look and saw that it was a live .45 cartridge, just like the one that would have left the barrel of my revolver and hit Sam. It was unusual for ammunition, especially live ammunition, to be lying around like that, and it did make it look like someone had been careless, or distracted, or in a rush. I went to pick it up and then—I suppose in crime-scene mode from reading the Christie book—stopped myself. Could a cartridge pick up fingerprints? I didn't see why not, so I left it there.

Still no one was nearby, and it occurred to me that, with the shooting, much of the *Prairie Princess* crew might have taken advantage of the confusion to leave the lot and were now discussing the incident over drinks at one of the local bars. Or maybe Vernon was off having a serious talk with the person who was supposed to have loaded the gun, if it wasn't him. Maybe he was giving some employee the heave-ho to protect himself from being given the heave-ho.

Nothing else seemed out of place that I could tell. Not that I'd necessarily recognize it if anything were different. Too bad I didn't have a giant brain like Hercule Poirot, I thought. He would probably draw all sorts of inferences based only on these inanimate objects and his knowledge of human nature.

Again I realized I how little I knew Vernon. Someone had told me he had tried to make it as an actor when he first came out from New York, but eventually found props and sets more interesting as well as providing more steady pay.

A vague memory floated up from today: I had seen Vernon leaving the commissary after lunch at the same time I did. There was nothing in this memory to have aroused suspicion or even much interest. Just another guy heading back to work, chatting with a dark-haired young woman.

He had been explaining something about an antique gun being used in the Kipling picture, and I had heard the girl say, "Guns? I would be too afraid!" or something like that. I just remembered it had been the kind of cotton-headed comment some girls make so that their male companions feel big and strong and smart. I hadn't seen him after that.

I wasn't seeing him now, either. I stood there for a moment, wondering if anything in the room could possibly be a clue, but nothing in there was telling me much. I picked up the fallen pillow, tossed it back on the sofa, and left.

The assistant director, John, was waiting for me outside my dressing room. He was accompanied by another man wearing an ill-fitting dark suit, a gray fedora, and the impassive expression of a cigar-store Indian. This other man might as well have been holding up a title card that said DETECTIVE.

"Oh, there you are," John said, sounding relieved and as though he'd been surprised not to find me where he had left me.

"This is Detective Robert Jameson," he said. "Fixx says it's okay to talk to him."

I nodded, and John left without a word. I turned to the man in the dark suit. He tipped his hat to me, a bit awkwardly, and said, "Miss Franklin."

"Detective Jameson," I said, and let him follow me into the dressing room.

Without a change of expression, Detective Jameson took in the details surrounding him: the skirted table with its mirror framed in lights, the satin-covered chairs, and the vases of white roses that were replaced daily when I was on the lot. The roses were put there by the same unseen hand that replaced my towels, unwrapped fresh bars of soap and would, today, make a bloodstained robe disappear.

"I don't guess I should offer you a drink?" I asked, motioning him toward one of the armchairs.

He smiled ever so slightly. "No, thanks," he said.

"You're a detective?" I asked. "But it was an accident. A stupid one. Wasn't it?"

"Could be," he said.

We regarded each other for a moment, and I realized he was letting the silence lengthen, perhaps to let me get uncomfortable enough to start talking. I wasn't uncomfortable, but I started talking anyway.

"How do I know you're really a cop? Maybe you're a bit player I never met and Fixx just sent you over to make me feel like they're doing something about this. Or maybe you're just going to report back to him."

He smiled tolerantly, reached into a breast pocket and produced the badge. It looked real enough.

"We found out about Mr. Harvey being at the hospital and my boss gave me the go-ahead to ask some questions," Jameson said, putting the badge away. "Just between you and me, the chief likes to make the occasional gesture to indicate that the studio doesn't own us completely."

"And maybe he wants to find out if I really did have anything to do with it—on purpose, I mean," I said. "Which I didn't."

Detective Jameson had pulled a notebook and pencil from the same suit pocket, and now he asked the usual questions, though more of them than I expected.

When the shooting occurred (that's how he put it, I suppose to avoid saying "when you shot Mr. Harvey"), was that the first time I'd touched the gun?

Yes, I said.

Had I seen anyone handling the Colt who shouldn't have been? Anyone other than the prop man, Vernon Stone?

No, I said.

Did I know how to shoot a gun?

14

Yes, I said. My father and I often did target practice with both handguns and rifles when I was growing up. (The impassive face registered a flicker of surprise: one slightly raised eyebrow.)

Did I have any suspicion that there was something different about the Colt? No, of course not.

Did I know of anyone who would do this on purpose? No.

Did I know of anyone who would want to harm the actors involved? No, I answered. Not even me, although Raymond—the one who wasn't shot—was my ex-husband.

This time both eyebrows went up and the pencil paused in mid-air before he began to write again. This information, known to the motion picture community but not the general public, would come out anyway; why not get it out of the way now?

A little glimmer of heightened interest. "Was he the one you were aiming at?"

I stared at him for a moment before answering, trying not to sound defensive.

"No," I said. "I was cheating the barrel to the side slightly for the camera. So it would look better on the screen."

Jameson nodded and wrote. "Did you have anything against the victim?"

"No," I said. "He's a good kid." Sam was maybe two years younger than me.

Jameson wrote some more, asked if there was anything I'd like to add. I told him about finding the .45 cartridge in the prop room.

"I didn't pick it up," I said. "I thought there might be fingerprints on it from whoever loaded the gun. Even if it was just Vernon."

Jameson twitched a grin I can only describe as indulgent, making me feel like Nancy Drew, girl sleuth, then wrote some more in his notebook and put it and the pencil back in his pocket.

"I do have a question myself," I said.

"Please," he said.

"How is Sam? Do you know?"

"In surgery last I heard," he said. "That's all I can tell you."

If Detective Jameson had ever been starstruck, he had gotten over it by now. I sensed no desire from him to find ways to prolong his exposure to my exalted presence, and liked that about him. When he'd gotten whatever information I could give him, which wasn't much, he put his fedora back on, touched the brim and said thanks and good-bye.

Before closing the door I looked up and down the studio streets to see if John was on his way back, hopefully dragging Vernon by one ear, but only saw a group of British soldiers slouching along the way I don't think British soldiers ever quite did; a film editor, a woman I liked, who waved at me and gave me a sympathetic look; and a couple of scenarists who had left their tiny offices, apparently summoned to some set to rewrite lines, judging from their worried scowls and animated gestures.

There was still no sign of John with Vernon when I heard a familiar knock on my dressing room door: *rat-tat-a-tat-tat, tat-TAT.* It was Raymond doing his signature knock, which dated back to his 1926 picture, *Good Old College Try*, where he played a football star in love with two coeds.

In that movie, as in all his movies, Ray did the right and noble thing, choosing the poor-but-sweet coed over the rich-and-scheming one.

That was the picture in which a hopeful-looking Raymond rapped out this rhythm on his sweetheart's door, followed by a title card reading "SHAVE AND A HAIRCUT!" This was followed by a shot of the sweetheart looking ecstatic, and knocking "TWO BITS!" from the other side of the door.

Audiences found this to be so charming and funny, it became a fad. Raymond couldn't go out without people knocking out *rat-tat-a-tat-tat* at him everywhere he went: on his restaurant table, on a nearby wall, or, once, on the shiny fender of our Duesenberg when we were stopped at a light. Then they would grin and wait for him to answer with the *tat-TAT.* He always obliged and they went away happy. Eventually, it became the way he always knocked. Like he was doing now. Except he added the *tat-TAT* himself, knowing I wouldn't play along.

I opened the door, remembering I'd promised that we would talk. "Hi, Ray."

16

There are lots of men six feet tall, with chiseled features, blue eyes and wavy, reddish-blond hair, who look fantastic in any costume. But not all men have that presence, that larger-than-life quality that makes people want to look at them: that thing some people called "It." Besides being a great actor, when not drunk, Raymond had It. He was a star.

I guessed I had It, too, in some measure. You couldn't succeed on the screen without this indefinable quality, though my theory was that it was just an accident of biological geometry, the way our faces reflected light, the way we moved, and the way the camera caught our images, that made audiences want to watch us. Having It could make you crazy because It can't be earned or bought or copied. All you can do is work hard, hold out for good roles, treat your fans right, and hope It lasts for a career.

Though Ray's career was on rocky ground just now, he still had It. He made quite a handsome picture standing there, his background the landscaped gardens in which our bungalows were set, both he and the landscape clothed in the glamorous golden light of the afternoon sun. Many women—and some men, too, I guess—would have swooned to find Raymond Sinclare on their front step.

I had swooned once, myself.

Chapter Three

Now I just sighed in resignation. To be fair, I couldn't blame him if he felt anxious. Shocking as it was for me to have pulled the trigger, he was the one the bullet had narrowly missed. That would be haunting him.

He smiled down at me. "Darling," he said. I'd never been able to get him to stop calling me that. I had finally decided it was just a habit and didn't mean anything,.

"Darling, are you all right? I thought you might've gone home, but then I saw Monty with the car."

"Come in, Ray," I said, stepping back into my dressing room and mentally giving him points for asking about me first. "Let's not play a scene on the stoop."

Stepping inside the dressing room, he turned to face me, a look of dismay on his face.

"It's not a scene," he said reproachfully. "I just wanted to know, well—first of all, how are you, darling?"

"About like you'd expect," I said, standing aside so he could come in. "Tired. I would like to go home."

"Of course you would," he said.

He paced around a bit, looking ridiculously handsome in a red silk brocade dressing gown over his tailored trousers, him and his still respectable supply of It. Objectively, I could see it. Subjectively, I just wanted to accomplish whatever level of comforting he required, and then get him out of my dressing room.

Raymond stopped in front of me with a pained expression. Searching for words. Doing his best to make me see that he was searching for words.

"What is it, Ray?"

"Well, I keep replaying the scene in my mind, seeing you aiming right at me."

"Which I wasn't."

"Yes, of course. Still, I can't get it out of my mind."

"What I can't get out of my mind is Sam," I said. "You know: the one who was actually shot."

He paced around a bit more, then stopped at my dressing table and looked down at the unopened pack of Lucky Strikes. "I thought you'd quit."

"I keep them around to remind me I don't need them," I said.

He smiled faintly, and absently pushed the little packet of coffin nails back and forth, this way and that, on the glass tabletop.

Finally he said, almost apologetically, "There's a thought haunting me."

I waited.

"Although I know it's utter nonsense, and I don't want to think it, it keeps coming back … I can't help wondering … could you, in any possible scenario, have actually really wanted to shoot me?"

"What?" I said sharply, more surprised than offended. Ray had always been prone to anxiety, which I knew, but I was irritated anyway—and annoyed with myself for being irritated.

I sighed, went to a side table, poured water from a cut-crystal decanter into one of its matching glasses, and handed it to him. He sipped gratefully. I sat on the arm of one chair.

"Ray," I said, "who was my father?"

He smiled wanly. "Hick Hickenlooper, the stunt man's stunt man," he said.

"That is correct," I said. "And how old was I when I got my first rifle?"

"Seven."

"Raymond," I said, "If I had ever really intended to shoot you, we would not be having this conversation, because I wouldn't have missed."

I saw him trying to figure out how to take this.

"And I sure wouldn't have done it on camera. Or arranged it

so that the blame fell on someone else."

His strong, cleft chin trembled. Oh god, he wasn't going to start sobbing, was he?

I got up hastily and put a consoling hand on his arm. "Ray, listen to me. It has been ages since I've wished you were dead."

He looked alarmed.

"I mean—sorry, that came out wrong," I said lamely. "You know what I mean."

The right words were escaping me. I really did feel tired. Even though he was older than me, I had always felt like the world was just too much for Raymond, and that I needed to make things easier for him. Even now. Even when I needed things made easier for me.

But he rallied and developed a ghost of a grin and an almost sheepish look. I smiled encouragingly.

He composed the handsome face into a more hopeful expression, meant to show he was now going to be all right, that he would buck up and soldier on. It was a look of heroic resolve his fans would have recognized from *Song of the Desert, Highland Rebel*, or *Mr. Masterson*.

"You would have been sad if you'd shot me," he said, almost happily, smoothing his silk lapels.

I sighed. "I'm sad I shot anyone."

He smiled a more genuine smile. He did feel better.

"Darling, you're so good for me, even now. You're so … down-to-earth."

"Thanks, Ray," I said. I'd been called a lot of things, sometimes by him, during the divorce. That wasn't the worst.

I had cared about him, once. Quite a lot, too.

We had met when I showed up as Dancing Girl #2 in one of his biggest silent-film hits, *Oasis*. Only the week before, I'd been helping the wranglers with some of the Arabian horses needed on the picture when the director spotted me and offered me a screen test.

My father was working steadily coordinating stunts of all kinds and had no illusions about the business or the people in it, and had to be persuaded. The pictures, silent or sound, had been

20

good to him, and he didn't mind my fooling around with horses and even riding as an extra myself sometimes. But he knew too much about what could happen to innocent young girls once the studios got hold of them.

"Frankie? She's not even that pretty," he said to my mother.

"You haven't been paying attention, dear," my mother said over my head, like I wasn't even in the room. "She has grown into a striking young woman—especially when captured on film."

She showed him a photo she had taken of me, which she had just picked up from the camera store on Sunset. I had to admit I didn't look half bad in it, sitting by the pool in my bathing suit, hair wet and dark from the water, pretty good teeth showing as I laughed at my mom for some silly pun she had just made, I forget what. The picture did show how much the camera loved high cheekbones, deep-set eyes, a pointed chin and what some Hollywood reporter would later describe as "a straight, slightly arrogant nose."

My father had just grunted, said he supposed he couldn't stop me, and added to my mother, "I'd like to be there to watch when they try to wrangle her into a dress."

So I did the screen test, for which they did wrangle me into a dress. With my hair curled and my face sporting more makeup than I had ever worn in my life, I was asked to sashay around a set meant to look like a country club, smiling at nothing, just to see if I could move, and how I looked on film. It was a ridiculous lark. And then they signed me.

The next week, there I was on Fortune Pictures' Soundstage Four, dressed in harem pants and a midriff-baring top, striking what I hoped was an alluring pose next to a plaster-and-plywood column between Dancing Girls #1 and #3, waiting to entertain the sultan.

I don't know if the character actor playing the sultan noticed me, but the star did. Raymond was playing an English adventurer, and we had a brief scene in which he asked me kindly if I had come to the desert by choice, and I giggled and ran away. The interest he showed in the scene turned out to go beyond the script—in part, I think, because he was intrigued by the idea that I didn't seem to be taking any of this seriously.

By that time he wasn't taking much seriously either, except for his commitment to alcohol. I'd never known a true drunk, and at eighteen, I thought I was in love, and was too young to know that I couldn't change him. We were married up the coast in Santa Barbara and I knew almost immediately it had been a big mistake.

Within three months I found him in our bed with Dancing Girl #3. She apologized to me, and he and I quarreled. A month after that, another starlet called our house demanding to talk to him and seemed surprised that I'd answered. I kicked him out, telling him to come back when he could keep his wedding vows.

We went on like that for a while. He would move out for a few days, then come back contrite, with charming apologies. A few weeks later, he'd do it all over again. In between affairs, he would drink—apparently to forget that he'd promised not to have any more affairs. His attempt to erase his memory worked too well. Eventually, he couldn't even remember their names.

Meanwhile, I threw myself into learning to act and dance and sing, never complained when we were still shooting scenes at three in the morning, and did whatever the studio told me to do. I even climbed barefoot into the rigging of a three-masted schooner for publicity photos once, though I don't care for heights. As a result of all that, plus the studio's relentless promotion of me and my pictures, my own career took off.

And now, at twenty-four, I could hardly believe my luck. The career changed my life dramatically, dizzyingly. Costume fittings, voice lessons, dance lessons, interviews and photo sessions with magazines and newspapers—all these were worked in around shooting schedules that took up most of every day. We would be finishing up shooting one picture, while doing retakes for the previous picture and rehearsing the next one.

I found the whole process to be fascinating, and turned out to be pretty good at memorizing lines and understanding what directors wanted. I discovered I loved wearing beautiful dresses, and the more feathers and sequins, the better. I found the people, especially the crew, fun to be around.

But then there was Ray and our ill-considered marriage. After a while, I tired of his shenanigans and told him that he could keep the Sunset Tower apartment, the scene of most of his infidelities, but that his presence was no longer required at my Beachwood Canyon home. We had been divorced now for two years.

Ray kept drinking after the divorce, and I suppose kept womanizing, too, although I was glad that wasn't my business anymore. As he drank more and more, becoming unreliable and difficult to work with, the studio had used him less and less, and six months ago had warned him that they would drop his contract if he couldn't stay sober.

Though his private life wasn't my business anymore, I felt bad about this setback and when I argued for him to be given another chance, playing the evil banker in *Prairie Princess*, I got my way.

Now here he was, looking older than his thirty-six years and working only because his ex-wife had promised the studio he'd behave. One of us had to be down-to-earth, I figured. I wanted him to be successful somehow, in some way—mainly so I could stop worrying about him.

He gave me the hero look again.

"Thank you, darling," he said. "I do feel better, having talked. Maybe I'll call over to Hank and Jimmy's to see if they're doing anything for dinner."

"Well, now, there's an idea," I said brightly.

It would be good for him. Fonda and Stewart were roommates, best pals, and wholesome, by this town's standards. The friends who dropped by for dinner might end up doing nothing much more scandalous than building an elaborate kite or model airplane. Considerably cheerier as he considered this course of action, Raymond kissed my cheek in good-bye and went off to his own dressing room.

By now I had given up on John producing Vernon for me to talk to, and I had to admit I was probably not that high on the list of people the studio and the police thought he should see. Maybe he was even under arrest, I thought. I stared at the door for a moment, wondering if I should keep waiting, then snagged my pale blue beret off the hat rack. I was tugging it on and placing it at a rakish angle, which, under the current circumstances, felt frivolous, when there was another knock at the door.

My new visitor was Arthur, our director, dapper in his customary tweed suit, tweed vest and tartan tie.

"How are you, my dear?" he asked sympathetically. "I apologize for not coming to see you earlier."

"I'm doing all right, Arthur, considering," I said. "How long will we be shut down for?"

"A few days," he said. "Wiseman didn't build this studio up by being the sentimental type, and his New York accountants sure aren't."

"Have you talked to Vernon?"

He shook his head. "I know John was looking for him, but so far, no."

"How is Sam, do you know?" I asked.

"I sent Betty with them to the hospital," he said. "She telephoned to say Sam was in surgery." No more information than Jameson had. "We'll know later today or tomorrow how he's doing."

I nodded, taking this in. "I should go see him."

"You should send flowers."

"But Arthur –"

"If the gossips get wind of this, they'll ambush you at the hospital. But you will have thought of that yourself, my dear."

I had not thought of this myself. But I had made up my mind. I had to see Sam, see for myself that he was all right. I'd deal with the gossips later. Maybe they wouldn't show, after all.

"I imagine Mr. Fixx is doing his usual good job of playing it down and paying people off."

"Yes, but even so …" Arthur said. He glanced at me to see if I was being swayed, saw that I wasn't, and said, "I'm not your boss off the set. But I want you to be aware that the gossips won't always be on your side like they are now."

"Thanks, Arthur," I said. "I do appreciate it."

I saw him to the door and watched him walk away, heading back toward the soundstages. I had the luxury of going home, but Arthur, the captain of the ship that was this picture, the producer as well as the director, was going back to work.

It even felt odd to me to be leaving in the late afternoon, but there wasn't much else for me to do at this point. I left the bungalow and found my driver, Monty, waiting outside with the Packard. Monty was about nine feet tall and never spoke. At least that had been my impression when I was a kid and he had first come to work for our family. He was very large, and very kind, and when he did speak it was quiet and to the point.

Tipping his billed hat to me, he opened the door and I slid gratefully onto the soft pale leather of the back seat. The door closed with a muffled, reassuring thump, and soon my big, cream-colored motorcar was rolling in stately fashion toward the studio gates.

At the main intersection we paused to let the usual parade go by: more red-coated British soldiers, several extras in powdered wigs and knee breeches, another in a fringed buckskin shirt, two workmen carrying a ladder and paint buckets, six giggling girls in white togas, and a man in a robe, leading a camel.

Outside the gates of Fortune Motion Pictures, the atmosphere was nearly as fantastical. In this town, when you were hungry, you might walk in the door of a restaurant shaped like a coffee pot, a shoe, an airplane, or a hat. If you had a job, your ride to work certainly took you past tall, spindly palm trees, but also palm readers, oil derricks, oily characters of all stripes, and the odd movie star.

After all the costumed players on the lot, the "civilians" on the street—women in flowered dresses and sensible shoes, men in suits, most people wearing hats—looked slightly foreign to me.

The traffic was already getting congested around the studio, and I leaned back, closed my eyes and listened to the soothing purr of the Packard's powerful engine. I wanted intensely to be home, where I had been planning to have a few friends over for dinner, now called off.

"Monty," I said.

I saw his eyes flick to meet mine in the rearview mirror. "Yes, miss?"

"Have you ever—" I stopped myself. What I wanted to ask was, had he ever shot anyone, and how it had made him feel. Even as I opened my mouth, though, I realized I was about to say something thoughtless, even cruel, just to make myself feel better.

Of course he had shot someone. He had left his native Alberta and gone off to the Great War, been wounded in the battle of the Somme, and come back shell-shocked, nearly mute.

I couldn't ask him to relive those experiences just to make myself feel better. Quickly I amended it, lamely, to, "Have you ever … been to Niagara Falls?"

His shoulders twitched—for him that was laughing out loud—and he said, "No, miss. Were you thinking of visiting?"

"Oh," I said. "No, no, it's just that someone mentioned it today on the set." A lie, but for the right reasons, I thought.

He nodded without speaking. There was no way he didn't know what had happened today, but he wouldn't talk about it unless I brought it up.

I didn't bring it up, but sat silently looking out the window as we crossed Wilshire, Beverly, Melrose, and eventually Sunset Boulevard, and headed into the hills, where shadows were gathering in the canyons as the sun went down. My home, way up in these hills, just off Beachwood Drive, felt worlds away from the strange community in which I worked—even though from my driveway I could see the four-story-tall lighted sign high on Mount Lee that said "HOLLYWOODLAND."

The sign had been put there to advertise a housing development, not the town where motion pictures were made. I had moved there with my parents when I was about thirteen, and within weeks I had claimed the brush-covered canyons and draws around our house for my own scrubby paradise.

I loved these hills and my rambling Spanish-style house. That was why, once I'd done the screen test and it looked like I had a chance in front of the cameras, I actually got serious about my

26

career. Few people came into this kind of luck, I knew, and if you were this lucky, no other profession could bring you so much money so fast. You would be crazy to throw it away.

I was grateful that it had all worked beyond anyone's wildest dreams, not just mine—because it meant that now, with my father gone, and my mother moved to the little ranch up north, I could keep the house. It meant I could stay here, and pay the people who worked for me, even during this awful time people were calling the Depression.

Dusk had filled the ravines with shadows that were creeping up to the ridgetops when the Packard's headlights swept the garden's whitewashed walls and the wrought-iron driveway gate, standing open. Monty would close it for the night now that I was home.

"Good night, miss," he said as I slipped out of the back seat and went up the steps to the heavy oak front door.

Chapter Four

My house was set in gardens planted with lemon trees, orange trees, succulents and herbs which I'd never learned the names of but which my gardener tended with loving care. There was a fishpond where lily pads floated and provided hiding places for any goldfish wily enough to escape the raccoons and cats. There was an outdoor fireplace where my parents' friends used to gather, and where mine now did. Tonight, though, I was glad to have the place to myself.

It was not as grand a house as some of my colleagues owned or rented, or had been provided by the studios. But it was welcoming. Its thick-walled rooms offered cool respite from California's hot summers, and were snug and cozy when nights turned chill. But best of all, it was mine.

The bedrooms, dining room, and living room looked out through a columned ramada to the pool surrounded by low palm trees and spiky cactus in large pots where alligator lizards liked to bask in the sun. In the purple of early evening, now, though, they were all somewhere else.

As I went down the hall, I heard a radio announcer's voice, faintly, coming from the kitchen, and picked up the tantalizing aroma of roasting chicken. Mrs. Monty would be in there now, busy with dinner. This tiny, gentle Frenchwoman, whose given name was Mireille, was the only good thing to come out of the war for Monty. He had come to work for us after the war, and she had followed soon after.

In some ways it felt like any other day, and I pushed away the thoughts of Sam. If no one called tonight with bad news, that would be good news.

It was odd that I hadn't seen Major Bowes yet. He was usually the first to greet me when I came home. I thought he might be napping in one of the big leather chairs in the library, or possibly—ah, I heard the sound of the Steinway coming from the living room across the hall from the library. That explained it.

The tune was "Lady Be Good," an old Broadway hit, being played in a saucy way by a guy who should have gotten the message that I didn't want company tonight. I knew Mrs. Monty would have let my friends know I wanted to be alone, but he clearly had thought that this didn't apply to him for the simple reason that he often shared my bed.

When I came into the living room, Major Bowes meowed and flowed off the piano bench like a pale cloud, coming over to wind around my legs. I picked him up, so as to make it more convenient for him to shed all over my sweater, and cooed, "How's my beautiful boy?"

And to the piano player, I said, "Oh, Max. Do be a dear, and go away."

Max was my … well … boyfriend? Too light. Lover? Too dramatic. Just Max, that would have to do. It was enough for me. But right now I didn't want company, even his. Even though I loved him. Even though, every time our eyes met, I thrummed like a plucked cello string.

"Nice to see you, too," Max said, playing a dark minor chord with a comic scowl, and then grinning up at me. He stood up from the piano bench to give me a kiss while simultaneously scratching Major Bowes behind the ears.

Max was about five-foot-six—my exact height—but with broad shoulders and large, square hands that looked more suited to chopping down trees or laying bricks than to teasing new popular songs out of a piano. He had thick, curly black hair, an aquiline nose, and dark brown eyes you could lose yourself in. Did I mention I found him irresistible? Except in the matter of marriage, which he kept proposing and I kept rejecting. I'd done that, I'd say.

"It's because I'm short, right?" he would ask.

"You're not all that short," I would say, sometimes throwing in a suggestive look somewhere south of his alligator belt.

"Is it because I'm Jewish?" he would ask.

"Max," I said to him once, "not that it matters to me, but you're not even observant. Your favorite lunch is a ham sandwich. You only made your bar mitzvah because your father promised you a piano. Not to mention, I have a Jewish agent—a far more important position than husband."

These discussions usually ended with a kiss that was meant to be playful and quick but then turned into something else that took a lot more time.

I had met Max about a year ago at one of Arthur Janeway's boisterous parties in Bel Air, on a late spring day when the air was warm and bright as honey. These affairs started with drinks and canapés around the pool, and continued into the evening or even the next morning when the gardeners might find some actor sound asleep on a pool chaise or curled up in the middle of one of the velvety green lawns, while a poker game still went on full tilt in the cardroom.

Arthur's parties always featured good food, even if the talk was mostly gossip and could become boring. I planned for them like a general planning for an engagement with the enemy. If I deployed too many of my allowed calories on a creamed lobster canapé, for example, that meant I wouldn't have any left for an assault on the tiny sausages in puff pastry, or anything with cream, or cheese. Or cream cheese. Dessert? I never even considered it. Well, maybe on Thanksgiving.

The party was well under way when I arrived on Arthur's sun-drenched pool terrace, following the sound of animated voices, glasses clinking, and the splashes and shrieks that went with people jumping or being pushed into the pool. The smell of hot cement, cool water, cigarette smoke, damp lawns, and various brands of French perfume filled the air.

I knew most of the guests, some famous, some not. Everyone seemed to be wearing dark glasses, and many of the women added wide-brimmed hats to protect their priceless faces from the sun. As I went by, hands holding cocktail tumblers went up in greeting, ice cubes tinkling. Tallulah, reclining in a lounge chair, gave me and my navy-and-white backless beach pyjamas an appraising look as I approached. She seemed to approve.

"Dah-ling," she drawled, raising her glass of bourbon in salute. "You look good enough to eat."

I smiled cheerily back at her, "Thanks, kiddo."

Arthur, in his host outfit of red silk shirt worn untucked over white cotton trousers, saw me from across the pool, excused himself from the conversation he was having with two producers, and approached, arms spread wide.

"Ah, there she is!" he exclaimed, taking my hands and kissing me once on each cheek. "My, you are radiant today!"

It was the typical way he greeted all of us. He loved actresses, and knew we were generally quivering masses of insecurities inside, always needing reassurance. In return, we acted our hearts out for him. I gave him a kiss on the cheek, and he gestured for a waiter to bring me champagne.

A few minutes later, holding my glass of bubbly, I peered over the tops of my own sunglasses, looking for anyone else I felt like talking to. They were mostly picture people, some of whom worked in front of the cameras, many more who worked behind the scenes.

A quick motion caught my eye and the lithe form of Kath Hepburn came into view, dressed in a waiter's jacket and pants and carrying a tray of drinks. It was a favorite prank; I think she liked to see how many party guests never bothered to look at the servants and to startle the ones who did.

"You should see them trying to remember if they said anything juicy that I'd repeat," she once told me.

She loped by me, her tray tilting alarmingly, jerked her chin in the direction of the pool and said, "There's a live one." Then she winked and darted off to spill gin rickeys on some poor unsuspecting partygoer.

A live one: That was our shorthand for a good-looking man, which dated back to another party by another pool, where she'd caught me gawking at Johnny Weissmuller. The muscular Olympic champion and former men's underwear model had become Tarzan the Ape Man for Metro. He had seen me

31

looking, given me a grin, flexed his muscles, and dived into the water in perfect form. I knew he was in a tumultuous marriage with the volatile actress Lupe Velez just then, though, and I had no intention of getting in the middle of all that. But I had appreciated the view.

This time it was different. When I shaded my eyes from the afternoon sun and looked, all I saw at first was a sleek, dark head moving through the turquoise water. The head turned out to be accompanied by a set of powerful tanned shoulders and arms executing machinelike strokes with no wasted motion. Intrigued, I watched until he reached the edge, pulled himself out in one graceful motion and looked about for a towel, rivulets of water sparkling and slipping down his flat abdomen, over white trunks and muscular legs. He looked absolutely comfortable with himself and the world.

Drying off, he had caught me staring, much like Tarzan had, but his grin didn't say "Look at me." It said, "I see you." A darkly handsome face with a devilishly charming smile and eyes that looked me over as a man, not a fan. For the first time since my divorce from Raymond, I felt something inside spark and flare, like the embers of a fire thought to be long dead.

I wasn't ready for that. I pushed my sunglasses up my nose, and fled down some wide limestone steps to another broad terrace populated with good copies of Greek statues and a handful of hard-drinking writers. Pale and rumpled, most of them looked misplaced, like bedroom slippers accidentally left outdoors. They were witty and biting, often total malcontents, and I found them the most interesting guests.

Joe Mankiewicz removed the ever-present pipe from his mouth and gestured me over with it. He was a writer a couple of years older than me, and responsible for some of the cleverest lines ever spoken by Gable or Crawford—or any number of others we'd never know about, since he didn't always get a credit.

"Frankie, who do you like in the Derby this year?" he called.

Relieved, I was happy to talk about horse-racing rather than examine the feelings that bronzed swimmer had stirred up in me.

"I like Cavalcade," I said. "He looked good as a two-year-old."

I went on for a bit about horses, as I tend to do if not stopped, and the writers nodded sagely. The talk then switched to boxing, which I cared less about, and then to complaints about their agents who were bleeding them dry and not getting them enough work, about the studios which didn't know what to do with them, and, always, how much they missed New York.

Entertaining as it was, after about twenty minutes I realized I was still hungry and went on a reconnaissance of the buffet table. Deviled egg? Or ham and olives on a cracker? I could have only one, so I had to make it count or eventually I wouldn't fit into my costumes.

Just as I made the decision, I heard an unfamiliar but pleasantly deep voice at my shoulder.

"Excuse me—I'm looking for Mrs. Gold?"

I nearly dropped the egg that had been the result of so much consideration, and turned to see the swimmer standing next to me, looking expectant. He was now, mercifully, dressed in fashionably roomy white linen pants topped by an aloha shirt that seemed to depict an epic explosion at a banana plantation.

"I don't think there's a Mrs. Gold here," I said.

"Oh," he said, looking disappointed, and then hopeful. "I thought for sure I'd found her."

I looked at him. He looked at me. There went that feeling again, like the strike and flare when you light a match, but this time the heat went right down to my toes. He smiled, and the temperature went up about a hundred degrees. I took a deep breath.

"At least don't reject the idea right away," he said.

"The idea?"

"The idea that we should get married," he said. "See, then when I say I'm looking for Mrs. Gold, you can say, 'I'm right here.'"

He grinned encouragingly. It was an adorable grin; I couldn't deny that.

I put the egg down. His approach was so corny, I had to

laugh. And so did he.

"So," I said, "This is just a wild guess, of course—but you must be Mr. Gold?"

"Max Gold," he said. "From Indianapolis by way of Broadway. I wrote the music and lyrics for *Once More with You*." He stuck out his hand. I shook it.

"I saw that show last year at the Shubert," I said, impressed. "Everyone was humming that tune 'All the Hearts' as we left the theater."

"Yeah?" he said, his face lighting up. "Whaddaya know, Frankie Franklin saw my show."

I felt my own face lighting up, and the heat inside was about the size of a bonfire now as I took in those warm brown eyes, and that smile which was simply angelic. Unless it was devilish. I couldn't decide which. I also noticed that we were the same height, though he had me weight-wise by about thirty pounds with that muscular chest and shoulders.

While I tried to decide how to respond, my new acquaintance made a deft move toward the table and came up with a tiny, gold-rimmed plate bearing a diamond-shaped canapé with a swirly, cheesy, thirty-thousand-calorie topping.

Offering it to me, he said, "I wish this were a real diamond."

I chuckled and accepted the plate, the deviled egg forgotten. "So do I. Diamonds are less fattening."

He deployed the angelic-pirate smile again and said, "I think we should get to know each other a little, since we're going to be planning a wedding soon."

I felt eyes on us and looked around to see three of the writers, two men and a seen-it-all-looking woman, regarding us with naked interest. They were always on the prowl for ideas, scenes, and dialogue. I half expected to see them taking notes as we spoke.

"Okay, Max Gold," I said. "How about we start all this off slow—with a drink?"

The party was still going strong, with people splashing and shouting in the pool, or talking and smoking and laughing around it. The ping and pong of a cutthroat table tennis game could be heard coming from a nearby pavilion, and I heard Kath whoop in triumph—she must have just bashed a ball past someone. Sometimes you'd see people slipping off in couples or even threes and fours—men and women, men and men, women and women—to other parts of Arthur's estate, like the secluded cabanas or unused rooms, bent on more private pursuits.

We didn't do that. Instead, we strolled through the gardens and settled in two wicker chairs surrounded by roses, and tropical plants, and something sweet-smelling—jasmine, I think—where we talked and laughed until the warm California afternoon turned into a cool evening.

"Boy, when the sun goes down here, all the warmth goes with it," Max said. He took off the white linen jacket that went with the trousers, and placed it over my bare shoulders. "Not like Indianapolis at all. Or New York."

Max had done the songs for not one but two recent Broadway hit shows, and had been summoned to Hollywood by telegram with an offer of money, a fantastical figure he could hardly believe. He had only been in California for a few weeks, writing songs for RKO musicals and already finding Hollywood to his liking.

"I even bought myself a car," he said.

We talked easily, like we'd known each other for years, about the pictures and the theater, books and sports. I had never known a songwriter, and asked maybe a million questions about how he did it. Music first or words first? Did he always write the words himself? How did he know he wasn't writing a tune someone else had already written, and he was only remembering it?

He asked me what it was like to act, and I told him I didn't know much, myself, and that I'd only learned a few tricks, but was trying to really learn the craft. Soon there were more stars in the sky than there were around the pool, and people were falling asleep on the chaise longues, some cozily wrapped in the big blankets Arthur provided for guests.

A few hours before, I had called Monty and told him to go on to bed, because I had a ride home. And around two a.m., when our conversation started to consist of more yawns than words,

Max had his white Auburn Speedster brought around, and waved the valet off so that he could open the door for me himself. We zoomed along Sunset Boulevard past the UCLA campus and slipped by the mouths of the steep canyons—Benedict, Coldwater, Laurel—that separated Arthur's neighborhood from mine. Then we wound our way up Beachwood, the neighborhood dark and quiet, and came to my street and then my house.

"Here we are," I said, indicating he should go on through the open gate.

"It's nice up here," Max said, looking around at the garden with its palm trees and cactus and at the white walls and red tile roof of my house. "Casa de Frankie."

"It can get foggy at night," I said. "But it is nice, yes."

With unstudied chivalry, he got out and came around to open my door. I gave him back his jacket and did not invite him in. We kissed a discreet little kiss that would have raised no eyebrows at the Breen Office, and he said, softly, "Good night, future Mrs. Gold."

"Miss Franklin," I had said back, and then smiled and slipped behind the door, closing it firmly.

That was how it had started. And now here he was, looking completely at home in my house and saying, "You don't really want me to leave, do you?"

"I'm pretty sure I do," I said. "I'd like to be alone."

"After what happened?" he said. "I thought we could talk. You know, if you needed to."

"I'll be fine."

"You've had a traumatic experience. People need to talk after traumatic experiences," he said.

I didn't think I needed to talk. But maybe I needed a distraction. I felt my resolve giving way.

He moved toward the cocktail bar and picked up a bottle of Campari. "Negroni?"

"Thanks," I said, resistance gone. "Well played, sir."

He did make an excellent Negroni. And he had made it clear, he wasn't going anywhere.

Chapter Five

For a musician, Max was an early riser. That, along with his natural cheeriness, could make him annoying in the morning. But he hadn't been annoying last night. I had needed distraction and he was an expert at that. He had distracted me until well past midnight.

Now he stood in the doorway, already showered, shaved, dressed, and bringing coffee to me in my favorite blue, beehive-shaped cup.

"What's the story, morning glory?" he said brightly.

I was awake myself, technically. I blinked under the assault of the morning sun, and realized I was immobilized by sheets that had wound themselves around my body, and Major Bowes, who had stretched himself out along my back. I looked at Max pleadingly.

"Save me," I said.

Max set the coffee cup on the bedside table, deftly scooted Major Bowes over, and helped me extricate myself from the sheets.

"I have to get two songs finished by noon or I'd stay to keep you company," he said. "How do these titles sound? 'You're the Girl I Loved in Days of Yore,' and 'Chain Maille Medley.' Some comic knights are supposed to sing them, so I have to write funny."

I took the coffee cup, sipped, and admired the sight of Max in his workday outfit of dark pleated pants and white shirt with sleeves rolled up. A loudly patterned necktie featuring oversized purple and orange flowers was dangling around his neck, waiting to be tied.

We were at the point in our relationship where he kept a

couple of changes of clothes, a toothbrush, and some other things at my place. He'd just brought it all over one day from his apartment at the Garden of Allah, where he still mostly lived. Officially when he stayed over, he had a guest room. Unofficially the guest room was always available for someone else.

"Whose idea was it to set a musical in the Crusades?" I muttered. "They're already getting the DeMille treatment over at Paramount."

"No one asked me," Max said. "I'm just a tunesmith for hire. They say 'write,' and I say, 'How many bars and in what key?' How's the coffee?"

"Great, and thank you," I said, wiggling my coffee cup at him. "You have clearly figured out the key to my heart."

He grinned and started to do up his tie. I had a momentary urge to act like a good wife and help him tie it, but it passed. One, I wasn't his wife, and two, I enjoyed sitting back and watching the play of muscles in his forearms as he deftly whipped the patterned silk into a perfect Windsor knot.

"That's the idea, sweetheart," he said, adjusting the knot. "I intend to spoil you into submission."

He leaned down to give me a kiss. "Seriously, you all right?"

"Yes, I'm fine, really. I'm going to go visit Sam in the hospital."

"You're sure that's a good idea?" Max said. "He might think you've come to finish him off, and make a break for it."

"Wise guy," I said. "I just need to see for myself that he's OK. If he's in good enough shape to run away, I would cheer."

Max ruffled my hair. "Okay, sport, see ya later." And out he went.

I slipped a satin robe over my nightgown and went downstairs where Mrs. Monty would be waiting with my breakfast egg and more coffee. Mrs. Monty was as tiny and French as Monty was huge and Canadian. She looked at me sympathetically and gently took the coffee cup out of my hands. I knew Monty would have told her what had happened.

"I will have coming up ze soft-boiled egg, without ze toast," she said. "More coffee?"

I nodded. "Yes, please."

She no longer murmured in dismay that I only consumed "little bits of the this and the that."

As a teen-ager I had wolfed down everything she made, especially her baked toast and eggs with cream, my favorite breakfast. But now, I had explained to her, I had to go without, at least most of the time. Costumes and the camera were unforgiving. So, no toast for me. Or butter, either. She brought the soft-boiled egg over in its blue egg cup, and placed it in front of me, without even a sigh.

"Le voilà," she said. "An egg, *toute seule.*"

Standing, she was the same height as I was sitting, and I looked over to see a twinkle in her eyes, as though waiting for me to feel sorry for a lonely egg, all by itself.

I laughed. "It's all alone, but won't be for long," I said, picking up the spoon and tapping cracks into the shell.

Monty materialized in the kitchen doorway.

"The Packard, miss?" he asked, his long face impassive as always.

"Not for this trip," I said. "How's the Hudson running?"

"Tip-top, of course," he said. I had kept the eleven-year-old car for sentimental reasons. It wasn't impressive or imposing like the Packard, but thanks to Monty's meticulous care, it ran as smoothly as the day my father had bought it.

"Great, thanks!" As soon as I had dispatched the lonely egg, I nipped upstairs and changed into a low-key navy blue dress with a sailor collar. I went through the matching handbag to make sure all my essentials were there and, once outside, put on dark glasses.

The old car hugged the roads that twisted and turned down the hill from my house, and in maybe fifteen minutes I was parking on a side street near the hospital, Cedars of Lebanon, not far from the studios.

Except for the tourists, most of the people in the neighborhood were used to seeing our familiar faces out and about, and I walked from the car to the hospital mostly unnoticed, except for a man coming down the broad stairs who glanced up quickly and then looked down again, flustered. Probably new in town, I thought.

The young woman at the information desk was pleasant, and all business. "Hello, Miss Franklin," she said, as though she'd been expecting me. "How can I help you?"

She gave me Sam Harvey's room number and I went down the hall, wondering if I should have brought him something— flowers, like Arthur said, or, I don't know, a teddy bear. I realized I didn't know him very well at all, and in fact, even though I'd bristled at Max's teasing, I wasn't sure he would want to see me.

Outside Sam's room, I heard voices, one of them Sam's and, I realized, a second one that I recognized. I couldn't make out words, but the gentle baritone was that of an old friend who had also been one of the lucky winners in this business. Moviegoers would have recognized it, too.

Clay West was a singing cowboy, as well known as Gene Autry. He'd been discovered by Gloria Swanson when she visited the Army hospital where he was recuperating from appendicitis after returning from the Great War. He made a couple of pictures with her, and when the talkies came and he was given the chance to sing, he surprised everyone with his strong, mellow voice. "The voice that has a smile in it," one columnist wrote.

He learned to ride horses for his first Western—and that's where this Pennsylvania boy found his true calling. After a series of oaters that featured daring chases at the gallop, saloon fistfights and any number of songs about coyotes, cattle, and lonesome trails, Clay West was one of the highest-paid actors in Hollywood. Even after the crash of '29, people with hardly two coins to rub together would still manage to find the price of admission and get in to see Clay's reassuring presence on screen. He gave them hope.

I waited for a pause in the conversation, and then walked in to see Clay reaching out to smooth Sam's hair as gently as though he were caressing a kitten. Then he leaned over and kissed him tenderly on the forehead.

I stopped dead in my tracks, knowing I wasn't supposed to

have seen this, as Clay sprang backwards away from Sam with a look of sheer terror. Sam's face was a wan mirror of Clay's.

In a town full of good-looking men, Clay West stood out in his own way. He was tall, with broad shoulders, and strong features that shouldn't have gone together at all but somehow did, and especially on the screen. On and off-camera both, he had what people called star quality. In other words, he had It, too. In spades.

Of course I knew he liked men, and also knew that he was good at not stirring up talk—though in this company town, it wasn't exactly a secret. I hadn't realized he even knew Sam, though. The only thing that shocked me now was that he had let his guard down this much.

The look of alarm, even guilt, on Clay's face vanished when he saw it was me.

"Why, it's Frankie," he said warmly, looking pleased, and very relieved.

Sam was too tired and in pain, I could see, to care who was in the room, but he looked surprised to see me nonetheless. "Miss Franklin," he murmured.

"Frankie, please," I said, going to him and putting my hand on his. His torso was snugly bandaged. I could just see the top of the bandage above the hospital sheet.

"I'm so sorry this happened," I said.

"Aw, it's all right, Miss—Frankie," he said with some effort. "The doc said it'll be awhile before I can work again, couple of months."

He stopped, gathered his strength, and added, "Guess I'm off the picture."

I couldn't argue with that. We would have to re-shoot the hotel room scene without him, and he would simply be replaced by some other handsome, hungry young actor.

"If we had the time, we could shoot around you," I said, and then winced at the unintended irony of that phrase. If only I had. Sam noticed, too, and gave me a weak grin.

There was something I could do, I realized. I had enough power with the studio now to do it. "I'll promise you something,

Sam," I said. "The next picture I make, when you're well enough, you'll have a good role in it."

"I—I couldn't ask you—" he started.

I gave Clay a look, and he interrupted Sam. "We don't argue with Miss Franklin," he said soberly. "Looks like you're booked for your next job."

"It's the least I can do," I said. "You have the talent for it.."

Sam nodded and closed his eyes, too tired for more at the moment. Clay reached out and smoothed the young man's silky blond hair again.

I was about to say more but was interrupted by the loud clacking of heels and a chortling voice outside the doorway.

"Hello hello, have I found the party?"

With a sound as attractive as fingernails on a blackboard, her voice preceded her, and then she appeared in the doorway: Virginia Tuttle, powerful purveyor of Hollywood gossip. As always, she was a stylish vision in a fitted navy suit with a silver fox fur thrown over her shoulders. She looked ready to dine at Musso & Frank—or on us.

Chapter Six

Neither Clay nor I was fooled by her sweet smile. Above the red lips were the glittering, merciless eyes of a predator.

"Good morning, Virginia," I said, pleasant but neutral. There was no point in asking what brought her here. Her spies were everywhere. Just like Fixx's.

"Fancy meeting you here," she said, looking me up and down, making me glad I'd taken some trouble with my outfit. I didn't need her writing a story speculating that Frankie Franklin had stopped caring how she looked.

Virginia's sharp gaze then swept around the room, took in Sam, who had closed his eyes, and targeted Clay.

"I thought I might catch up with you and your—friend— here," she said. "I'd heard you had a new roommate. I just didn't expect him to be so … young."

She was not one of the studio publicity people, but a syndicated columnist whose writing appeared in hundreds of papers around the country, and she could kill Clay's career with just one insinuating item in tomorrow's edition. She happened to like me at the moment, although that could change at any time. She could like us, but we weren't her friends. She could like us, but what she loved was the power her words had to elevate or bury.

Now Virginia turned back to me.

"And you, Frankie dear," she said, as silkily as her gravelly voice could manage, "While Clay is coming up with an answer for me, do you have any comments about the, er—occurrence— on the set yesterday?"

It never was wise to drop your guard when Virginia was

around. Since she cared nothing for who any of us really were, it was best to present her with the studio-approved version, and play it to the hilt.

So now I smiled a smile that made the most of the studio's investment in my even, white teeth, as broad as it was artificial. And if she wanted a quote, I'd give her one that served my own purposes. And Clay's.

"I am so glad you asked, Virginia," I declared with that mid-Atlantic accent we all had to practice with our voice teachers. Really, it sounded great, I thought. Too bad she wasn't recording it.

"As you can see," I said, "young Sam here is doing fine, and we are all feeling awfully grateful and happy that he is on the mend. It was just a very unfortunate accident."

Virginia regarded me for a moment, then took out a notebook and wrote down what I had said.

"I had to come to see him, of course, once I knew he was out of danger," I continued, and paused to let her write that down, too.

I glanced at the sleeping Sam, knowing she would see my genuine look of concern, for what it was worth. The next expression on my face was not so genuine, but I wasn't an actress for nothing. Stepping over to Clay, I linked my arm through his possessively.

"And I'm just so very happy that Clay agreed to come with me to visit young Sam," I said, and looked up at him with soft, shining eyes and a look of adoration that stopped just short of cocker spaniel. "He has been my rock."

Picking up the hint, Clay covered my hand with his big mitt and smiled down at me fondly.

Virginia darted a look from Sam to me to Clay and back again, eyes bright as a sparrowhawk's. She shifted her shoulders under the fox stole, patted her marcelled hair and said, "Well, well, well, that's all very sweet. Very, very sweet. I expect I shall see you two around, then."

And she turned and retreated from the field, the battle conceded to us. We could hear the staccato clack of her heels
44

receding down the hospital corridor as she went. Clay and I heaved a mutual sigh of relief.

The next visitor was a large, no-nonsense nurse who filled the doorway in her starched whites.

"This young man needs his rest," she said. "It's time to leave him be for a while."

Clay let himself be herded out of the room, but looked back anxiously.

The nurse's expression softened, and she said, "You can come back when it's visiting hours tonight."

We made our way out of the hospital, walking side by side companionably, pretending we didn't see the stares of patients, even doctors and nurses, as we went by. I continued to smile brightly up at Clay, just in case any of Tuttle's tattlers might be watching.

On a windowed stretch of corridor that finally was empty of people, Clay stopped and turned to me. "Frankie," he said, "about the shooting: How do you think it happened?"

"At the moment, I have no idea," I said. "I just hope Vernon has turned up and explained it to someone. The answer has to be with him."

"I know accidents happen," Clay said, "but from what I've heard, Vern's not generally known for being—well, I just can't see it."

"Neither can I," I said.

"And the question is, was this done on purpose?"

"On purpose," I repeated, thoughtfully. I hadn't seriously considered that someone might have done such a terrible thing deliberately, not even when I was talking to Detective Jameson. "But why? Who? What did they think to accomplish?"

"Could be someone had something against Sam, or Raymond, or you … maybe even against the studio," Clay said. "Someone who wanted to make you or the studio look bad, maybe."

"I guess I did wonder about that, for a second," I said. "But that all strikes me as kind of silly. Melodramatic, you know. Something you'd see in a picture, but not real life. At least it felt that way when the detective was talking to me."

But now that Clay had said it, I did wonder again. Did I have rivals at the studio, other actresses who would go to these lengths to harm me or cause me to harm someone else, just to further their own careers?

"Maybe someone thought that just having this happen would upset you and that's wall all they wanted?" Clay offered.

"At the risk of someone else's life?" I said.

"I didn't say they'd have their saddle cinched on tight," Clay said. "It would have to be someone not thinking straight."

I couldn't imagine anyone well-known who would do something so evil, so—let's be honest—stupid. Carole? Constance? Jean? Myrna? The thought was ridiculous. Not even Joan, who could seem a bit, well, frighteningly driven to succeed. Not Kath, either. If you'd done something she disapproved of, she would take the most direct route and tell you to your face.

Things did happen between rivals, but they were usually off-the-cuff slights, a nasty comment at a party or premier or maybe a drink flung in someone's face. But not a planned "accident." With the work schedules most of us had, there was hardly time to sleep, let alone hatch a plan that could get someone killed.

Unless it was someone not a direct competitor, just someone else unbalanced enough, who had something against me. Something that would throw my career off course, make me look crazy myself, or make the fans come to dislike me.

"Or it could be something as simple as real bullets being in the gun for some other purpose—a close-up, or, I don't know, target practice for fun," Clay said as we started walking again. "And then for some reason it was not reloaded with blanks."

Live ammunition was not unknown in the pictures. When my father had made silent Westerns, they often had cowboys riding into town firing their guns into the air, with real bullets. Just a few years ago, real bullets were fired into the corner of a building Jimmy Cagney had just ducked behind in a gangster movie called *The Public Enemy*. But now, we were supposed to be more careful, I would have thought.

"So we have someone who's careless, or who has harmful

intent, or is … just crazy," I said.

"Or both the last two." Clay looked at me. "Either way, right now the important thing to me is that Sammy's going to be all right."

"Yes," I said. "He seems like a very nice boy."

Clay blushed in a way usually described as like a schoolgirl. "I like him fine," he said almost shyly.

It was my father, Hick Hickenlooper, who had taught Clay to ride. Before he became a stunt coordinator, my dad had been a riding extra who showed up in all kinds of movies, sometimes costumed as a bandit, an Indian, a knight, or a chariot driver. He had been hired for any scene you could think of that involved horses and needed people to handle them.

He also turned out to be very good at teaching novice actors how to ride, and Clay was one of these. Clay was twenty-two then, and very kind to eleven-year-old me, treating me like an amusing, if sometimes irritating, mascot. He also looked out for me like the big brother I never had.

We had never made a picture together, but I knew actresses loved being cast opposite him. Not only did women look exquisitely doll-like in any shot with him, he was a good scene partner. He actually listened, and made anyone he acted with seem cleverer, funnier, nicer, or more dangerous than they actually were.

Many actresses were sorely disappointed when Clay West the male ingenue became Clay West, the Knight of the Open Range, whose pictures only called for him to kiss his horse, Tornado.

I had had a huge crush on him, and in a way still did.

Outside in the bright sun, I put my dark glasses back on and scanned the area. There was Virginia Tuttle, planted on the sidewalk next to her big gray car, writing in her notebook. I nudged Clay, so he would notice her. I heard a deep "Mmm-hmm" and he took my hand.

"C'mon, pardner," I said, giving his big paw a squeeze. "Walk me to my car."

I turned away from Virginia and strode purposefully down the street.

"Is your car really this way?" Clay said, keeping up easily, hand still engulfing mine, and looking, I supposed, for the Packard and Monty.

"Yep," I said. "My old Hudson. Remember it?"

He grinned. "I sure do, honey. It was your dad's."

We turned onto the side street where I'd parked. "Can I give you a lift to yours?" I asked. People in passing vehicles were starting to crane their necks seeing the two of us.

Clay didn't look like a cowboy every day, especially when he was trying not to be noticed. Today, for instance, he had on a smart navy blazer and white trousers, and looked more like the commodore of a yacht club than an old cowpoke. Still, his face and mine were so well-known, heads were turning. I could at least give him the anonymity of my old, unstylish car.

Sometimes people let you go about your business and pretended they didn't notice you, but sometimes being a star was like living in a village where everyone knew you, and forgot that you didn't know them.

"I'm over on North Vermont," he said, getting into the passenger seat.

I made a couple of turns onto the side street and saw, not his "cowboy car," the Cadillac with the longhorns on the front, but his old Ford ranch truck. I glanced at him with a smile. "I see you came incognito, too," I said. "For all the good it did."

"I reckon I could have given that more serious consideration," Clay said. "But I was pretty worried about Sam."

It hit me again: I had done this, albeit unwittingly, to Sam.

"I'm so sorry, Clay," I said. "I'm glad he's going to be all right. He is, right?"

Clay nodded. "He'll need some time, but I've asked him to come stay at the ranch while he recovers," he said. "I'd been trying to get him to move in but he thought we'd both be likely to get in trouble for that. But I don't know that I even care anymore."

"The studio does," I pointed out. "You make them lots and lots of money."

He nodded, but didn't look particularly happy. "They hold

48

this over my head, you know," he said. "I am who I am, but I can't really be who I am as long as I'm in pictures."

"You're describing all of us, Clay," I said wryly.

Before he left my car, I had to ask him something else, though I didn't expect a terribly useful answer.

"Clay," I said, "did Sam mention if he noticed anything on the set before I—before he—before this … happened?"

"He hasn't been able to say much at all," Clay replied. "What he said to you just now was the most he's talked since I've been here."

"Oh," I said. "I hope I didn't tire him too much."

"It's okay," he said. "He'll be happy you came to see him. And when he gets out to the ranch, the fresh air and sun in the valley, playing with the dogs … that'll set him right."

I leaned over to give him a kiss on the cheek, and said, "I hope he deserves you."

Chapter Seven

Back home, I had the rare luxury of an afternoon off. Sort of. I would spend it in my office on the never-ending task of answering fan mail.

I got the same bills as everyone else, and magazines, and catalogs, and the occasional postcard from someone I knew who was traveling—and, each week, a thousand or so letters and cards from fans.

These items were addressed to the studio, mostly, though many also came to my fan club. The letters were overwhelmingly friendly and flattering. Some were odd, of course. There were a number of women and a few men who had advice for me about my hair, my makeup, my clothes, or my acting. There were some who thought I actually lived the stories they saw on the screen.

And there were some who thought they knew me, or even were related to me. Like the guy who wrote letters starting, "Dear Sis," and begged me to come home to him and Ma and Pa. It was all very strange, sometimes sad, sometimes heartbreaking, occasionally alarming. I answered most of them, sent out a lot of signed photos, and reported some to the police.

As I warmed up, making blue-ink loops and ladders on some scrap paper with my Waterman pen, Monty carried in three large cardboard boxes, one after the other. I could see they were filled with cards, letters, and even a few thick envelopes and a couple of small boxes. I couldn't fathom how anyone among the struggling masses could think I needed their gifts, but they sent them anyway.

In one box was a homemade stuffed doll with blonde hair and blue button eyes, wearing a gingham dress that was an impressively faithful copy of the one I had worn in my first starring role as "Little Sarry," a brave pioneer girl who used her wits to get out of all kinds of scrapes. Little Sarry did good deeds and outwitted bad guys in one of 1931's more popular ten-chapter serials, and gave me a chance to learn my craft.

The studio had realized audiences liked me in that kind of role, and my character in *Prairie Princess* was, in fact, a sort of grown-up version of Little Sarry. This reminded me that my next picture was a historical piece, too, and I made a mental note to turn down any scripts for a while where my character had to wear a long skirt or a sunbonnet, lest fans start thinking that was all I could play. I hoped some scenarist out there was writing a story set in a modern city and featuring a charming, deadly female villain.

Another box contained what turned out to be gift-wrapped cookies. I sighed and gave Monty the sign: throw them out. I didn't think I had any Borgias among my fans who wanted to poison me, but one couldn't be too careful. Sweets were always off the menu for me, anyway, and I didn't want to risk anyone else's health at Casa de Frankie.

Before Monty could pick up the box of cookies, Major Bowes padded over and gave it an inquisitive sniff. Then he jumped into the box and rolled around on the mail where the cookies were.

Monty looked down at the cat and raised an eyebrow, then looked at me.

"When he's done," I said.

The three boxes wouldn't have been so bad except that there were already three other boxes sitting in the corner that I hadn't gotten to. I tried to respond to all the letters, following Joan's maxim that the fans were what got us here, and we owed them at least an autographed photo. She followed her own advice, too. When I visited her, I would find her in her office, or maybe by her pool, writing notes and carefully signing "Joan Crawford," a name she'd been given by fans in a magazine contest.

Major Bowes continued to commune with whatever was in the box of cookies, and, watching him writhe around, I wondered if someone had put catnip in one of the envelopes, or even in the cookies. Why someone might put catnip in a cookie was beyond me. But wondering about that made me start wondering about other things, always leading back to the shooting. Wondering why people did inexplicable things sometimes.

What had Clay said? That someone might have done it on purpose, as a way of getting to me, for some reason? That still didn't sit right with me. Anyone on the set who had it in for Raymond would have known the bullet wouldn't have hit him, would have known I wasn't going to aim right at him. Would someone have been targeting Sam himself? Hoping that, in cheating the barrel to the side, I might actually hit him? It all seemed too unlikely.

So if those live rounds had been put in there purposely, I supposed it might have been just to scare me, or maybe to delay the shooting on *Prairie Princess*, something that would cost the studio money. Maybe that was it, I thought: a rival studio? Another director who was envious of Arthur? The more I thought along those lines the more it sounded like just a bad script. My mind threatened to tie itself into a knot, trying to make sense of it.

Hollywood was full of shady types, shysters, conmen, fly-by-night characters of all sorts, looking for people to exploit, running their own scams, not caring who they hurt.

And what if someone did want to hurt me? Threats of harm, of kidnapping, of killing actors and actresses were not unheard of, though they were dealt with as quietly as possible, and kept out of the papers for many reasons, one reason being that more crazy people out there might get ideas if they knew those things happened.

I looked at the boxes again. You'd have to be crazy yourself to assume any of it was safe.

Now Major Bowes was sniffing one of the envelopes with interest. Who knew, maybe there really was catnip in there. He had been seen in enough fan magazines, sitting regally on my lap or peering over my shoulder. Maybe some fan, knowing I had a cat, wanted to send him a treat. Major Bowes, who approached these sessions as though he was the main subject of the photos and the story, would have only seen these tributes as his due.

52

I picked him up, and he shoved the top of his head into my chin, purring.

"You don't get to try any of these, either," I said. Yes, just in the last couple of days I had become more suspicious. I was beginning to resent whoever had disturbed the quick, even rhythm of my days. I was even starting to suspect someone might want to poison my cat.

I picked up the envelope he'd been so interested in—it was from Albuquerque, New Mexico, not a center of catnip-growing as far as I knew—and set it aside with the cookies. We could dispose of them later.

Dealing with these items was also not making a dent in the pile of actual mail that needed to be opened and answered. I felt slightly resentful that I had to do it all myself, but didn't want to interrupt Mrs. Monty's constant stream of tasks to ask for help.

There had been an assistant for a few months, a pretty auburn-haired girl named Selma, sent by an agency, who I thought would work out. But she had turned out mostly to be interested in trying on my clothes and selling tips on my whereabouts and doings to the gossips.

In fact, eventually I discovered that Selma had a small side business charging people for pieces of my life—from my signature, my old laundry receipts, table napkins I'd used, even my used bobby pins, to tidbits of information to people like Virginia Tuttle for their columns. And I had made the mistake of letting her borrow one of my dresses to go out with a new beau—which she took as license to "borrow" other things of mine when I was not looking.

That wasn't all. When by sheer luck I happened to spot a necklace in a pawn shop that looked just like one my mother had given me—because it was the necklace my mother had given me—I realized she had to go. She seemed to have been expecting to get fired, for when informed that her services would no longer be needed, she merely shrugged and stepped into the taxi Mrs. Monty had called to pick her up and take her anywhere within a fifty-mile radius. Where she had gone after that, I didn't care.

The fan mail had piled up in the three weeks since then.

I was looking morosely at the boxes, elbow on desk, chin on hand, when I heard a soft cough. I looked up to see my gardener, Mr. Noguchi, standing in the doorway. That wasn't unusual. He was dressed in his khaki work shirt and pants, holding a basket full of lemons and limes, also not unusual. Like many California gardens, mine boasted several prolific citrus trees. The lemons and limes bore all year round, and Mr. Noguchi regularly brought baskets of them into the house for Mrs. Monty to cook with.

Mr. Noguchi was probably the most dignified man I'd ever met, short, slim and composed, his face and hands bronzed by the sun. He usually spoke with quiet confidence, though admittedly most of these conversations were about garden improvements, which, not knowing anything about gardening except that I loved white flowers, I always agreed to.

He was also always happy to talk to me about his daughter, Kitsuko, who had been studying French literature at Stanford. He was immensely proud of her.

Today, he seemed to have something on his mind. He paused there as though he wanted to speak, but wasn't quite sure how to begin.

"Mr. Noguchi," I said with a smile. "How are you?"

"Me, I'm fine," he said, glancing down quickly, shyly almost. "But you look like you might need some help?" His glance took in all the boxes around me.

I allowed as how I did, wondering if he was offering to help, himself. "But you have plenty to do outside, I'm sure?"

"I do," he agreed. Mr. Noguchi spoke in the flat accents of the Central Valley. He had been raised since the age of eight in Reedley, where his parents had been farming since they came to California, by way of Hawaii, at the turn of the century.

Mr. Noguchi went on, "But you know, Kitsuko has finished her degree, and …"

"Ah," I said. "Not a lot of jobs for a French literature major out there, I suppose?"

"Not a lot of jobs anywhere," he said. "And especially not close to her father. I told her I would miss her if she went far away for a job."

"Aha," I said. "And it's clear I could use some help."

We both glanced around the room, which would only continue to fill up with boxes as I got further behind in handling them.

"Is Kit around?" I said. "I'd be happy to talk to her."

Mr. Noguchi's smile lit up his face. "She's down at the house," he said. "I'll send her right up."

Chapter Eight

Kitsuko, known as Kit, had been away at college for four years, only visiting now and then, and I knew Mr. Noguchi wanted nothing more than to have her nearby—preferably back home—again. I knew he had been lonely since his wife had died, while Kit was in high school.

Not long after he left, I heard a breathless, "Hi!" in the doorway.

"Kit!" I said, and went to her.

Kitsuko Noguchi fairly vibrated with energy, from her stylish bobbed hair to her spectator oxfords, and I was reminded of this as I took her hands in mine, saying, "Let me look at you!" like some fifty-year-old character actress.

I had seen her only rarely while she was in college up north. But I remembered the girl as always in motion, black hair coming out of her pigtails, running anywhere she could have walked. Her parents had enrolled her in athletic pursuits of all kinds while she was growing up: dance, archery, swimming, even baseball, in high school, to channel some of her need to move. On one memorable trip to Malibu, she wouldn't stop pestering a famous surfer to teach her to ride the waves until he finally gave in and let her clamber onto his board.

And now here she was, looking all grown up and comfortable in tailored slacks and a sweater, smiling at me expectantly.

"Dad says you could use some help with the mail," she said, making a discreet effort to look around me at the boxes of packages and envelopes.

"You know, I could," I said, and stood back. "Can you start now?"

She laughed and strode into the room, surveying the task. She asked a couple of questions—does everyone get a note, can we just send photos to some?—and then dove right in.

Within an hour, there were neat stacks of envelopes on my desk, sorted into must-answer, only-wants-a-picture, only-wants-an-autograph, thinks-I'm-the-cat's-pyjamas, and not-sure-what-they-wanted-to-say but took four pages to say it, awaiting my attention.

She had also made several useful suggestions, such as assembling a file of notes, short and sweet, typed on a number of pieces of my stationery. I could sign a bunch of them at once, she could add a Dear Adeline or Jane or Bobbie at the top, and off they'd go. Because after all, Kit pointed out, how many ways could you say thanks for writing and how much you appreciated their coming to see your pictures and best of luck?

I saw the practical wisdom in this—but suggested that she vary the wording ever so slightly, just in case two fans who got identical notes met someday and compared their Frankie missives. It was odd, I thought: while I was going about my business here in California, strangers in Ohio or Kentucky or Vermont were discussing my love life or hairstyle or eye color or who knew what else. I tried not to think about that too much.

Most of my mail contained expressions of affection and admiration, though, and made me smile. There were some that prompted me to answer with a handwritten note. To the fourth-grader from Little Rock who wrote that she wanted to be just like me, I wrote a note thanking her and encouraging her to look to her mother and her teachers as people she should admire and emulate, not just someone she only saw as a twenty-foot-tall image on the screen. There was the ninety-year-old lady from Canoga Park who said she thought of me as the granddaughter she never had, to whom I wrote that I was sure any child would have been lucky to have her for a grandmother and perhaps there were children in her neighborhood who needed one.

I tried to answer these the way my mother would have: Help and care for those around you, because they were far more important than any of the celebrated people you saw on magazine covers. I hoped she'd be happy I was following her example, realized I missed her, and made a note to call her soon.

Kit handed me a small stack of letters that she thought I might want to answer myself. I evicted the catnip-addled Major Bowes from my chair, sat down at my desk, and picked up my pen.

But as we worked, my mind kept returning stubbornly to the shooting and the moment when I fired the gun and saw Sam fall. I kept imagining a different outcome, as though it was a scenario I could rewrite. What if I'd cheated the barrel the other way? What if we had blocked the scene differently? What if I had just checked the gun carefully myself, not trusted entirely to Vernon?

It was a pointless endeavor, but not until Kit had cleared her throat twice, discreetly, did I realize I had stopped and was staring out the window.

She was too polite to ask me directly what had happened on the set. I knew her that well, at least. I also sensed that, if I wanted to talk to her about it, I could.

I did want to talk about it to someone, I decided. I found Detective Jameson's card where I'd thrown it on my desk, gave it to Kit, and asked her to call him. Feeling like I'd done something, anyway, I went back to the letters while she did so.

"Miss Franklin, to what do I owe the pleasure?" said the genial voice when she had gotten him on the line. I was a little surprised. On the phone, he was remarkably more animated than he was in person.

"Have you remembered something that might help with the investigation?"

"Oh—no," I said. "I just—I just want to know if anything further had turned up today."

"These things can take time," he said. "There are a lot of leads to track down. You're sure you don't have anything you want to tell me?"

"Like what?"

"Like maybe it really was you?"

"What?" I exclaimed.

"Well, think about it, Miss Franklin. You were pointing a gun at your ex-husband. Maybe you still have it in for him. Maybe he said something that was just the last straw. Maybe you got

58

someone to stick live rounds in the piece, or maybe you even did it yourself. And then all you had to do was swear convincingly that you didn't know how they got there."

"I never—I—well, I don't, I mean –" I sputtered. I wondered if Raymond had floated that idea with him.

"Maybe you're not that good a shot," he said. I bristled at that. As I had reminded Raymond, I am an excellent shot.

"But detective, there's someone out there who really did this. Maybe by accident, but –"

"Oh, you did it."

"I did not!" I snapped. "Well, I mean, yes, I did pull the trigger, but—"

I heard him chuckling. "Don't worry; you're not a suspect. Whatever else we might discover, your bosses have informed my bosses that you are not a suspect."

That rubbed me the wrong way. I knew I was innocent, of course, but Mr. Fixx would have done the same thing, squashed the investigation, whether or not I was innocent. It bothered me that there might be any doubt about it.

"Everyone loves you," Jameson said. "Even your ex-husband. I sure can't say that about my ex-wife. I just wanted to illustrate the dangers of pushing too hard and making assumptions. And why slow and methodical is the way we have to do these things."

I considered that, then asked what I had called for. "Have you talked to Vernon yet? The prop master?"

"No," Jameson said. "We visited his home. He wasn't there. Neighbors hadn't seen him either coming or going, but because of his irregular and long hours, they often didn't."

"Will you call me if you do talk to him?" I asked. "I'm beside myself wondering."

"No, I'm afraid I can't do that," Jameson said, matter-of-factly. "This isn't the only investigation we're working on, you know. And we wouldn't be able to share the information with you anyway."

"But—"

"I'm sorry, ma'am," he said. "I can tell you're not used to being told no, but no."

I felt frustration welling up, but also slowly realized he was right. I had no formal part in the investigation, unless I knew something I could tell them.

"I'm sorry, Detective," I said. "I feel responsible. Not because I was the one who did it, but because this was—is—my picture. And Sam is a good guy. And I do get impatient with uncertainty."

"Well, patience is essential in my line," he said, not unkindly. "That's why it's a good thing I'm the gumshoe and you're the movie star."

And as such, I thought, I'd better get back to the work of handling the fan mail.

It took us an hour or so to write notes to a dozen fans, Kit tapping away at the Royal typewriter, handing the notes off to me to sign with my fountain pen. Of course I had practiced my signature long ago, settling on one with two intertwined capital Fs, one above the other.

I signed the last note and said, "Kit, would you like to help me learn my lines for the next scene we'll be doing when we get back to shooting?"

"Sure," she said.

I picked up my copy of the sides, the pages with my lines, and thumbed through them.

"Where were we?" I said to myself. "Where the head of the Dupree gang threatens me with burning my house and barn down?" Raymond was playing Dupree. "Okay, yes. Here, you read his lines, and we'll see if I've learned mine."

"Right," Kit said, sitting a little straighter in her chair and clearing her throat.

"Nice place you've got here, little lady," she said, lowering her voice to sound threatening. "We wouldn't want nothin' bad to happen to it."

"Mr. Dupree, I think I have said just about all there is to say to you," I responded assertively. "You will find that, as with my father—"

"—Uncle—" Kit corrected.

"Right. Uncle," I said. "You will find that as with my uncle, I do not respond well to threats."

I suppose anyone looking in at us would have laughed to see the slim Japanese girl with the Louise Brooks bob growling her way through the bad guy's lines. But she was warming to it.

Kit gave a sinister chuckle. "It don't have to be a threat. I can be real nice." Then she made a face and in her own voice said, "This Dupree is a real creep."

I ignored the side comment and went on.

"You know your problem, Dupree?" I said with determination. "No one's ever stood up to you, not really. But someone's got to. And it might as well be me."

I stopped, thinking. Distracted again.

Kit said, "The next line is, 'So clear out now.'"

"I know, Kit, sorry," I said. "Hang on a second."

The line was sticking with me: It might as well be me. Jameson said they hadn't talked to Vernon yet. They hadn't yet found him at home, and had other investigations to conduct. But if no one else had been able to find him and talk to him, I thought, it might as well be me.

Chapter Nine

"**O**w!" Something was poking me in the back.

The costume designer winced in sympathy. "Sorry," he said around the pins between his lips. He took them out and added, "You were slouching."

I gave an impatient sigh. "My mind's on something I need to do after this," I said. "I guess I slouch when I think."

Fittings were essential but not my favorite part of the job. It meant standing still for too long. And sometimes getting stuck with pins. I did like wearing beautiful things, though, and especially those made by Charlie Torres. The bearish, bearded Texan, who was never seen without his signature polka-dot bowtie, created the most beautiful costumes.

"Oh, actresses are being paid to think now?" Charlie said.

I stuck out my tongue at him and tried to stand straighter in the diaphanous white silk gown. We were in the wardrobe department, surrounded by racks of costumes, sketches on worktables and bins of fabric and trims. High windows let in the daylight Charlie demanded, the better to see true color and texture.

"I don't like this one," he said to an assistant, handing her the silk ribbon he had been working with. "Bring me that gold braid there."

This was the gown I would wear to play Napoleon Bonaparte's wife, the Empress Josephine—at least, my version of her, in a picture they were calling *Martinique's Rose*.

We had been having a trying time finding an actor to play the short Emperor, because none of the really short ones wanted to reveal their lack of height onscreen. Meanwhile, the other preparations continued. I wouldn't really feel the character until the costumes were fitted, the wigs styled, and I also had tried on the shoes. The shoes were usually what helped me most: so much of the character was in the walk.

"How much longer is this going to take, Charlie?" I asked.

"It takes as long as it takes, honey," he said, now fiddling with the way the yards of gauzy fabric fell around me. "They want to shoot all the costumes on you right after *Princess* wraps, and we've still got to work out details on the coronation robe."

I suppressed a groan. I had found that Vernon hadn't shown up to work this morning, and I had decided to visit his house, telling myself I was just concerned because *Prairie Princess* was my picture and I needed to be concerned with everyone on my pictures.

Detective Jameson had said Vernon wasn't home when they'd visited. But, I thought, maybe the police simply hadn't been there at the right time. Like the detective had said, this wasn't their only investigation, and, after all, no one had died. No one at the studio seemed to be concerned. It could be that Fixx had bribed the police to the point where Jameson was just stringing me along, or that the publicity people had spirited Vernon away so that no one could talk to him.

"Frankie?" Charlie said, startling me.

"Oh, sorry, what?" I asked.

"I said don't worry about the color of this fabric right now," the designer said. "It's not the white I would use if you had your own hair color. But when they put you in the brunette wig, it will be stunning."

"Oh," I said again, a little absently, thinking I should really care more about that sort of thing. "I'm sure it'll be great."

Finally Charlie released me from the onerous task of standing still while being measured for some of the most beautiful gowns in the world, and I jumped off the fitting stool and made a beeline for my own clothes, then dashed out to the curb and my trusty Hudson.

In direct defiance of my contract, which demanded I dress beautifully whenever leaving the house, I had thrown on khaki trousers, loafers, and a brown sweater, hoping the combination of the old car and this outfit might be a sort of camouflage.

I eased the convertible onto Santa Monica Boulevard and drove past antique shops and filling stations, empty lots and billboards. The town had changed since I was a kid. Now there were buildings and oil wells sprouting up where fields of beans used to grow. There was even an oil derrick in the middle of La Cienega Boulevard, put there right in the middle of a bean field before the street was extended from Santa Monica to Sunset. But not that many of the people who lived here now remembered the old city. Now, almost everyone came from somewhere else.

People from other places liked to complain that there were no seasons here. But the signs were there if you knew what to look for: shorter or longer days, warmer or cooler nights, slight changes in the sky, different kinds of clouds. In the fall, there was the smell of burning leaves from the trees people planted if they really wanted to see fall color. The fires added to the general haze in the basin, but it smelled good. Almost as good as when they were baking over at the Wonder Bread factory in Beverly Hills.

Like many of those who worked in pictures, Vernon Stone lived near the studios, in Culver City. Even some bigshot producers lived close enough to walk to work. Monty and I had given Vernon a ride home from a party once, and just to be sure I had the right place, I checked the address Kit had looked up for me, without my even asking her, in the phone book.

The homes in Vernon's neighborhood featured houses in every style imaginable, just as mine did, but only smaller: tiny Italian villas next to Spanish adobes next to half-timbered Tudors, and a few New England saltboxes thrown in for good measure.

I knew I had the right place when I saw what appeared to be several cottages out of a Grimm's fairy tale. Except for the driveways and garages, they could have come from a medieval village—if the medieval village had gardens full of big-leaved tropical plants, flowers in hot reds and yellows, and even a cactus or two.

Vern's house had a round turret with a conical roof housing

64

the stairway, painted brown like the rest of the house. I had to smile when I saw it. I parked and got out of the car, looking around for signs of life as I went up the walk to the front door. The afternoon *Call* was on the front step, and I picked it up and knocked on the door. No answer. I stood there, thinking. I didn't have any idea where he would be if not at home, but was unwilling just to turn and walk away now that I was here.

I stepped off the front porch, wondering if he might be in the back yard, and went around to the side of the house, which was bigger than it looked from the street. The late afternoon quiet spoke of kids herded indoors to do their homework, mothers making dinner, fathers coming home from jobs they were lucky to have. There went some of them now, cars driven by tired-looking men wanting dinner.

Stepping stones were set in crushed rock along the side of the house, where everything seemed quiet. I don't know what I expected to find; it just seemed like any other place, closed up while its occupant was at work. As I stood there thinking, I heard a small sound from inside. A cat? I heard it again. Definitely a cat. Maybe Vernon was at home after all, hiding out. Or had left his cat there … for how long? It might have been days. The little guy would be hungry.

The front door of the house next to Vernon's opened with a squeak and then closed with a bang, and a woman's voice called, "Ratto!"

That was an odd name for a kid, I thought. The voice was loud, so loud that it brought the term "fishwife" to mind. I walked out to the sidewalk to see who had a set of pipes like that.

A small, round woman strode purposefully toward me in sturdy black oxfords. Her clothes were remarkable for the way her flowered housedress clashed with her plaid apron. Her gray hair had been wrangled into a bun at the back of her neck, and she wore steel-rimmed glasses that magnified dark brown eyes and gave her an owlish look. Getting closer, she stopped and smiled a surprisingly sweet smile. Sometimes it's okay to be recognized.

"You're Frankie Franklin," she said in a voice I could have

heard a block away. She had an accent I couldn't quite peg—not Spanish, not Italian. She finished drying off her hands on a cotton towel she was carrying, and extended the right one to me. I shook it.

"I'm Fernanda Botelho. Are you and Vernon friends?" she asked.

"I—yes, you could say that," I said. "We've worked together a bit."

"But you're not the girlfriend."

"No." She didn't seem to find it odd that I was there, so that saved me any further explaining.

"Yeah, I saw in the gossip rags you have a boyfriend already, writes music," she said. "He's good-looking. Short."

"Thanks. And he's about my height."

"Vernon and his girlfriend, *ecch*, they make a lot of noise," Fernanda Botelho said, nodding her head. "A lot."

"Like ... parties?" I wondered how loud talking could bother her, considering her own natural volume, which seemed pitched to be heard over the noise of a freight train or large machines on a factory floor.

She chuckled. "Party of two, maybe. It's a good thing I have an open mind and am a woman of the world. Nothing embarrasses me."

"Oh," I said, and then, as I realized what she meant, "*Oh*."

She nodded, happy I'd finally caught her drift. "You neither, I guess, in your business," she said. "It's like a two-person Garden of Allah in there. Even when they close the windows."

Now I chuckled, picturing the Garden, the slightly scandalous place on Sunset, where Max, in fact, lived. With villas and bungalows set among lush plantings, Allah's sometimes seemed like a zoological garden habitat for creative types, where they could either live quietly or behave as outrageously as they wanted, away from most of the public's prying eyes.

Tenants and visitors at the Garden kept an all-day, all-night party going, threw themselves or each other into the pool, called down to Schwab's for more booze ... I imagined the debauchery scaled down to two, and got Mrs. Botelho's drift.

Mrs. Botelho hastened to add, "It's all right with me," she said. "He's never had more than one girl at a time after his wife left him."

"So you've never complained to the landlord," I said.

Mrs. Botelho laughed. "I am the landlord," she said. "Landlady, whatever you want to call it. Nah, he's a good tenant otherwise. And my house is the closest, so if it doesn't bother me …"

I nodded. "What about the girlfriend?"

"The brunette? Skinny little thing," she said, adding something emphatic in her own language, which I now realized was Portuguese. "She hasn't shown up for a while either. Not for a couple of days."

The day of the shooting, I wondered?

"What was that, Wednesday? Maybe they ran off to Reno to get married, him and … Annie, I think that's her name."

Mrs. Botelho shrugged.

"It sounded like she made him very, very happy," she said. "At least until a few days ago. There was a commotion. They even came outside yelling, but I was on the telephone with my sister in Providence, long-distance, bad connection, so I was thinking about that and didn't hear what they were saying."

"Really?" I said, intrigued, and glad I that I didn't have to urge her to keep talking. She seemed to have no problem with talking.

"All I could tell was, Vern sounded like he was trying to get her to talk to him, you know how men do when you don't feel like talking, won't leave you alone? But loud. Like he was mad. Like maybe they'd kiss and make up later, and run off and get married."

"Did you say anything to them?" I asked.

"Nah, I don't care, live and let live," she said, with another shrug. "They didn't see me anyway, got into his car still arguing. I left right after to go spend the night with my other sister, she lives in Torrance, she's sick all the time."

She shook her head, then shrugged and chuckled to herself. "Vernon pays the rent on time, wasn't a nuisance at all until this girl came along, so I never got in the habit of asking him questions. We'll see, we'll see … "

She shrugged, having exhausted all speculation about her tenant for now. She looked up and down the street. "Now I need to find Ratto."

"Ratto?"

"My cat. He leaves for five minutes and I get a mouse in the house. I need him to do his job, what does he think I keep him around for?"

I'd heard a cat in Vernon's house, I told her.

"Oh yeah? No big surprise to me," Mrs. Botelho said, starting off toward the house, exasperated. "He fed Ratto. I told him, if you feed him, he'll lose his taste for mice. But Vernon would just give me that sweet smile and keep doing it. I better go in and see where he's hiding out."

She went to the door and tried it, found it locked, then pulled out a skeleton key and let herself in. I stood on the walk for a moment, consumed with curiosity and new questions. Had Vernon even been on the set when the accident happened? I had just assumed he had been. Maybe he'd left even before that, if there was trouble with a girlfriend.

I had never been inside his house. Curiosity consumed me, and I went inside.

Chapter Ten

Mrs. Botelho had left the door ajar—perhaps she didn't want to be seen to have slammed it on me—and I made a show of joining her, calling, "I'll help you look for Ratto!"

The house was cozy with dark, shadowy corners and nice, clean-lined furniture arranged with precision, no dust or clutter anywhere. There was a half-finished jigsaw puzzle, a landscape, on the dining room table, but no other indications that anything had been left unattended or undone. Magazines were stacked neatly on the coffee table, books organized by subject and author on the bookshelves flanking the cold fireplace. If a very disciplined elf happened to live in Culver City, I could imagine him living here.

Mrs. Botelho had gone to the back of the house, calling the cat. I poked around downstairs for show, until I couldn't stand it anymore. To be honest, I was as fascinated by her description of Vernon and his paramour's activities as any of my fans were about my own love life. I went up the stairs and into the bedroom, calling Ratto, too, mostly to cover the fact that I was blatantly snooping.

If I had expected signs of a wild orgy, the bedroom would have disappointed. Oh, there were scarves tied to a couple of the bedposts and I could guess what that was about, but after listening to Mrs. Botelho, it didn't shock me. Otherwise, the bedroom was as neat as the rest of the house. Not even a used teacup or cocktail glass left on a table. I was about to leave when I heard a muffled meow.

"Aha," I said, getting on hands and knees to peer under the bed. When my vision adjusted to the darkness, I saw two glowing yellow eyes an arm's length away–and a hat box, closer than that. There was no good reason for it, but unable to stop myself, I pulled the box out and lifted the lid. I felt myself blush as I saw the stack of magazines, the one on top featuring a girl falling out of her lingerie under the words "Bedtime Tales." I replaced the lid hastily and shoved the box back under the bed.

I spoke to the glowing eyes. "Ratto, you naughty boy. You're way too young to be reading this stuff."

Continuing to talk nonsense to the cat, telling him he was actually a very good boy for staying where he was, I reached farther under the bed, hoping to grab him by the scruff of the neck. But he edged away. I reached more. He edged more.

And then my hand encountered something else on the hardwood floor, something silk—I knew that texture by touch.

The cat forgotten for a moment, I pulled the bit of fabric out and held it up. It was a camisole, dark green silk with deep red roses embroidered along the front and back top borders and intricate lace edging the bottom hem.

It was fine silk, and a lovely piece of workmanship, hand-sewn with nearly invisible stitches, with a small, perfect honeybee embroidered on the back, below one of the shoulder straps. It was more ladylike and much nicer than anything on the covers of those magazines in the hatbox. And at least as nice as anything I owned.

As a kid, I had protested strenuously against every frilly, fancy item of clothing my mother tried to put on me. But a few months of dressing up for work had changed that. I had not only come to appreciate the finest costumes Fortune Pictures had designed for me, I also found that I loved custom-made lingerie. What a revelation: It didn't all have to have itchy lace! All my "unmentionables" now were sewn by a lady with a shop on Pico Boulevard. Camisole, bras and tap pants, slips … I even had fittings for my nightgowns. I loved the feel of silk and satin under my hand and also how it looked and felt, and never ceased to marvel at the skill it took to hand-stitch those seams.

So I immediately recognized that this camisole wasn't something a shop girl or bit player could afford, not unless they saved up for months. Maybe Vern bought things like this for his girlfriends? I suspected this had been part of a set, and that there had been something like tap pants to go with it. With Mrs. Botelho's description of Vernon and the girlfriend's rather, er, strenuous relationship, I could easily picture the delicate bit of silk being flung off and kicked under the bed during a night of passion.

Hearing Mrs. Botelho's solid tread on the stair, I shoved the camisole back under the bed and called over my shoulder, "I've found him!"

I made another grab for the cat, who hissed and burst from his hiding place, a striped, orange blur streaking past Mrs. Botelho just as she reached the doorway. She stomped her foot at him as he disappeared down the stairs.

"That's right, you better get home and catch that mouse, you good-for-nothing!"

We went down the stairs to the front door and she turned to me with a smile, one cat-wrangler to another. "Don't ever treat cats too nice. Makes them lazy."

With a sense of relief I realized she hadn't asked why I had turned up on Vernon's doorstep. And now, after finding that Vernon wasn't around to be talked to, I hadn't even learned anything useful about the accident or even where he was.

I watched her go up her own walk and shake her fist in mock anger at Ratto, who rubbed against her thick-stockinged ankle when she got to him, clearly unimpressed by her shouting and stomping. As I drove away I saw her in the kitchen window with the cat in her arms, letting him shove his head up under her chin. At least one of us had found what we were looking for in Vernon's house.

The sun was sinking into the Pacific as I drove up the winding streets of Beachwood Canyon, and the windows of my house were aglow and welcoming when I arrived home. I could hear Mrs. Monty in the kitchen as I went through the house to the pool patio and found Max in a wicker chair, staring thoughtfully out toward the dusky hills, pipe in his mouth, pencil in hand and several pages of sheet music on his lap.

He looked up when I neared him, and then, eyes on mine, tossed the papers onto the chair next to his. His comic timing was perfect, and I had to laugh.

"Do we make too much noise?" I asked, throwing a leg over his lap and sitting facing him.

He put the pipe down and pulled me close. "What, you mean like this?" He growled playfully in my ear. "Probably."

Further developments were interrupted by Mrs. Monty appearing at the patio doors.

"Madame, ze phone is for you. It is Philomena Mink."

I gave Max a quick kiss and got off his lap, ignoring his groan. He started tidying up the crumpled sheets of music, grabbing one page that had been caught by a breeze and was heading for the pool. I took the phone Mrs. Monty had brought out from the house on its long cord.

"Hey, dollface."

No one sounds like my studio publicist, Philomena Mink. She was from New York, but from Australia before she was from New York. Her accent was a strange collision of sounds and sayings. Though no written word can quite capture the sound, "dollface" came out sounding like "dole-fice."

"Hey, dollface, how are you?" she asked. "I'd be there in person but I'm on the massage table and you know how Sven hates when I cancel an appointment."

Mass-age table. I pictured the tall, blond, muscular Sven having to work around her elbow as Philomena grasped the receiver in her perfectly manicured fingers.

"I'm fine, Phil," I said. "Sam's also doing better." Just in case she cared.

"I heard. I talked to Mr. Fixx a little while ago. Mr. Wiseman called him."

Sam wasn't her client, so Phil was only so interested. But if Mr. Wiseman, the head of the whole damn studio, had called Phil's boss, the head of publicity, that was something to which she'd pay close attention.

My guard went up. "And how is dear Mr. Wiseman?" I asked.

"Worried, I'm told," Phil said. "The gossips are sniffing

around. They know Clay's spent considerable time at the hospital with Sam."

"I saw Clay there myself," I said. "And Sam. I think we gave Virginia Tuttle, at least, something else to think about."

"We heard," Philomena said. I wondered who snitched. "But she's not the only one snooping around now. That's why they need your help, doll," Philomena said. "They need your help tomorrow."

"My help?" I said. "I should think I've done enough, shooting Sam."

"It was an accident."

"How do you know?"

"By the time Mr. Fixx is done fixing, believe me, it'll officially be an accident," she said.

"Well, then, everything's jake," I said, glancing over at Max and rolling my eyes.

"Except for what they need you to do."

Here it comes, I thought. They'll have Clay and me look like more of a romance. We'll be ordered to go out to be seen at the Trocadero, go riding in the hills, or take a fishing trip where I can "accidentally" fall in the stream and he'd pull me out, or —

"They want you and Clay to get married."

"Excuse me?"

As though addressing a particularly dim child, she repeated slowly, "They want you and Clay to get married. Tomorrow."

"Phil, Clay likes boys."

"Precisely."

"Phil, I don't think this is a good idea," I said, wondering why I was even arguing the case, or even particularly surprised. "Lavender marriages" were quite common in our community. They were one of the ways in which the studios carefully managed the stories of our private lives. The studios would do anything to keep those rivers of audience money from drying up. Usually they would find a relative unknown to marry off to a star, but I had gone and given them ideas with my performance for Virginia Tuttle at the hospital.

Our contracts dictated how we could dress and how we

should behave. Everything we did was supposed to fit the life stories the studios fabricated for us and peddled to *Photoplay* ("Clay West, Real-Life Cowboy") or *Modern Screen* ("The Frankie Franklin You Don't Know!").

Mostly, we played along— it was the price of success. I had played along since the beginning, because I had never felt the need to rebel—until now. Going along with this just felt wrong. I knew Clay wouldn't agree to it, either.

Over my protests, Philomena kept talking.

"They'll have the Honeymoon Express revving up on the runway tomorrow at ten," Phil said. "I'll be at your place at nine."

"Phil, if Clay was going to marry anyone, it would be Sam," I said. "If Sam was a girl. Or if they could get married anywhere. Or if—you know what I mean."

"It was the best arrangement I could come up with on short notice," Philomena said. "And Sam won't mind. Be ready at nine."

And Philomena hung up.

I put the phone back in the cradle and handed the whole thing back to Mrs. Monty. As she walked away, I stood there biting my lower lip, thinking. It was true I had given Virginia Tuttle the best impression I could of being smitten with Clay, and it would make a great story. I could see it now: Frankie Franklin suddenly discovers true love with a man who was actually a childhood friend. It would be the perfect way to preserve Clay's image, whether or not he wanted to do it.

But Clay, while being discreet, had never tried to present himself as something he wasn't, and I felt sure he wasn't about to start now.

Clay might be at the hospital visiting Sam, or out at his ranch in the Valley, where he'd moved because Hollywood was getting too crowded.

I ran after Mrs. Monty, took back the telephone, and dialed the ranch. Clay's housekeeper, Mrs. Garcia, answered and said he was meeting with his architect on plans for the new barn.

"Hi, Clay," I said when he came on the line. "How's the horse palace coming along?

"Just fine, honey," he said. "We'll have a barn-warming shindig when it's done."

"You seem awfully calm, considering," I said. "You heard from the studio?"

"I did, honey," Clay said. "I love you and all, you know I do, but —"

"There's something to be said for having your own standards."

"Right. I couldn't do that to you," Clay said.

"I couldn't do that to you, either," I said. "Marrying me would be the biggest mistake of your life."

"That's what I thought, too," he said kindly. "No offense, you understand."

"None taken," I said. "And I want you to know, I think I have a way out."

"You do?"

I did. A plan of my own had presented itself, fully formed, surprising even me.

"Yes, but I'll have to tell you later. A bit later," I said.

"Don't do anything foolish, now," he said, with a chuckle.

"Who, me?"

I hung up the phone and walked over to Max, who was looking at me with narrowed eyes. "You look like you're plotting something," he said.

"Indeed I am," I said. I got closer, and closer still, until I could smell his pipe tobacco and see the ironing creases in his shirt. I put my arms around his neck, nuzzled the stubble on his chin and breathed into his ear, "So, big boy, you know the question you've been asking me every week for a year?"

"What question would that be?" he said, brow furrowed as though thinking hard. "Oh! Right, now I remember."

He cleared his throat, and said, "The one that goes, 'Frankie Franklin, will you marry me?' That you always say no to?"

"Yes, that's the one," I said. "Ask me again."

Max cleared his throat, and asked me again. "Frankie Franklin, despite all the times you have told me no, dashing my hopes week after week ... will you marry me?"

"Yes!" I said, and surprised myself with my own enthusiasm. Now that it had been said out loud, I realized being married to Max was something I really did want.

He gave me a skeptical look. "You've always said no," he said. "Is this a trick?"

In answer, I took his face between my hands and kissed him, then went off to find Kit. Max followed. He had gotten the main drift of my conversation with Philomena, and now was asking things like when and where, and what would we do when Philomena showed up here at nine tomorrow morning?

"We won't be here," I said. "Just leave it to me."

I found Kit on the tennis court in a trim white tennis outfit, slamming balls against the wall with powerful swings of her racket. She stopped when she saw me—normally she'd be off at this hour, but now all her attention was for me. The ball bounced off into a corner.

"What's up, boss?"

"Kit, do you know if Pancho's in town? We're gonna need her and her plane."

Sometimes it's good to have a friend with a plane, who can fly fast. Pancho Barnes was that kind of friend. She was a few years older than me, and we had ridden horses together and gotten into and out of some hilarious, sometimes scary, situations. She had no fear on a horse or in the air, and had even become a stunt pilot, flying in pictures like *Hell's Angels*.

She had bought 180 acres of land out in the desert a few months ago, and had big plans for the property. I thought she might be out there, but I hoped Kit could reach her, and that she was near her plane and had time to help me out.

"Panch, it's Frankie," I said when Kit had gotten her on the line.

"Hey, kiddo, when are you gonna start up flying lessons with me again?"

"Soon, I promise," I said. "But now I need your help."

"Name it, sugar," she said.

"Can you fly me and Max to Yuma? I need to get married."

"I thought you were always careful, kiddo," she said, sounding disappointed in me.

"Oh—no. No, no, no, it's not like that," I said hastily, blushing a little. I explained the pickle Clay and I were in. Pancho caught on quickly.

"So you're going to get the jump on them," she said, with a chuckle. "Sure, I can do it. When?"

"Tomorrow morning?" I asked. "Burbank, at seven? There's a grand in it for you."

"Don't insult me like that," Pancho said in mock indignation. "I'd do it for free just for the hell of it—or maybe for the price of the fuel. Either way, you got it, babe. Seven, tomorrow morning, Burbank airport," Pancho said. I could hear her laughing as she hung up.

Now, where was Max? I heard a tune being picked out on the piano, the way it sounded when he was working out a musical idea. When I came in he glanced at me with a small smile.

"What's that?" I said. "Something new?"

"Yeah," he said, looking off into the middle distance and adding chords to the tune, which had a sound I could only describe as wistful. "I'm thinking of calling it 'Frankie's Not the Marrying Kind.'"

He played a few more bars while I tried to think of what to say to that. Finally I asked, "Do you not want to do this?"

"Oh, I do," he said, stopping and fixing me with the big brown eyes. "It's you I don't know about. Is this just a quick way to get out of a tight spot? Is it something you'll come to regret?"

I swallowed. Having realized I really did want to marry Max—how could I not have said yes sooner?—I was surprised and a little hurt to think he might not want me.

He regarded me for a moment, not unkindly. "Oh, I'll go through with it; it's what I want. But … this is not quite the way I'd pictured it."

I looked down at my shoes. It hadn't occurred to me he'd be anything but delighted. He had asked every week for nearly a year. And he was right that I wouldn't have thought of it if Philomena hadn't called. But now that I knew I wanted it, I also knew that I wouldn't change my mind.

Sitting next to him on the piano bench, I watched him play a few more bars, and finally said, "One thing you need to know about me: If I make a promise, I keep it. When I promise … all that stuff … tomorrow, I will mean it. And I will mean it forever. Do you see?"

Max stopped playing and gave me a rueful grin. "With you, sweetheart, I'll take whatever I can get."

But he wouldn't stay the night. A few minutes later I heard the Auburn's engine start up with a growl, then grow fainter as Max took the twists and turns down the hill, and then fade away completely. I knew he was on his way to the place he still kept at the Garden of Allah just a short way up Sunset. Maybe he just needed to think, regroup, or turn the Garden's twenty-four-hour cocktail hour into an impromptu bachelor party. He could find any number of companions—Bankhead or Benchley, Flynn or Colman—willing to help him celebrate. And if he indulged in anything besides drinking, singing and swimming on his last night of freedom, I didn't want to know. On the other hand, deep down I knew he wouldn't. He wasn't Raymond, after all.

Chapter Eleven

Yuma, Arizona, was where people in the pictures went when they wanted to get married now, today, immediately, without waiting the three days required in California. The three-day waiting period was also known as "the gin law," the purpose of which was to give people bent on instant matrimony the chance to sober up and change their minds.

Loretta Young had started it. She was practically a child, just seventeen, when she eloped to Yuma and entered into a marriage that lasted about a minute. Others had found it convenient, and a good way to pretend you didn't want attention. Just across the state line, Yuma was close enough to fly in, get married early in the morning and be home in time for a late lunch and the morning papers' deadlines.

Pilot Paul Mantz ferried so many couples to Yuma for quickie weddings that his plane had become known as the Honeymoon Express. And if Philomena wanted to please her boss, Clay and I would be the latest.

We were supposed to be collected by Philomena at nine and meet Mantz at Burbank, but instead it was Max and me being driven there at all deliberate speed, just as the first rays of the sun crept toward the HOLLYWOODLAND sign.

We arrived at the airfield right at seven, and, true to her word, there was Pancho, waiting next to her Lockheed Vega, a chunky silver dragonfly of a plane, like Mantz's. She was dressed in her customary jodhpurs, leather jacket and beret, and had a big black cigar clamped between her teeth. Her round face lit up when she saw me. She gave me a bear hug in greeting and nodded at Max appreciatively. I'd forgotten she hadn't met him yet. Max grinned at her affably.

"He's mine, sister, so don't be getting any ideas," I said.

Pancho grinned at me. "You don't have to worry, Frankie," she said. "Possession is nine-tenths of the law. And if you're ready, let's mount up."

We boarded the plane, and found a bottle of whiskey and another of champagne tucked into a picnic basket. Pancho grinned. "One for before, and one for after. The bubbly will have to be chilled, of course. My best stuff—consider it a wedding present."

Pancho was one of a kind. Rather, one of many kinds: a former debutante, a former gun runner, an excellent horsewoman, and legendary party-thrower, she had an eye for good-looking young men. Sometimes she liked to arm-wrestle them before she pounced.

She had even formed the first stunt pilots' union a few years ago. Thinking of her sense of humor as well as skill, I hoped she wouldn't throw in any barrel rolls or loop-the-loops into this trip just to celebrate. I wasn't sure you could do that in a plane like this, but I wouldn't put anything past Pancho.

"Hey kiddo," Pancho shouted as the Vega's propeller started rotating, slowly at first and then picking up speed, roaring. "You gonna tell him your real name?"

"You mean Frances?" I shouted back.

"No—Hickenlooper!"

Max gave me a startled look.

I saw him mouth, "Hickenlooper?" but the sound was drowned by engine noise. I thought we'd talked about everything, but I guess there were some things I had left out.

The Vega rumbled down the runway, left the ground and took to the sky, and the awakening city dropped away beneath us. Feeling the exhilaration I always did when a plane took off, I looked out the window under the broad awning of the wing, watching the houses and roads get smaller and smaller and fewer and fewer until there was only desert below, unrolling to the soundtrack of the sturdy plane's purring engine. We seemed to be making good time, and why not: Pancho didn't fool around when she had somewhere to be.

I was feeling wound up. It's a given that brides are nervous on their wedding day, but this was different. Most brides weren't eloping to evade a different marriage altogether, proposed not by the groom but by their bosses. I wasn't worried much about the studio's reaction. They would work it into the story they'd created for me, and look elsewhere for a willing starlet or somebody's secretary to marry off to Clay—if he would go along with it. I didn't expect he'd go along with it any more than he would have with me, but you never knew.

As the silver plane winged its way over the desert, I also thought about Vernon, worrying that mental splinter, wondering about the girl, Ann or Annie. Maybe they really had taken off together. Maybe that's why Vernon couldn't be found on the set, because he'd eloped.

I chuckled suddenly and Max looked over. "What?"

"Vernon's landlady was speculating that Vernon and his girlfriend might have run off to get married," I said. "She said Reno, but wouldn't it be funny if Vernon and his girlfriend were also going to Yuma to get married, and we ran into them there?"

"That would be quite the coincidence."

The valleys and mountain ranges slid by, mile after mile, with Max looking out the window on one side and me on the other. We were dressed for the photographer who would capture the wedding: him in his stylish gray pinstripes, me in my shawl-collared navy suit and a white ascot with a swirly "F" embroidered on it. The bottles of booze lay stashed, untouched, in their picnic basket under a seat. I appreciated Pancho's gesture, but it was a little early to start drinking, wedding day or no.

Eventually, Pancho sighted the airfield at Yuma, and soon we were on the ground with the car and driver Kit had arranged waiting to take us to the courthouse. When the car pulled to the curb, Max took my hand and kissed it, then smiled encouragingly at me. I found myself smiling a huge, giddy smile in response. He got out and opened the door for me. I clamped my cloche hat onto my head, got out and strode with purpose to the courthouse, nearly dragging Max along by the hand.

The building was appropriately imposing and dignified, but the master of ceremonies for this solemn occasion made me think of one of the old medicine-show fellows who would bark at the crowd and sell them bottles of elixirs.

Judge Freeman, we had heard, had performed thousands of marriage ceremonies and he had it down to a system. He was tallish, with what had once been red hair, now fading with age, and would have done well portraying small-town dignitaries in the pictures. When he met us in the courthouse he clasped my hand in a slightly damp grip and looked into my eyes with a practiced sincerity and said, "My dear, I am so pleased to meet you, and especially on this momentous day."

Then he turned to Max, and gave him the same treatment. Max looked as though he were trying very hard not to laugh.

"Now I understand you two are here to conduct some important business with me?" he said solemnly but brightly.

The important business took about five minutes in which we said all the usual things about promising to love and honor— though I balked at "obey."

"I'm not saying that," I said, and even though Max looked unperturbed, I said, "Sorry."

He was taking it well, I thought. It occurred to me just before the do-you-take-this-man part that I had never asked him what kind of a wedding he had imagined when he asked me every week. I was pretty sure it wasn't this.

It wouldn't have been my first choice, either. Other, more romantic settings flashed through my mind: a picturesque French village, a summer garden, the ballroom of a grand hotel ...

"Do you take this man to be your lawfully wedded husband?" the judge said, breaking into my reverie, and I realized it was the second time he'd said it. He now paused, eyebrows raised.

Max was also looking at me with the beginnings of alarm, as though wondering if, after having gone to such lengths to get him here, I was going to back out.

"Oh!" I said. "Yes! I mean, I do!"

Max grinned, and turned to Judge Freeman. "You didn't ask if there was a ring," he prompted.

Judge Freeman stopped, and raised his bushy eyebrows expectantly.

I hadn't even thought about that part, not even to ask if there was somewhere nearby where we could obtain them. It wouldn't have surprised me to see a wedding-ring concession stand right there in the courthouse.

But Max had planned a surprise of his own. He held up a hand like a magician alerting his audience that he was about to pull a rabbit out of his hat, then reached into his breast pocket and produced a small velvet-covered box.

He fumbled only a little bit as he opened it, and inside was not one ring but two: a hefty gold one for him and a slimmer, smaller one for me, with an intricate filigree design around the outside.

"I hope it fits," he said almost shyly, taking the larger ring out and handing it to me, then holding out his left hand. "Yours, I mean. I gave the best guess I could."

"But when did you—"

"I'd had my eye on these for a while at Joseff's," he said. "And when you hit me with this idea, I thought I'd better come prepared. It was late when I got there, but he opened up the place for me."

So he hadn't spent the entire evening at a wild bachelor party. To my surprise I found myself choking up as I slid the ring onto his finger. I didn't get a clear view of him putting mine on. Things had gotten pretty blurry by then. I sniffed, and Pancho, standing next to me, produced a pristine white handkerchief from the pocket of her jodhpurs and gave it to me. I nodded a thanks and dabbed at my eyes and nose.

"Well, you're all good and legal now," Pancho said as we were driven back to the airfield. "You know, next time you get married, you'll need to come out to Rancho Oro Verde, and I'll throw you a proper party, a humdinger. It's just a ragged old alfalfa farm right now, but it already has an airstrip, and I know just what I'm going to do with it. It's going to be the West's first fly-in dude ranch!"

I snorted at the "next time" and assured her I'd love to see the place with my current husband.

"It's going to have a pool and a rodeo arena, and guest rooms for, god, I don't even know how many. It'll be great. I'll fly you in," she said. "You'll have to come out and ride with me."

If it was anyone besides Pancho saying this, I might have thought it was all talk. But with Pancho, I believed it would happen.

"Thanks again for doing this, Florence," I said.

"After that caper in Pasadena, I owed you, Frances."

Max gave me a quizzical look.

"What were we, you about sixteen and me twenty-five? Something like that," Pancho said. "Old enough to know better, young enough not to care. I'm a bad influence."

She jutted her chin at me. "Have her tell you about it. I gotta get you guys home and then get me home."

Max looked at me again. "Florence?"

"I'll tell you about both things," I said as we boarded Pancho's plane.

Landing back in Burbank some time later, I saw my Packard with Monty standing beside it. And Philomena. And several photographers. And my agent, Zeppo.

When we got close, my agent, whose given name was Herbert Manfred Marx, gave me an eye-roll worthy of his big brother Groucho and said, "What are you, trying to give me a heart attack?"

Then he smiled and gave me a hug, and shook Max's hand, and said, "Mazel tov."

Pancho clapped me on the shoulder and said, "Frankie, great to see you. Keep your powder dry." Then she looked at Max and said, "Sonny, you've got a good one here. And if I ever hear you've done her wrong, I will hunt you down. There won't be any place in the world you can hide."

Chapter
Twelve

"She scares me a little," Max said as Pancho marched away.

"It's okay," I said. "I think she likes you. And wants to make up for not doing something awful to Raymond back when he was misbehaving."

Max and I arranged ourselves for a photo or three, and Philomena handed me a huge bouquet of mixed roses: pink, yellow, red, white. There was a white card among them with a note reading, "The best man won. Congratulations on your wedding! Love, Clay"

"The story is Clay cedes the field to Max," Philomena said. "It'll be the tale of a noble cowboy letting his girl go, because he knows she and this ... piano player ... will be happy together. Something like that."

"Thanks, Phil."

Soon we were in the Speedster, heading out to Laguna Beach and our oceanfront hotel, a cozy small Spanish adobe called the Casa del Camino. The honeymoon suite had been prepared on short notice—I expected they'd given someone further down the social scale the boot to a slightly lesser room, and I hoped they'd been well-compensated.

In the room there were candles burning, and a big basket of fresh fruit on the table. Philomena had made sure Pancho's bottle of Veuve Clicquot was on ice, and placed there just minutes before we came in: the ice was hardly melted. Philomena herself had done a disappearing act. I had to salute her ability to make the best of a situation in which I'd completely ignored her advice.

The big bed had snowy white sheets on it, and looked very

inviting. But Max, now changed into khaki pants and a polo shirt, said, "Walk on the beach?"

I changed out of my navy suit and into white sailor pants and a striped sweater, and threw a cardigan over my shoulders, protection against the ocean breezes that were picking up.

Soon we were leaving a double trail of footprints in the sand while the waves rolled onto the beach and slid back again, as though changing their minds, over and over, as they had since oceans began.

When I failed to respond to Max's observations on the golden-pinkness of the sunset and the beauty of the sea, he stopped and turned to me.

"Penny for your thoughts," Max said.

"Vernon. Sam. Clay. And you."

"Glad I'm in there somewhere," he said, in a tone indicating he took no offense.

I looked out to sea, where a line of brown pelicans glided through the air, just above the surface. One broke away, rose up and dove like an arrow into the glassy water, coming up with a fish. With their round bodies and long bills, they always made me think of dinosaurs.

"I hadn't known your real name was Hickenlooper," Max said at last.

I gave a short laugh. "Yeah, how would that look on a marquee?"

"Is that your maiden name or married name? Dazzled by your brilliance all these months, I never thought to ask."

I raised an eyebrow at him.

"Maiden. Raymond's real name is Raymond Sinclare. But hardly anyone else has the same names we were born with. Robert Taylor? Spangler Arlington Brugh. Joan was Billie Cassin, and before that she was Lucille LeSueur. Cary Grant was Archie Leach. Ginger was Virginia McMath, and Fred was Fred Austerlitz."

"But Bogie – his name has to be made up."

"Nope, he really is Humphrey Bogart," I said. "Humphrey DeForest Bogart, in fact. How could you improve on that?"

"Wow." Max said. "And I thought my grandfather was funny, changing his name from Goldberg to Gold between Bremen and Boston. So, who came up with Franklin?"

"Me," I said. "I always liked the story about Ben and that kite."

Back in the room, Max took the Veuve Clicquot from its ice bucket and said, "Sorry there's no saber handy. I'll have to do this the old-fashioned way." He worked the cork out of the bottle slowly until it emitted a soft sigh. He poured, and we clinked glasses, sitting side by side on the bed.

"So what is the story about you and Pancho in Pasadena?"

I chuckled. "Well, there was this horse of Pancho's, a nice coal-black quarter horse named Rum Runner," I said. "One of the up-and-coming cowboy actors rode him in one picture and decided this would be the perfect horse for when he became a big star. So he bought him from Pancho. Only he never did become a star, so you've never heard of him. And worse, he never paid Pancho for him. Instead, he needed some quick money and sold him to Hoot Gibson."

"A real cowboy star."

"Uh-huh," I said, sipping champagne, the memories coming back. A night with a full moon, a horse trailer and truck waiting down the road, me pretending the Hudson had broken down in front of the house …

"Hoot Gibson's house?"

"No, the guy who bought the horse. Or who, I guess technically at this point, had stolen him. His name was Orville Cotten. I have no idea what ever became of him, or how he explained it to Hoot, who was expecting the horse to be delivered the next day."

"So what happened?"

"We stole him back." I said. "I stopped the car across his driveway like it had stalled there, unbuttoned my blouse as far down as I dared, went up to the house and knocked on the door, and created this big scene about my engine dying and could I use his phone, except I didn't know who to call … I think that was where I discovered my love of acting."

Max chuckled, and I went on. "Anyway, while I was doing that, Pancho, calm as can be, went and took Rum Runner out of the corral, loaded him up in the trailer and drove away while Mr. Cotten tried to decide whether he wanted to look under my hood or the car's. Before he could figure it out, I said I'd give it another try and, whaddaya know, the engine turned right over. I said thanks and got out of there pronto. I don't think he discovered the horse was gone until the next morning."

"What about the Florence thing?"

"Oh yeah, that," I said. "It's Pancho's real name. I just call her Florence sometimes when I'm trying to be serious."

"Hm," Max said. "I don't suppose he realizes the girl who came to his door turned out to be Frankie Franklin?"

"I doubt it," I said, with a short laugh. "The studio took that girl, put her in at one end of the assembly line and at the other end, somewhere between Lombard and Colbert, I popped out."

"I think I would have liked that Frankie … Hickenlooper," Max said with a smile.

I smiled back. "You actually get to see that one from time to time," I said.

Now it was dark and the water was mysterious, shining black and silver under the night sky, the rollers rushing in, collapsing on the beach and whispering back out again. I was glad to be inside and warm, wearing a luxurious slide of a silk nightgown and hearing my new husband brushing his teeth in the bathroom. The world felt safe and secure in this moment, not a place where people just disappeared, any more than Pancho's horse had just disappeared out of that corral.

People were always somewhere. Where was Vernon, the guy with the answers? Holed up in a friend's empty beach house, drinking, consumed by guilt? Being hidden by someone trying to protect him, or talk him out of killing himself? Or just enjoying his own wedding night?

Still staring out the window, I felt Max come up behind me, and worry left me as though carried away by the waves outside. He had a funny way of making that happen.

I leaned back and felt nothing between our bodies but the

88

thin silk of my gown. Sleeping in the altogether was a slightly scandalous habit he had. His chest hair tickled my back and I leaned more, feeling him breathing, strong, warm, and solid against me.

"Excuse me," he said softly into my ear.

"Hm?" I said, over my shoulder.

He gently slid one finger under the silk strap of my nightgown.

"I'm looking for Mrs. Gold," he whispered in my ear. "Mrs. Max Gold?"

I felt his breath on my neck, felt my heartbeat quicken. He had a funny way of making that happen, too. I turned in the circle of his arms and pressed myself against him. He smelled of pipe tobacco, aftershave, champagne and … just Max.

"She's right here," I said.

Chapter Thirteen

I was feeling pretty good as we zipped up the Pacific Coast Highway, the Speedster's top down and the wind whipping through my hair. There would be tangles, but I would throw myself on the mercy of the hairdressing department later. The day was diamond-bright and warm, with a breeze off the big blue expanse of ocean off to our left, which today was looking as peaceful as its name.

For a couple of days, I had managed to put aside my thoughts about Vernon, even convincing myself that he might have returned home soon after I left Mrs. Botelho. Maybe he had been back for days by now, sneaking food to Ratto again and doing some heavy thinking about safety procedures on the set.

As Philomena had said, Mr. Fixx very likely had arranged things so that the accident was buried, erased, never to be mentioned again, and the best thing was to forget it myself. This was nothing, compared to the kind of misbehavior and mayhem he was usually called in to handle. After all, nobody had died, nobody was inappropriately pregnant, and no members of the general public had been hurt.

Soon we were in town, and then climbing into the Hollywood Hills. We rounded a turn, and there were the white walls and the gate to my house … our house, I realized now. At least I thought that was how it was supposed to work. I made a mental note to talk to my lawyer. Details, details. I suddenly had someone else in my life to think about, now that he was no longer just The Boyfriend.

"So are we supposed to feel different, now that we're married?" Max asked as we went up the broad tiled steps to the door, which he opened for me. "I thought you'd know because you've done it before."

"Badly," I said, dropping my handbag on the hall bench. "From my experience, starting tomorrow, you should get bored with me and start chasing other women, and drinking too much, and making me regret I ever did it. On the other hand, I have heard that there are people who find lasting happiness and remain faithful until death do them part."

"You've heard that, eh?" Max said.

By now the members of my household had heard us arrive and started to appear in various doorways: Monty from the back, Mrs. Monty from the kitchen, Kit from the office. They all looked serious and Kit came forward, already assuming the role of spokesperson for Casa de Frankie.

Kit, as usual, was straightforward. "Bad news, boss."

I looked at Max and back at her with an expression that said, go on.

"Vernon is dead."

I'd always heard of people's knees buckling in shock, though I hadn't ever seen it, and now I felt mine going. I put my hand on a nearby chair back to steady myself. Even as I did it, I realized a part of me had been expecting this, somehow. Why else would he have been out of sight and communication for so long? It didn't make it less shocking.

"When? How?" I said, knowing I wouldn't retain much that she told me.

"I'll get some drinks," Max said. I walked, numb, into the living room and sat on one of the leather sofas. Max came back with two whiskeys-and-soda and Kit gave us the rest of the story, as far as it was known.

"Drowned," she said. "They think it might've happened the night of the shooting, but they found his body by the pier in Santa Monica only a couple of days ago."

We'd been in the air on the way to Yuma. And then on the road to Laguna.

"Why didn't anyone—"

"It was your wedding night," Kit said. "We didn't want to call or wire and ruin it. There wouldn't have been anything you could do."

Kit handed me the morning paper, folded to the page with the story. Handing it to me, she said, "I'm sorry, boss. Were you close friends?"

"No," I said, starting to read the story. Kit had folded the paper so my eye went right to it. "I just feel … responsible."

According to the *Examiner*, the body of Vernon Stone, prop master at Fortune Pictures, had been found near the Santa Monica pier a couple of days after an accidental shooting on the set of *Prairie Princess*, starring Frankie Franklin.

I still felt a small shock seeing my name in print. I expected Philomena, in her calculating publicist's heart, considered any mention a success.

The story speculated that perhaps Mr. Stone, known to colleagues as a perfectionist who stressed safety above all, had gone into the waves on purpose, consumed by guilt, to drown himself. That's all it could do, speculate. He had left no note in his house or his car, which was parked near the beach, and no one had been found who had talked to him. In an ironic twist, the writer noted, had he lived he would have known that the shooting victim, young Sam Harvey, was recuperating and in no danger of dying from his wound.

I read the story over again, trying to picture Vernon's last hours. You never knew how a catastrophe would affect someone, what their actions would be. Vernon had seemed quiet—at work he did, anyway—and maybe that was a sign of how seriously he took it. Had he gone straight to the beach from the studio? Maybe just to think? And when thinking about it got to be too much, had he just walked into the water, still in his work clothes, and kept on going until the bottom dropped away, making no attempt to save himself?

And where had the girlfriend been? How had the poor woman received the news? What had they been arguing about when Mrs. Botelho overheard them? Maybe he had been despondent, guilt-ridden, and she was impatient with him, urging him to buck up, it couldn't be that bad. I knew people who had little tolerance for the sadness or worry of others. Maybe she was one of those.

I thought of Vernon, a lifeless body in the cold ocean even while I snooped around his house, seeing his unfinished puzzle, his carefully organized belongings, the racy magazines in a box under the bed. It made me feel small, and disloyal somehow. Even though he wasn't a close friend, any kind of friend, really, he was part of the studio family. And it really was like a family, right down to the squabbles and pranks and the feeling that the director, your temporary mom or dad, was playing favorites.

There was the studio family, and the Casa de Frankie family: Mr. and Mrs. Monty, Mr. Noguchi and Kit. I was lucky to have them, especially since for some time, in terms of actual relatives, there had only been my mother and me—and Raymond, briefly. Now, though, I thought with a warm glow, there was Max.

A sudden twinge of guilt replaced the glow. My mother! I'd been so occupied with outsmarting the studio by hightailing it off to Yuma, I hadn't told her about the wedding. I couldn't let her find out about it in the papers.

"Kit," I said. "Can you get my mom on the phone? I need to tell her I'm married!"

Kit's astounded look, as though she couldn't imagine I'd overlook such a thing, didn't make me feel any better. But without a word, she ran for the phone.

My mother would understand. We didn't talk every day, but didn't have to. We both loved time alone when we could get it, and up at the ranch she often spent all day by herself in her art studio. My parents had bought the place in the 1920s and she was in her element there. She wasn't precisely alone, what with her housekeeper Soledad there, along with a colorful crew of rough-looking ranch hands, any of whom would lay down his life for her.

A Snow White beauty in her youth, she was still beautiful, her hair at fifty nearly as dark as it had been in her twenties. She had never remarried, saying she was happy with her life now and that she'd had a good marriage already. Any fellow who had it in mind to be a bother to her, if she didn't want to be bothered, would have to contend with the ranch hands, who felt no man was good enough for their Rose.

"Married?" she said in surprise and delight. "Married? Why, Frances!"

"Sorry I didn't tell you before," I said. "It was … kind of sudden."

"But how romantic, darling!" she exclaimed. "Is it that nice boy Max you've been seeing?"

I laughed, wondering if she thought I changed boyfriends weekly. And I also realized I was very happy to hear her voice just now.

"Yes, Mom. Max. We'll come up for a visit soon."

"You know there's a guest room for you any time," she said.

I pictured her standing at the phone in her paint-smeared smock, probably still holding a brush and anxious to get back to her easel, no matter how much she enjoyed hearing from me. And I got a wave of longing to see her.

"I'll come visit as soon as I can, with Max," I promised.

"I hope you do, darling!" she said.

I didn't tell her about Vernon, or the shooting. I knew talking to her would make me feel better, and it did, but that didn't mean I had to make her sad for someone she didn't know. Though I'd tell her all about it eventually, this didn't seem like the best time for it.

Over the next couple of days, I went back to the set of *Prairie Princess*, and Max went to let the Garden of Allah know he was moving out, and that the rental company could come pick up the piano he'd been using. Watching him and Monty bringing in the rest of his clothes, and his books and other belongings, I had the time to think about what this actually meant. He would be here all the time, now … what was that going to be like? I guessed I'd find out.

And on Wednesday, instead of going back to the set, I went to Vernon's funeral.

Chapter Fourteen

had told Max he didn't need to come with me. Word of the wedding had gotten out and I didn't want this to be our first public appearance as a couple. In a black crepe suit and a simple black hat with a short veil over my face, I hoped to blend in with the other mourners.

After the autopsy, Vern's body had been cremated, and interment would be after a ceremony at Forest Lawn. It felt more like a vast, serene park than a cemetery, with emerald green lawns and shade trees, under skies that were clear and sunny more than 300 days a year. The dead could rest in peace knowing they … well, whatever the dead knew. None of them were talking.

It was mostly picture people, I noticed, in the pews of the Wee Kirk o' the Heather. It was not a big crowd, but the few friends and co-workers who were there looked sad and thoughtful. Among them was Detective Jameson.

"So," I said, as we got far enough away from the chapel so that we weren't part of the crowd.

"So," he said, looking like he was willing to talk, "What do you want to know?"

"I guess that was your last, what do you call it, lead? Vernon was?"

"Yeah, no one else handled the gun before it was hung on the chair for you. No one saw anything useful."

"I should have checked all the rounds," I said. "I've been thinking about that."

"Only two of them were live," Jameson said. "Even if you had, you weren't expected to do that job, and all you would have seen may have been the blanks, if those were all that were showing in the cylinder. You would've assumed they were all blanks. Wasn't your job to do any different."

I considered this for a second and said, "That's not what my dad would say."

"Was he in pictures?"

"Yes, he was a stuntman, after being in the rodeo, and a riding extra. He taught me to shoot. Sometimes it's easy to think on a set that the guns are as pretend as everything else."

He nodded. "But you know better."

"I should," I said. "So is the investigation closed?"

He nodded. "The studio has been anxious for it to be declared an accident, and now it is."

"Do you think he really killed himself?" I asked. "There was speculation that he might have been overcome with guilt about the shooting."

Jameson gave a wry chuckle. "There are always a lot of opinions out there," he said, "but only a certain number of facts that can be verified. He didn't say that to anyone, and there was no note. Not a thing that could tell us why. Sometimes that's how it is."

I remembered Mrs. Botelho's account. "Did you talk to his landlady, Mrs. Botelho?" I asked.

He shook his head. "She was unavailable the night we went to the house," he said. "And now there wouldn't be much point. No one we could find noticed him on the beach that afternoon. There were a lot of people in the water, a lot of horseplay."

I considered that. "She said he was having an argument with his girlfriend," I said. "That would have been before he went to Santa Monica. Maybe she went with him?"

"If she did," Jameson said, "she hasn't come forward and we have no one who thought to mention her. And there didn't seem to be a girlfriend type here." Meaning the funeral.

He regarded me quietly as I stood there, trying to think of any reason he should keep looking into both the shooting and the death. Finally he smiled, and said, not unkindly, "There could have been something else going on in his life that no one even knew about." He waited to see if that had sunk in before going

96

on. "Sometimes, Miss Franklin, people take a lot of secrets with them when they die. Most times, in fact."

I looked at him and nodded, giving the subject up. We were at my car now, with Monty standing nearly at attention next to a graceful fender, staring off into middle space but really keeping his eye on the crowd. A few people with cameras, some fans, and photographers for the magazines who hadn't made it to the airport to catch Max and me returning, now crowded around my chauffeur and me. Excited, like kids around a Christmas tree.

"Is it always like this?" Jameson asked.

"If I go out as Frankie Franklin," I said. "Sometimes I just want to be plain old Frances Hickenlooper again."

"Is that your disguise now? Impersonating your old self?"

"It doesn't always work," I said.

He smiled. "Don't be too hard on yourself, Miss Franklin," he said and shook my hand. "It's been very nice to know you briefly. I'll be looking for you in the pictures."

As the detective walked away, I turned to the crowd and started signing autographs—in books, on photos, on scraps of paper—with Monty looming just behind me. I never called him my bodyguard, but then again, I never needed to: his imposing presence was warning enough to anyone with bad intentions. My fans tended to be well-behaved anyway, and, once they'd gotten a bit of attention and my scribbled name (it never looked as pretty done on the spot as it did signed at my own desk), they started to drift away to wherever they needed to be next. But one young man stayed behind, and came hesitantly up. His bony wrists showed from the sleeves of his neat, inexpensive suit, and he looked anxious.

I recognized him as one of the crew from the *Prairie Princess* set.

"Stanley, isn't it?" I said, with a smile, feeling as though he'd dart away like a spooked calf if I moved too fast.

"Yes, ma'am—Miss Franklin," he said, twisting his tweed cap in his hands. "I know you've been wanting to know more about Mr. Stone and what happened that day."

I looked at him with interest. "Did you have something to tell me?"

It wasn't much, he said. When the shooting happened, he'd been getting some props ready for the next scene on the list. He had heard the shot, and knew that, in the story, Sam was supposed to have been just behind Raymond when they broke through the door, and that it was Raymond who was supposed to fall when I fired the gun.

"I didn't know what to do," Stanley said. "Sorta like everybody else, see? But then everyone ran to where you and Mr. Sinclare and Sam were, except me. I didn't want to be in the way."

And another person had hung back, too, and had caught his attention.

Stanley said he had seen a slender woman, with long, curly brown or black hair, walking swiftly toward the sound stage's exit doors.

"And right after, I saw Mr. Stone run that way, too, and he yelled after her a couple of times," he said. "Then they went out to the cars."

"Did you get a good look at the girl? Did you know her?" I asked.

"I think it was this girl he'd been seeing for a while. I'd seen her around on a couple of pictures before this one. She was an extra and I only noticed because he was talking to her, seemed real sweet on her. But I don't think she was working on this picture. She wasn't in costume or anything, just seemed to be visiting the set."

"The girl he was seeing? Do you know her name?"

"I never heard it, ma'am. I only heard she was staying at the Studio Club before. And one day a few weeks ago, I heard Mr. Stone on the telephone saying he'd meet her there. Or, I guess it was her. He just called her something like honeybun, like he did when I saw her on the set before."

"Did you tell the police any of this?"

"No, I—you see, I—well, the truth is, Miss Franklin, the police and I don't get along so good, either," Stanley said, looking furtively at me, waiting to be judged, I supposed.

I remembered seeing him off in corners, in hushed exchanges with actors and crew. He was probably one of those people who supplemented his studio income with a side business as a bookie or drug provider. But if it was my judgment he expected, he'd be waiting a long time. People did what they had to do to get by, especially these days.

"Why are you telling me this?" I asked.

Stanley shifted uncomfortably. "I'd heard you were trying to find out about it," he said. "And I know you're a straight arrow, and, well, I thought this might help you sort it out—you know, for whatever reason you wanted to."

"Thank you, Stanley," I said.

"I don't know how the girl fits into it," he said, "but Vernon, he was real good to me. Gave me a chance when nobody else would. It just don't seem right that he's dead. It would be good to at least know how it happened."

And he turned and slouched away, having taken his anxiety and transferred some of it, at least, to me. Monty let me into the Packard and then got behind the wheel. I sighed, but it only released part of the tension I had built up.

"Home, miss?" he asked.

"No, Monty," I said. "Santa Monica."

Monty drove us out to the beach, and stayed with the car as I went out onto the wooden walkway by the pier. The late afternoon sea breeze was bracing, but the scene was depressing. Though the beach still attracted those wanting sea and sun, the amusement park had fallen on hard times along with the rest of the country, and the pier now was used mainly as a landing for the ferries that took people out past the three-mile limit to the gambling ships anchored there.

I'd heard of people jumping from the ships and swimming to shore, either for a bet or drunk out of their minds. I looked out at the ocean, slate-colored in the early evening, clouds gathering, their lower edges glowing with reflected light from the setting sun. Even three miles was a long way to swim. It would take an hour to walk that far on land.

I remembered Vernon once had mentioned he liked the water,

99

but was not a strong swimmer. He must have been completely distraught, not himself, to choose that way of dying. If he had chosen it.

"Hey, lady," said a voice from behind me. I jumped, but realized Monty was close enough if needed. "Someone die?"

The man was standing at a respectful distance. One of the surfboard riders, maybe. He also didn't seem to recognize me. It happened sometimes, and I expected if you were on the beach all the time, you might not go to the pictures much. He just saw a woman dressed in black, expensive clothes.

"Yes," I said. "A friend. Right out there."

"I heard about that," he said, and I caught the odor of gin on his breath. He was wearing unremarkable work pants and a shirt. Maybe not a surfer, then. I didn't think you could stay upright on one of those big boards skimming along under the curl of a wave unless you were sober, but you never knew.

"I was wondering about that," he said. "I think I saw the guy."

"What did he look like?" I asked.

"Blondish, kinda slight guy. The girl had dark brown or black hair, long, a lot of curls."

"There was a girl?"

"Yeah, and she was slim, too. She was kind of flat-chested. Like the flappers always wanted to be. I don't understand that, but ..."

He stopped, darted a quick look at my own bust. Men, I thought. It's never far from their minds. I said, "So they were on the beach?"

"Yeah, if that was them that I saw," he said thoughtfully.

"At first I thought they were just fooling around in the surf, him chasing her, them pushing each other, falling down ... I couldn't tell what was going on."

I tried to picture this, as a breeze came off the water and made me shiver. I looked out at the waves, watching the gulls and terns skimming over it. He had seen a couple, Vernon and the girl with the curly brown hair ... It had to have been the girlfriend Mrs. Botelho and Stanley had seen.

Were they playing? Probably not. It sounded like they'd been having an argument of some kind at the studio, and then at the house, and that it continued in the car and down to the beach. Maybe they'd come here to make up? Maybe Vernon was so beside himself at what had happened that the girlfriend was angry at him, trying to talk him out of it?

"You say he was chasing her?"

"Maybe," the beach bum said. "You couldn't really tell. I couldn't hear what they were saying over the ocean, the splashing, and other people's voices. No one else seemed to notice, all busy with themselves, their friends. But I like to watch people. It was funny, you know? They were just dressed in street clothes, not bathing suits. But a lot of people come down and go for a walk, get their feet wet, in their regular clothes.

"Then, like I say, I thought that they were just fooling around at first, and then it got rougher. I looked around to see if anyone else noticed, but when I looked back, I couldn't see them anymore. I didn't think much of it—you know, like they could've just come back in. Later, I figured while they were horsing around, she might've gotten into trouble in the deeper water, and he was trying to pull her back."

I thought about that, about how people who think they're drowning panic and end up pulling their rescuers under.

"Anyway, then someone must have told the lifeguards, 'cause I saw them take off on their surfboards, but after a while they came back with nothing."

I looked out at the ocean and felt cold inside and out. Poor Vernon. I tried to put a story to these images. Had she been frightened of Vernon? Or frightened for him, if he was distraught over the shooting? Angry with him? Him with her? Had she, panicked or furious, gone into the water and tried to swim away, while he pursued her? But why? If it started on the set, it must have had something to do with the shooting, I thought. She didn't work in the prop department, as far as I knew. But maybe she had something to do with it that I wasn't seeing.

"I thought I dreamed it," he said, interrupting my thoughts. "I was a little crocked, fell asleep here under the pier. I hoped I dreamed it. And then they found the man's body, couple of days later."

"What about the girl?" I had seen no one fitting her description at the funeral. But she also hadn't turned up at the beach. It seemed likely that she had drowned, too, and also taken her secrets with her.

"I expect they'll find her eventually, too," he said. "On the other hand, sometimes that big blue just swallows people up."

I shivered again as another breeze swept in. Some people said cold drafts meant a ghost was near. I never believed it. But I did notice how the sea, which had looked so peaceful to me a few days ago, now seemed brooding and dangerous. Even though it was the same ocean, the same blue, under the same sun.

"Thank you for telling me about this," I said. "I had wondered."

"Sure thing, pretty lady," he said. And then, "Hey—are you in the pictures?"

"Yes," I said.

"I thought you looked familiar." Without another word, he turned and walked away, slowly, like he didn't really have anywhere he needed to be. I wondered where he lived, and had the odd feeling that maybe he lived right here, and slept under the pier.

Chapter Fifteen

A few days later, the *Prairie Princess* crew was back at work, on location about thirty miles north of my home, where everyone was focused on me and the team of two gray horses I was about to drive down Main Street for the seventh or eighth time. The Santa Clarita sun beat down on the hills, the frontier town set, my buckboard, me, and the grays, who stood calmly in their harnesses, used to all this.

At least I had some shade, thanks to the parasol that Bobby the production assistant was holding over me while we waited for Arthur to call action.

"I feel bad for the horses," I said. "They'd like shade, too."

Bobby chuckled. "They're not wearing makeup that would sweat off their faces."

I closed my eyes, enjoying the scent of sun-warmed pines, horses, and leather. I imagined myself in the Western town of the story and prepared to ignore the group of people in modern dress and sunglasses gathered nearby. These included Arthur, perched on the bed of the camera truck, chatting with the camera operator.

Arthur never really called, "Action!" He felt it tended to scare the horses—and sometimes actresses. So he would just lean forward intently and say, "OK, go ahead."

He said it now, and I took a deep breath, and when I let it out again and opened my eyes, I was once again Charlotte McCord, brave cowgirl, about to head off into the sunset. I let the camera see me gazing resolutely down the rustic main street toward the hills. I had run the bad guys out of town and now I was heading off to a new adventure.

Looking down from the wagon seat, I smiled at my co-star, a craggy character actor named George, who was playing the town's new sheriff.

"You're going to make a great sheriff, Abe," I said to George. "I'll write when I get to San Francisco."

George looked admiringly up at me as I gathered the reins and clicked my tongue at the grays. They twitched their ears, and then started off at a smart trot, hooves kicking up picturesque puffs of dust. We passed the saloon, a couple of ladies in sunbonnets, two little boys playing marbles, and the town doctor in his buggy, the camera truck rolling along beside us.

A few seconds Arthur called "Cut!" and I pulled up the team before we ran out of Main Street.

"Good boys!" I told the grays, and turned them back to our starting place, where the wranglers came and took their reins.

"Give them an extra carrot each for me," I told the wrangler. "Eight takes just to get me out of town—they earned it."

Except for being trussed up in a corset and a gingham dress, I liked shooting at the ranch. It was only an hour away from home but felt far from the city. The air was clean and fresh, there were trees and hills, and it usually meant I got to ride horses, or drive a team, or do something else that was fun.

Today was even better because it meant we'd almost finished principal photography on *Prairie Princess*, and it always felt good to wrap up a picture. In a few weeks I would move on to *Martinique's Rose* with a lot of the same crew, only having to remember *Prairie Princess* when the publicity push and premiere came. I'd be asked the same questions over and over: How much was I like my character? Did I actually like horses? No one would ask about the accident, not if they wanted to have continued access to me and my carefully rehearsed ad lib answers.

At least I didn't have to remember too many lies about my life, because my studio biography was close enough to the truth. It said I'd grown up as a wealthy rancher's daughter, and was able to ride, rope, shoot, and also make a fine apple pie. Some of that was true. My father had been a cowboy and then a stuntman,
104

but certainly was never wealthy. The smartest move he'd ever made, after marrying my mother, was buying the ranch up in northern California near Niles, where he'd worked on silent two-reelers.

The truth was, I was fair with a rope, and pretty good with both rifle and six-shooter, but could not bake an apple pie to save my life or anyone else's. Or do much other cooking, which was a good thing. If I'd known how to cook, then I'd just want to eat.

When we were done for the day, and Monty was driving me home, I thought about the beach bum's story, which haunted me. Together with Stanley and Mrs. Botelho's accounts, it was clear there was a girl who had been with Vernon when he died. Where was she now?

"Drowned. That's the simple answer," said Max from the piano bench a bit later, after hearing me going over all the possibilities, including that one. "She was seen in the water with him, right?"

"Yes," I said. "But it still bothers me, Max. Who was she? Mrs. Botelho said he had a number of girlfriends but she'd been the latest. Why was she with him when he died? And why did she die herself, if she did?"

"The ocean is big, and stronger than any of us," Max said. "Which is why I prefer swimming pools."

I made a frustrated noise. "I talked to one of the crew about it," I said. "He said she was an extra at one time, which is how I guess she met Vernon. But I can't very well ask to see a roster of all the Anns or Annies working as extras in the past year. Even I'm smart enough to know that would make me look a little crackers."

"So …," Max said, knowing if he didn't let me talk it out now I'd never let it go.

"So I wonder if she has any connection with the shooting? Did she distract him that much before the scene? Did she do something with the gun herself, without him knowing? But why?"

"Was he really that smitten with her?"

"I told you what Mrs. Botelho said about them making

noise."

"You did," he said. "And I can sympathize. I can sympathize enough to say I'm glad she's not our landlady or neighbor."

"Maybe he was upset because she wasn't supposed to be visiting him on the set? And he got angry and distracted at a critical time?"

I had all kinds of theories. Actors—good ones, anyway—are students of human behavior. Preparing for a role, they not only learn their lines and the action, they make up detailed personal histories that help to make sense of what their characters do in the story. For me that was one of the most interesting parts of the job, figuring out what made my characters tick. Now I found myself wondering what had made Vernon tick.

So on Saturday afternoon, I dressed in dungarees and a loose sweater and drove to the storybook cottage once more. It was that time of day when the shadows deepen and the colors start to go gray. Lights were coming on in the neighborhood's windows, people going about their lives. Cars came and went down the street, their engines rumbling, a procession of big round headlights and running boards, and no one noticed me as I adopted an I'm-nobody walk and posture, trying to look like just another harried young mother anxious about paying this month's bills.

Vernon's house had that silent, closed-up feeling that tells you it's empty before you even knock on the door. I hesitated on the sidewalk, wondering if I should just go over to Mrs. Botelho's and ask to be let in. I had prepared a story, but I didn't really want her following me around in there.

As I stood thinking, I heard a small "Prrt?" from the bushes at the side of the house and found Ratto under the mullioned window, looking up at it like he wanted to get in. I could see that the window was slightly ajar, and wondered if that had been his usual way in when he wanted a handout from Vernon.

"Hey, Ratto," I said, approaching in what I hoped was a friendly way. "Read any good dirty magazines recently?"

The orange cat turned big yellow-green eyes on me and meowed again, then looked back at the window in a pointed fashion. When I didn't move fast enough, he came over and ran himself along my ankles.

"OK, I get your drift," I said.

I looked around and, seeing no one nearby, scooped Ratto up, pulled the window open and poured him over the sill. Then I trotted over to Mrs. Botelho's and knocked on her door.

"Why, it's the famous face again," she said when she saw me on her porch. "What can I do for you?"

She was wearing a different plaid apron and a different flowered housedress today but it was all still a perfect clash in both color and pattern. I wanted Charlie Torres to meet her one day. She would provide him with years of costume inspiration, I was sure.

"It's the silliest thing, really," I said, my expression sheepish. "But I think I may have lost my charm bracelet when I was helping you find Ratto the other day. Also, I think I heard him in there again just now."

"Oh? That little pest," Mrs. Botelho said. "I didn't see a bracelet in there. But I know how those things can slide into a crack or under a pillow. Here, I'll let you in and you can look for it."

"Thanks so much," I said enthusiastically. "It's not expensive, but it was something my mother gave me, so, you know—"

"I wish my daughter was so sentimental," Mrs. Botelho said. "Maria, she says she don't want anything of mine when I go. They're too old-fashioned. And you know, my things are good, rose gold, from the old country!"

"I'm sure she'll feel different … er, eventually," I said, suspecting that we'd stumbled upon a topic that Mrs. Botelho would be happy to expound upon at length, once she got warmed up.

"I don't have much chance to wear my good things," Mrs. Botelho said as she opened the door with her skeleton key. "At least the ones we had left—I've sold a lot, you know. Anything to get by these days."

I made a sympathetic noise and then did one of those, "Hark! I hear a noise" poses, saying "Oh, you know, I think I just heard

Ratto. Off that way."

I motioned toward the kitchen and Mrs. B stumped off, shaking her head and asking herself, "Now, how did he get in here?"

Ratto meowed twice, grumbling because no food had been forthcoming after all the trouble he'd gone to, getting me to let him in. Mrs. B called him in a voice that could be heard by the cats out on Catalina Island, and I dashed upstairs to Vernon's bedroom.

Everything was as I'd seen it last, except for the bedposts, which were now bare of scarves. I pictured Mrs. Botelho, woman of the world, shaking her head and removing them so Vernon's family or friends wouldn't get the wrong idea about him should they show up here for his things. I thought it was nice of her.

Under the bed, everything looked the same as it had before. I left the naughty magazines where they were but grabbed what I had come for: the green silk camisole. The fine fabric bunched up to almost nothing in my hand. I slid it into my pocket, and took my charm bracelet out of my other pocket where I'd stashed it before leaving home.

"I found it!" I called, skipping lightly down the staircase and waving the bracelet like a trophy.

I thanked Mrs. B for letting me in, and we chatted for a while about her efforts to contact Vernon's family.

"He mentioned a brother in Oakland," she said. "But I don't have a name or address. It didn't sound like they were in touch very much."

We stood there with Vernon's empty house behind us, and were quiet for a stretch. Then Mrs. B said, "If you happen to think of a way I can reach that brother of his, if he wants to come and get any of Vernon's property, let me know, will you? The girlfriend hasn't shown up again, either, so I can't ask her. And I gotta rent the place out soon."

I promised I would get in touch if anything occurred to me, and drove home thinking about how houses were like movie sets: just spaces filled with stuff, the backdrop for stories, real and imagined. Soon the house would be the setting for someone else's story. I wondered what would happen to all his carefully chosen and carefully cared-for things, including the half-finished jigsaw puzzle on the dining room table. And the naughty magazines.

Maybe I should have felt odd about grabbing the green camisole, but any guilt I might have felt about taking this wisp of silk was outweighed by the prospect that it might lead to this Ann-or-Annie—which might lead to answers about Vernon. That's what I told myself, anyway.

Back up in the hills off Beachwood Drive, I left the Hudson next to the Speedster in the garage and went into the house. Maybe it was just another place filled with stuff, but it felt more like home than ever with Max there, officially part of the family, with his music and his splashing in the pool and his silly jokes, not to mention his appreciation for Mrs. Monty's cooking.

My tiny cook practically fizzed with delight every day, now that she had someone who did justice to her culinary skills. *Coq au vin*, crepes, fish *en papillote,* chocolate mousse ... he exclaimed over each dish, asked how she accomplished it, and cleaned his plate.

"I'd better start swimming a lot more," he said one evening, having dispatched steak with bearnaise sauce, creamed spinach, and *pommes frites.* "I may not have to fit into the same outfits you do, but I do want to be able to get through the door."

Chapter Sixteen

"I used to wonder what it felt like to be shot," Sam said. "When she came to visit yesterday, my acting teacher told me I really didn't have to go in for that much realism next time. I think she was trying to make a joke."

I smiled but also winced a little. We were sitting in two of the dozen or so matching rocking chairs that sat in an inviting line on the broad veranda of Clay's ranch house. The hundred-acre estate with its house, stables, riding trails, and even a full-size polo field, was one place where Clay seemed truly happy and relaxed. I loved visiting him here, especially on a beautiful, cloudless day like today.

Sam looked right at home himself, in his pyjamas, slippers and a lap robe, with one of Clay's German shepherds, Lily, napping peacefully at his feet. She had adopted him the moment he arrived, and only left his side to play with her brother, Prince.

I was glad that Clay had persuaded Sam to come to here. A few weeks after the shooting, Sam was bandaged for the wound and the broken rib he had sustained and was moving about slowly under the watchful eye of Clay's housekeeper, Mrs. Garcia, and Lily.

"You know," Sam went on, "It wasn't at all like I used to imagine. At least I didn't blubber and make a fool of myself, did I, Miss Franklin?"

"Frankie," I said. "And no, you did not."

I didn't say I was sorry yet again. He already knew. I had come to visit, and to let him know that he had a not-so-small speaking part in *Martinique's Rose,* the Empress Josephine picture. Rehearsals would begin in a few weeks, about the time Sam's doctor said he could think of returning to work.

"You're Jean-Pierre, a young courtier to Napoleon," I said, handing him the script. "He's witty and charming and her friend ... at first. You'll see." I gestured to the pages. "You can start memorizing your lines while you're here, keep from getting bored."

Sam looked around with a smile I could only describe as bemused, then down at Lily, who raised an eyebrow at him. He reached down with his good hand and stroked the big dog's head. She sighed and closed her eyes.

"I don't know how anyone could be bored here," he said. "There's a library with I don't know how many books, and all kinds of interesting birds. And when I can swim again, the pool. And the tennis courts."

"And the horses?" I offered.

Sam grinned. "I'm not much of a horse fan," he said. "They're kind of big and unpredictable. But they are beautiful."

From where we sat, we could look down the gentle slope of broad lawn to the drive and, beyond that, the polo field. Clay was out there working one of his swift, agile polo ponies. They looked toy-size from here, the pony rocking along at a steady canter, Clay hitting the ball forehand and backhand, from both sides, with precise, powerful swings, never letting it stop. He sat a horse better than anyone I knew, and I watched admiringly for a few minutes as he crisscrossed the field, mallet swinging, he and the bay pony moving as one.

A bit later, after handing the pony and stick off to one of his grooms, Clay came up the hill, with Prince at his heels. Lily noticed, and trotted down the hill to join them. Striding toward us in his tall boots, white breeches and polo shirt, his dogs hanging close, Clay looked like a man who was exactly where he should be.

Sweaty and smiling, he bounded up the stairs. "Hey, boy," he said to Sam.

"Hey, boy," Sam said back, color rising to his cheeks.

I had to smile at the way both Clay and Sam lit up when their eyes met.

"And you!" Clay said, turning to me with a broad smile. "You

111

look terrific. Marriage agrees with you."

"I guess so," I said, feeling self-conscious. "This time around."

We moved to the table nearby for lunch: Clay's favorite Mexican meatloaf sandwiches and lemonade, brought by Mrs. Garcia and a helper. Warm breezes played about the veranda, the dogs lolled around our feet or gazed longingly at us, hoping for handouts, and birds were making lazy, mid-day calls in the oak and eucalyptus trees. I felt like a kid on lunch break from school. Carefree, almost.

"I could get used to this," Clay said, with a grin. He felt it, too. "Are you coming to play next weekend? Walt's going to be here. Dave Niven. Maybe Spencer."

I nodded over my half-sandwich. A lot of people in pictures had taken up polo. Will Rogers also had his own polo field at his ranch and if people weren't playing there, they were playing at Clay's or one of the more than two dozen polo fields in the area. After Will had gotten Disney into the game, the animator began to play every chance he could. Spencer Tracy practiced almost daily.

Many folks in town played with more enthusiasm than skill and it was surprising there hadn't been more accidents or even deaths.

"I've seen sacks of potatoes ride better than these blighters," Leslie Howard, a really skilled player, had whispered to me between chukkers one day.

Clay and I talked polo for a while, Sam doing his best trying to follow along, and then Clay said, "I was really sorry to hear about Vernon."

"Yes," I said. "I just keep thinking, I wish he'd waited and found out Sam was going to be all right."

"Some folks would see it that way," Clay said. "Others, well, just thinking that their negligence almost killed someone, couldn't live with themselves. He also might have had something else going on that was weighing on his mind, maybe for a long time. Some people do, and then it just takes one thing that's the last straw."

I nodded, and thought. "There was a girl with him," I said. "At the beach."

Both Sam and Clay looked up. Curious.

"I've been asking around a little," I said, trying to sound casual. "I feel responsible."

"That's funny," Sam said, putting his glass of lemonade down on the tray next to his chair.

"That I feel responsible?"

"That you said there was a girl," he said. "No, not because he didn't like them. I think he did. I think his girlfriend—a girl, anyway—was visiting him at lunch. I saw her come out of the prop department, looking sort of ..."

Clay and I waited while Sam searched for the word.

"Happy? Sad?" I asked ... like we were playing charades.

Sam's pale eyebrows knitted for a moment, then went up. "Pleased," he said. "You know, like sort of a little bouncy, like she was ... pleased with herself."

Sam had been going to see Vernon for pointers on handling his own gun, a Colt like mine, since he wasn't used to them. But when he approached after the girl had left, the door to Vernon's office was closed, and the response to his knock was a terse, "Just a minute!"

I considered this. So many questions. But it seemed obvious to me the girl had to be the one Vernon had been seeing, who had been at his house. "What did she look like?"

"Very slender, and she had dark, curly hair," Sam said, remembering. "I haven't thought of it until now. Not a face you'd really remember, but very pale skin. Like too pale for her hair. And wearing a summery dress."

"Had you ever seen her before?" I asked.

"Not before that day," Sam said. "She was there before we started the scene, though, just watching, like some of the other people. I didn't know whether she was a visitor or working."

We waited for more. Sam thought a bit and said, "But everything after I took my place for the scene ...." He looked up, and shrugged. "That's all a blank."

"Vernon's landlady said there was a girlfriend," I said. "She thinks her name was Ann, or Annie."

They looked at me. "His landlady likes to talk," I said.

They looked at me with interest, almost amusement.

I sipped lemonade. "And a guy at the beach said there was a girl there, too," I said. "His description sounded the same."

"You really were curious, weren't you?" Clay said, impressed.

"Yes," I said. "I just kept wondering, even though the studio insists it was just an accident that turned out not to be so tragic, for Sam, anyway. Still … maybe Vernon expected to be fired."

Clay chuckled. "Only if it made a picture come in over budget, or he actually killed a star or something." He glanced fondly at Sam. "Which you're not, yet."

"I'm also alive," Sam said. "I'm happy about that."

"So am I," said Clay.

I pondered the mysterious Annie, as I'd come to think of her, as I drove home. I realized she also must have been the girl I saw leaving the commissary with Vernon after lunch, a girl whose face I hadn't even seen. I doubted she, whoever she was, wherever she was, could tell me anything about how the accident happened, but maybe she would have some insight into Vernon's state of mind at the time, and then at least I'd have the story, such as it was.

Or maybe she was dead, too, taken by that big, beautiful, deadly ocean. Which meant I could wonder for as long as I liked, and would never have an answer.

Chapter Seventeen

$\mathbf{B}$ack home, I saw Monty's reliable old black Ford waiting in the driveway. I had persuaded him and Mrs. Monty that things wouldn't fall completely apart if they went away for a weekend once in a while. I had urged Kit and Mr. Noguchi to take the weekend off, too, and knew they would probably spend it puttering about their small house beyond the garage or going for a hike in the hills.

"You're going to be okay flying solo, boss?" Kit asked as she sealed an envelope containing an autographed eight-by-ten glossy photo addressed to a fan in Chicago, one of the last batches of fan mail we had decided to handle before the weekend.

I put down the fountain pen and flexed my fingers. "Of course," I said, and gave her my best Garbo impression. "I vant to be alone."

Kit chuckled.

"Except for Max, I mean."

Max and I had talked about going to Catalina, always out there beckoning us from the strip of haze on the horizon. We could probably have found someone to yacht us over to the island for a stay at the St. Catherine Hotel and dancing at the Casino. But when it came right down to it, the idea of being home appealed most. The thought of having the house all to ourselves for a weekend sounded, in fact, like extravagant luxury.

Mrs. Monty was skeptical. "Perhaps I should 'ave made ze meals to leave for you," she said, brows knitted in concern over her prominent nose. "In ze icebox."

Monty, meanwhile, stood patiently, towering, by the door, not in his chauffeur's uniform but in a comfortable-looking tweed suit that gave him the air of a country gentleman. They were going to visit his brother and his family in Ojai.

"We'll manage fine," I said airily. I hadn't really considered how we'd eat—we only had to fall down the hill to find any kind of restaurant we liked—but I knew there were things in the cupboards or being kept cold in the snazzy new Frigidaire that all of us still called the icebox.

"Of course we will," Max said after they had left. "Although if there's cooking to be done I expect I'll be doing it. One thing I know about my new wife is that she doesn't cook."

As it happened, we found other ways of amusing ourselves and didn't think about eating until much later that afternoon when Max declared he was hungry and that he could no longer live on love alone.

"What ever shall we do?" I asked, lolling about on the bed, watching him dress in casual dark trousers and a checked shirt. With the collar open, revealing just a tantalizing glimpse of neck and chest, he looked somehow even more attractive than with nothing on at all.

"Leave it to me," he said. He left the room, and after a few minutes of luxurious stretching and enjoying having the bed all to myself, I grabbed the pale blue silk robe I'd flung over a nearby chair, slipped it on and followed him.

In the kitchen, I discovered Max had found the eggs, the stove, and a small, flattish pan with a handle. He had gotten the cheddar cheese and a large dill pickle out of the refrigerator and was carefully cutting them into small squares. I watched with interest.

Done with the pickles and cheese, he took the pan by the handle and held it up like a prize.

"Omelet pan," he announced. "We are in business."

"You know how to use that?" I asked, preparing to be impressed.

"Yes, I do," he said. "I am a man of many unsuspected talents. Now I need butter."

"Not too much!" I said.

116

"Enough," he said, "Or you cannot get your omelet out of the pan."

He turned on a stove burner and left the butter melting in the pan, then broke two eggs into a bowl and beat them with a thing made of wire loops.

"It's a whisk," he said, seeing me studying it. "I've seen them in France but never here."

"Mrs. Monty," I said. "She's French, you know. She must've brought it from there."

I hadn't known we had such an item, and had to admit that there were probably all kinds of things I didn't know about in my own house.

Beating the eggs, Max said, "When I left home, my mother told me I needed to know how to cook at least one thing so I wouldn't starve. Hence, omelets. The pickle was my own invention."

He added salt and pepper. "Tallulah loves my omelets," he said. "I mean, loved."

"For breakfast," I said. Not a question.

He kept beating, not looking at me. Not looking guilty, but still not looking at me. Well, that was all right. It was before us, I figured. And Tallulah Bankhead, well, few men—or women— could resist her.

Max sneaked me a glance. "At least I don't go around stealing people's underwear."

"It's not underwear," I said. "Not exactly. It's a camisole. Really, some of them are so pretty they could be worn out in public. Maybe one day girls will do that."

"And you took this one from Vernon's house, why?"

"It's custom work," I said. "I thought if I could find out who designed it, I could find out from them who it was for. This work is really beautiful, but I don't know whose it is."

"And if it's the girlfriend's?"

"It might help me find her, or at least figure out her role in all this."

"And what will that accomplish?" Max asked. "Especially if she turns up dead, too?"

117

"I don't know," I confessed. "I guess that would be where it ends. But I'm not ready to give up yet."

"So you're going to find her family and appear on their doorstep with their possibly dead relative's underwear—"

"Camisole."

"—camisole, and say you found it under a strange, dead man's bed?" Max said.

"I wouldn't do that," I said. "I haven't thought it through that far. But I'm not ready to give up yet. Even if there was no crime, there were two accidents that never should have happened."

"Isn't that kind of the definition of an accident?" Max said. "Something that never should have happened but did because of stupidity, or fate, or … whatever?"

"I'd like to think someone would care if something like that happened to me," I said, "and would want to get some answers."

"You're Frankie Franklin," he said. "Your face is on the cover of *Photoplay* this month with a story about how you overcame your severe shyness as a little tyke to become an actress and beloved star of the motion pictures. Half the country would go into mourning if something happened to you. FDR himself would order an investigation."

"Well, I care what happened to Vernon. And I'm going to find out what I can."

He considered this, and nodded. "Not that I could stop you. But I just have to play devil's advocate."

"Every Nick needs a Nora. Every Holmes needs a Watson," I said. "Just call me Sherlock. Or Shirleylock. Or something."

Max inspected the eggs he was still tormenting, and asked, "Do you know if Mrs. Monty has an herb garden?"

"Yes, that I know," I said. "There's um, parsley. I think I can identify parsley."

"Yeah, it's the stuff that comes on the baked potato you never eat. Can you go pick some?"

"I think I can manage that," I said, and went out to the garden where I knew Mrs. Monty grew herbs. I was usually too involved with other things to pay attention to what they were, but I saw that next to each little plant was a wooden stick with its name—
118

sage, tarragon, rosemary—neatly written on it, and found that I could indeed recognize parsley, from having seen it on my plate. I plucked a few stems and brought them in to Max like a bouquet.

Max grabbed a knife and a cutting board and expertly chopped the parsley into little green bits and put them aside. I watched in fascination as he turned up the flame under the pan, waited until the butter foamed a bit, then poured in the eggs and swirled them around until they coated the bottom and gradually became pale yellow and opaque. A minute or two later, he picked up half the cheese cubes and dropped them onto the eggs, followed by the pickles. My stomach growled.

A couple of minutes later the omelet was done to Max's satisfaction, and he folded it neatly with a spatula and slipped it, plump and golden, onto a plate he'd had warming in the oven. It looked great.

"OK, doll, now scatter the green stuff over the eggs, while I make a second one," he ordered. I did.

"This is heavenly," I said when we finally sat down and tried the actual product. "You do have talents I knew nothing about."

"I don't want you to get bored with me," Max said, pouring me more white wine. "In fact, I was just thinking—"

He was interrupted by the sound of a car gearing down outside to make the turn into my driveway, a sharp squeal of tires, and then a sputter and silence. Then the engine being cranked up again. Then silence.

"That did not sound good," he said.

I was already up and heading for the door.

We were brought up short by the sight of Raymond's enormous silver Duesenberg, which had come to rest at a haphazard angle across the driveway. Inside was Ray himself, disheveled and draped over the steering wheel, looking out and up into the branches of one of the olive trees, as though he'd never seen one before.

"What's that noise?" I said, hearing a hiccupping sound like a bad radio coming from inside the car.

"I think he's singing," Max said.

We smelled the whiskey the moment the car door opened. Raymond felt for the running board with his foot, missed it, and more or less fell out onto the driveway, grabbing the door to steady himself. He was wearing the pants to a nice linen suit, and one of his expensive, custom-made shirts, but no tie and no jacket. He reeked of Scotch, his favorite, Glenlivet. He was humming to himself and smiling blurrily at us.

"Frankie and Maxie were lovers," he sang. "Oh lordy how they could love—" And then his knees started to go.

Max grabbed Raymond's arm and ducked underneath it, keeping the taller man from falling down. "Hey, pal," he said. "Can you walk? We'll get you into the house."

"Can I walk?" Raymond said as though it had been a challenge. "Can I walk? I can dance! I can … I can … fly …"

I stood there aghast. This was as bad as I'd ever seen him. I dashed for the front door. Max half-dragged, half-walked Raymond up the steps and into the house, depositing him on one of the living room sofas. I liked that sofa. I hoped he wouldn't throw up on it.

Raymond regarded me blearily. "What is the matter, my darling?" he asked, slurring. "Is it not past cocktail hour?"

"Well past for you, Raymond," I said. "What on earth are you doing, drinking like that again?"

"I can't stand it anymore. I was almost killed! By my ex-wife!" He shook his head and then grimaced. "Even though … washn't her fault …"

He groaned. "I couldn't even go to Vernon's funeral," he said. "I'm horrible. You're horrible. Everything is horrible."

We tried to get him to lie down on the couch, but he kept popping up to a sitting position, reminding me of one of those children's toys. He finally stayed sitting, but clutched his head in his hands, moaning, "I'm the worst of the worst. No one is worse than me. And they keep coming back to haunt me."

"Who, Raymond?"

"Women. The ones I'd forgotten. Only now I'm starting to remember them. Mary, Peggy, Ellie, Virginia, Joanna … Oh my god, Joanna … I told her she was, she was a … a golddigger!
120

But she wasn't." He jabbed a finger in the air in Max's and my general direction. "She was a sweet girl… they were all sweet girls… I'm worse than nothing …"

His head lolled, and his eyes closed. Max and I shot a glance at each other, disgust mixed with pity.

"I'll go make some coffee," Max said, and went off to the kitchen.

Raymond snapped to attention on the sofa, still sitting, though. "I didn't remember any of them for so long and now they're haunting me!"

There was no use in talking to him. He sprawled back again on the sofa and was not making sense, and clearly would not be making sense for the next several hours.

Max and I got one cup of coffee into him, and then another. "You're lucky Max knows how to make coffee," I said.

Raymond was hunched over the cup, staring into it as though it held tea leaves rather than coffee.

"Blue Willow," he murmured, studying its blue-and-white pattern. "Like at Willie Hearst's castle … We had such fun there … such fun … The zebras! D'you remember the zebras?"

Several cups later, it was becoming obvious that he couldn't sober up enough to drive. But I didn't want him to stay here and ruin a perfectly good weekend with Max. That would be too much—my first husband ruining a weekend with my second.

"Max, let's get him into the Hudson," I said as we retreated to the kitchen for a quick discussion of logistics. "I just want him out of here and to keep the Duesie away from him for now."

We got him into my little car and drove him home, which was a few canyons and many winding, steep streets away from our house. Raymond moaned at every turn that he was about to "heave," as he said. I drove grimly on and finally got to the Tudor-style, half-timbered residence. His houseboy, Gabby, came to the door looking sorrowful, and took possession of him. Gabby hardly talked—even less than Monty. He was small and dark and competent, and if he was disgusted by his employer's condition, he didn't let it show.

"Come on, Mr. Raymond," he said, "let's get you into bed."

"Can we help?" I asked, hoping he'd say no.

"No. He's been like this a few times lately," Gabby said.

We watched as the door closed behind the small Filipino houseboy and his sagging employer.

"I guess we're lucky he didn't throw up in my car," I said.

"You have a gift for looking on the bright side," Max replied, holding the Hudson's door open for me.

I started the car up as he got in on the passenger's side. "I think I'd better come here tomorrow to check on him, and bring the Duesie back. Maybe I won't leave his keys, though," I said.

"Will you need me?"

"Always," I said, giving him a smile and a sideways glance. "But not for that. I'll just call for you to come pick me up later."

Chapter Eighteen

The 1930 Model J Duesenberg is a large, stately motorcar, and I could swear this one looked embarrassed to be found, in the bright morning light, looking abandoned rather than properly parked in the driveway.

"Sorry, old thing," I said, patting the wire-wheeled spare tire mounted on its sleek side.

Raymond had bought this impressive auto soon after we were married. He'd seen one at the Paris Motor Show and wouldn't rest until he had bought one. For me, he said—although everything about it was custom-made to suit his taste, from the length of the chassis to the pale gray brocade-and-leather interior, to the hood ornament, which was a glass falcon's head by Lalique.

The two-ton car was ridiculously fast. We'd tested its speed out in the desert once, and it had easily topped 100 mph, with Raymond driving and both of us roaring with laughter. We had had fun, every now and then.

"He doesn't deserve either of us," I said as I slid behind the wheel. I had always loved to drive the Duesie myself, and had had second thoughts about letting him keep it in the divorce.

I ran my finger along the dashboard: no dust. He'd had the car kept up nicely—or rather, his assistant, Tony, had. Raymond didn't have a staff at home anymore except for Tony and Gabby.

The Duesie's powerful engine sprang to life when I started it up, with a sound that made me smile: like a lioness gently awakened from her nap, stretching, ready to run.

Annoyed as I was at Raymond, I was looking forward to the twenty-minute drive to his place, just because I had missed driving her. We started down the hill, on the twisting, turning streets in my neighborhood.

"All they did was follow a snake and pave its trail," my father used to say about the way down.

I knew these roads by heart, and probably could have driven them blindfolded. Usually I took the curves like a slalom skier, swooping left and right, knowing exactly the top speed that was safe. And at first, that's how I started off.

It was a beautiful spring day, the sun slanting through the trees and making dappled shadows on the road, the air fresh, the birds singing all around. A fox darted in front of me and I said, "Oh!" in delight and tapped the brake.

Delight quickly turned to alarm.

The Duesie responded under protest, barely slowing. Not a welcome feeling on a road like this. Two or three curves later, it became clear that the brakes were failing.

When I realized what was wrong, a surge of adrenaline made my palms tingle, and I geared down, hoping that would help. It barely registered, as the Duesenberg plunged forward, like a horse with the bit between its teeth, ignoring me. I tried the parking brake. That didn't help, either. Normally I gave no thought to what lay beyond the downhill edge of the street: houses, stone staircases, nearly vertical drop-offs into the brushy canyon. Now the edges loomed in my mind. I could almost feel what it would be like for the giant car to hurtle off the road, with me inside. The brief moment of flight, and then the crash.

I fought to keep the car on the pavement as the tires squealed and then sprayed dirt and gravel, taking each turn too fast, knowing it was only a matter of moments before we broke free and went over.

Heart pounding in my throat, I looked desperately for a means of slowing, short of crashing headlong into a tree, a rock or a house. I saw everything that flashed by as something I might be able to steer into, hit at an angle and stop before we went over, or killed somebody. I knew I couldn't be choosy, but my mind recoiled at the thought of bashing into any of the things I could see. Another car: no. A stone wall: no. A eucalyptus tree:

124

God, no. Soon steering would do no good, and all that would be left was the speed, and the headlong plunge.

And then I saw it: a driveway straight ahead, one that I wouldn't even have to steer for as the road took off to the left. Palms and native trees flanked it, and the wrought-iron gate across it was, by some stroke of luck, standing open.

It wasn't like I had a choice. I was going too fast to make any kind of turn, and the Duesenberg went for the drive as though of its own accord. I could only hang on.

The car hit the bottom of the driveway too fast, and its front bumper struck the rising ground with a jarring thud and then bounced back up. Even with my hands braced for impact, my forehead hit the steering wheel. Please, no scars, I thought wildly, and counted myself lucky that I felt no blood streaming into my eyes.

But—it felt like a miracle—the big vehicle had slowed, just a bit. A small beam of relief broke through the storm of fear that had seized me. I prayed the drive was long, and steep. It was. The Duesenberg jolted roughly at every bump, but kept slowing as we climbed.

And then, reaching the top: Paradise. Or at least an earthly version of it.

As the car continued to roll, slowly, a panorama of emerald-green lawns, clipped hedges, spring-flowering shrubs, and more palm trees unfolded before and around me. My heart's wild pounding was starting to slow, but I had another leap of alarm as I realized my heavy chariot was moving steadily, dumbly, toward an ornamental fountain of polished stone that sat in the middle of the circular drive, its water burbling and splashing like diamonds in the sun. The fountain looked pretty solid and certainly not like something I wanted to run into, even at five miles per hour.

The brakes would do nothing, but the steering was still responsive. I wrenched the wheel to the right, and saw, over the glass falcon's head, a small tree with a beautiful spreading canopy. It was the only object around I thought might stop us, and I steered for it.

The Duesie continued its slow progress, and the tree got

closer, and closer, and then, with bark screeching and trunk groaning, it bent under our front bumper. And we stopped.

We hadn't flown off the road. I almost couldn't believe it. We weren't at the bottom of a canyon. I wasn't dead, crushed in a tangle of steel and glass.

I fought the urge to throw up or faint, and closed my eyes, hoping to prevent either, with my hands still in a death grip on the steering wheel. Outside the open window, I could hear birds singing. I made myself breathe slow and deep.

When I did dare to open my eyes again, I saw a gardener in a black smock, standing frozen a few feet away, his face a horrified mask. He was not looking at me, but at the pretty tree bent over in front of the Duesie, like a maiden protesting the advances of an unwelcome suitor.

I gave him what I hoped was an apologetic look and slowly began to notice other details of my surroundings. The circular drive swept up to a grand house, a graceful confection of white stone that looked like a fifteenth-century French chateau. That wasn't possible, of course—it had been here since 1923 at the earliest—but still, it looked like someone had sent a gigantic dirigible to pluck the prettiest dwelling in the Loire Valley, bring it dangling across the Atlantic and deposit it right here in the Hollywood Hills, at someone's whim. There were people in this town who would do that, were it possible.

As I entertained myself with this fantastical idea, one of the chateau's grand double doors opened and the tiny figure of a woman emerged. Word of the invading Duesenberg must have been relayed to the house.

The little figure paused a moment, then descended the stone steps and came toward me. She didn't seem to walk so much as float across the ground in her slim black trousers and black ballet slippers, with a long gray-and-white kimono fluttering around her.

She paused again to take in the sight of her stricken gardener, the tree, the Duesie, and me, then came closer.

I shut my eyes again, still trying to fight down the feeling that I was going to be sick. When I opened them this time, she was

126

right at my window, peering inside with a look of acute curiosity in her dark eyes.

She was maybe in her mid-forties, though with one of those oval, serene faces that look ageless, all strong features and dramatic, swooping black eyebrows. What she saw, looking in at me, was probably more along the lines of a drowned rat.

She looked me over with a hint of a smile, took a thoughtful puff from a cigarette in a slim silver holder, exhaled a cloud of smoke off to the side, and spoke.

"Well, Miss Franklin," she said. "That was one hell of an entrance."

Of course she knew who I was; most people in town did. But, I realized now, I also knew who she was—even though this was the first time I had ever heard her voice.

Dinah Merriwether had been one of the biggest stars when the movies were silent, when actors emoted away unheard, the audience finding out what they said only when a title card popped up on the screen.

Audiences had loved her, clamored for her, had run out to see her latest picture every few weeks. DeMille had engaged string quartets to play for her as she arrived on the set. Some sultan or other had sent her a female tiger cub, which now resided at the zoo.

At the peak of her career, she had made a dozen or more pictures a year and was mobbed by fans wherever she went, from New York to Rome to Buenos Aires. She had had worldwide success, and famous lovers of both sexes; Raymond, I was sure, had been one of them.

Thanks to breathless news coverage of her every move, we all felt that we knew her like we knew our own families. She traveled with mountains of baggage and a retinue of servants. Reporters followed her and wrote about her trips around the world, and her several marriages. She was rumored to have hired doubles as decoys when she tired of the attentions of rabid fans and unwanted reporters. She lived with such panache and in such luxury, she was known as "the Empress of Hollywood."

And then, at the height of her fame, a few months before

the stock market crashed, the Empress had dropped from sight, a disappearance as neat and complete as anything planned and executed by the great Houdini himself. Only the rumors had remained: She had married minor royalty, was living in Tibet, had lost her fortune and gone mad, had died.

But now here she was: quite alive, not broke, and not visibly mad—standing just outside my disabled car, in fact, as though waiting for me to make a move. When I didn't, paralyzed by, well, everything, she spoke again, briskly.

"Well, get out of there, girl," she said. "Come in and have a whiskey—or tea, if you don't indulge."

Her voice was low and musical, not squeaky or strangely accented and clearly not the reason she had left the pictures when sound happened. She waited as I slowly unclenched my hands from around the steering wheel, groped for the handle of the door, and stumbled out of the car, croaking, "Whiskey."

Miss Merriwether gave the gardener a sympathetic pat on the shoulder and set off for the house, not looking back, with the air of one who simply expects to be followed. I did, on wobbly legs.

Up the stone steps and through the double doors, I tagged along like a puppy as Miss Merriwether led the way past potted palm trees and feathery green ferns, onto and off of patterned Persian carpets, to a cozy library where every bit of wall that wasn't a door or tall window was covered with bookshelves. Many of the books had worn covers, like they had actually been read, and a couple of chintz-covered armchairs looked like the perfect places to read them. Bing Crosby's voice was just crooning the end of "Stardust" from a phonograph in the corner.

Besides books, there were photographs on a desk and side table: Miss Merriwether with friends, maybe family. They looked fairly recent; this was not the home of a woman stuck in the past. Obviously, a lot of people knew where she had been for the last decade, but had protected her privacy.

A few of the photos dated back to her days in the pictures, and I recognized one as a still from *Sergeant Pearl,* one of her last films, a Civil War tale about a girl who masquerades as a boy to join her brother in the Union Army.

128

I remembered, oddly enough, that one of the few times I had talked to Vernon, he had mentioned working on that picture when he was still an actor. In fact, there he was in one of the other photos, among a group of people clowning around on location somewhere. It was a jolt to see the person I'd been thinking about so much, whose death was haunting me. A young Vernon, with more hair. He was not unattractive.

Miss Merriwether had paused near one of the tall windows, in front of a cocktail table which held an impressive number of bottles of expensive booze. She reached for a Kentucky bourbon, and poured generously into two short glasses, then added a splash of water from a crystal decanter. She handed me one and tipped her glass toward me.

"*Santé,*" she said, and took a sip. "It's times like this I really appreciate the end of Prohibition, don't you? I don't usually do this in the morning, myself, but then I don't have starlets driving their cars into my rarest plants every day, either. That's a golden medallion tree you may have murdered, by the way. I had it brought from Brazil."

I said I didn't know, and that I was sorry and would pay for the damage or to replace it.

"No doubt you could, and would," she said, taking a seat in one of the chintz chairs. I did, too. "But it's not necessary. I'd rather hear the story."

She leaned forward and almost whispered, "I'm very curious to know, what happened? Is someone trying to do you in?"

"Why, no—I—I don't think so," I said. "It's not even my car. Not anymore, I mean. It's Raymond Sinclare's."

"Ah, Raymond, yes," she said. "The one you very nearly shot last week."

She smiled at my look of surprise. "Oh, don't worry—I hear everything, or almost everything, up here on my perch. It's all much more amusing at a distance." The Crosby record had reached its end, and she went over, lifted the tone arm off the record and replaced it in the bracket.

"I didn't like it so much when I was in the thick of it," she said, returning to her chair. "The tension, the hours, the intrigue—the diets! Anyway, I was glad to hear you hadn't actually killed Raymond. We made four pictures together, you know."

I said I did know.

Her smile was sympathetic. "I also heard about poor Vernon." She sighed, looking over at the collection of pictures. "He was a good man. There are rumors that it looked like he was trying to save a woman from drowning that day."

I didn't ask how she'd heard that. She had already said she heard everything up here.

Continuing to look at the picture rather than me, she said, almost to herself, "It's strange but, I always thought it would be a woman—getting involved with the wrong woman—that would be his downfall. He was an addict."

She gave me a look. "Sex, you know. We had a fling." She shrugged. "But he fell in love easily and became obsessed and demanding. It's why his wife left him."

"I didn't know," I said. "I knew he was no longer married, but—"

"If one was involved with him, he would want to have ... encounters ... three or four times a day," she said, nodding her head slowly. "Every day. Even when one had an early call the next morning. I know, he didn't look like he'd have it in him. But you know what they say about still waters running deep."

Once more I tried to picture this, and failed, even though it fit neatly with Mrs. Botelho's description of him and his girlfriend.

"I hadn't thought of Vernon in years," she said. "You wouldn't think it to know him just in passing, but he had a certain, what would you say, magnetism about him. And I also could see him risking his life to save someone else's. He was, in some ways, selfless."

Something about her look made me bold enough to ask, "Did you love him?"

"I loved anyone I was involved with—at least when we were together," she said with a wry smile. "I was very good at convincing myself I was in love. But with Vernon, well, we only had the one thing in common, and frankly, the late nights with him were starting to affect my work. I remember sitting in makeup and Ada telling me, 'These black circles under your eyes will become permanent if you don't start getting enough sleep.'"

She chuckled at the memory. "So, as much fun as he was, I had to break it off. Because of that, and also, well, I knew Vernon couldn't provide me with the life I knew I wanted. Needed."

Miss Merriwether looked around the beautiful room, at the antiques, books, and art, and then back to me. "Yes, I'm not the first woman—or man—to trade sex and youthful allure for security. And I won't be the last."

She caught me thinking and added, "It's the same thing you do—and what all of us do in front of the cameras—isn't it? In the pictures you just do it on a more impersonal scale, making millions of people love you, instead of just one. And if you're smart, you know it won't last, and you make your plans for getting out."

Her smile was warm, and genuine, and I liked her despite of, or maybe because of, her blunt way of speaking. She was a woman who didn't—didn't need to—worry about saying the wrong thing and ending up out of work or on the street. An enviable position.

"My plan involved a financier named Paul Arondale. And if I do say so myself, I made his declining years very pleasant." She nodded, as if to herself, and then, looking out to her garden, not at me, said, "Do you think it was an accident?"

"What?" I asked, taken aback by the sudden turn in the conversation.

"The shooting," she said, now regarding me keenly. "Do you think it was an accident? Was Vernon's drowning? And, while we're at it, whatever just happened to your car?"

I thought for a moment. I didn't have the answers to any of those questions, though I was trying to find out the ones to the first two. It could be that the shooting and Vernon's drowning were both accidents. Or one accident and one guilt-shadowed suicide. If Vernon was obsessive about love and about his job, why wouldn't he, if he felt guilt, be passionate in his reaction to that, too? Both could be crimes, but with what purpose? If

131

someone had wanted me to shoot Raymond, wouldn't Raymond have gotten a hint, from somewhere, or someone, that he was hated that much? As far as I knew, he had received no threats and his drunken episodes had, luckily, hurt only him.

And the brakes … I wouldn't have been surprised to find that Raymond had been trying to save money by deferring maintenance on the car—putting effort mainly into its looks instead of its brakes or engine. As my father used to say, don't assume malice when sheer stupidity explained so much that went wrong every day.

Miss Merriwether was studying me. "You could have met a tragic end today," she said. "Which would have done wonders for your legend. Just look at poor Rudy Valentino."

Valentino, indeed. She raised an eyebrow, and, as her words sank in, I giggled. Then giggled some more. Then the giggle became laughing, and more laughing, until I couldn't breathe, and abruptly found myself in the grip of a full-on, unhinged, gasping, laughing fit. Something about having narrowly cheated death, having nearly killed my ex-husband, having run away to get married, and now having drinks with a living legend …

Afraid I'd spill it, I managed to jerkily set my bourbon down on a crystal coaster with the initials "DM" carved into it. It made a startlingly loud and sharp noise. Funny how you remember details like that.

Miss Merriwether quietly watched as I struggled for control, holding the arms of my chair. I wouldn't have been surprised if she'd given me a smart slap to snap me out of it, but she just sat calmly and waited for me to recover.

"I think it's time we got you home," she said sympathetically, when I finally was down to just hiccups, wiping my eyes, and apologizing for being such a mess in her presence.

"Now, now, no need for that," she said. "You have every right to be frightened out of your mind, and I think you've handled it bravely."

I coughed and had another go at the bourbon.

She regarded me a moment and then said, "I like your style, my dear."

132

I could only smile weakly back at her.

"All right," she said, getting up with the grace of a sixteen-year-old, "I'll have my driver take you back home, and we'll see about getting that hulk towed out of my landscaping and to your mechanic."

I realized it was past time for me to have called home to have Max pick me up—and that there would be quite a story about why I wasn't at Raymond's place instead. When I dialed my number, though, the phone just rang and rang, which was odd, even allowing enough time for Max to hear it from the living room, remember everyone else was gone, and get to the phone.

She looked out the window, where her gardener, still looking stricken, was conferring with a uniformed chauffeur.

"I think the tree can be saved," she said, watching them. Then she turned to me. "Do you like gardens?"

"I just discovered last night that thyme and sage look different," I said. "That was a new development."

"I'll tell you something," Miss Merriwether said. "It's not an overstatement to say that my garden saved my life. Gardens give us something to take care of and make beautiful long after our own beauty has faded."

Except hers was still present and accounted for, I thought. But she went on.

"What I mean," she said, "is that, even after our looks are no longer … what they were, when they're no longer something people will pay us for … we can still create beauty around ourselves, and for others to enjoy. So come with me, if you have just a few minutes, and let's see if I can't make you a convert. Philip—my driver—can wait a bit while I show you the plants that survived your siege."

Chapter Nineteen

Sometime later, Miss Merriwether's driver dropped me at my own front door and I went wearily inside. It was hardly noon on a Saturday, and I was exhausted.

Major Bowes seemed to sense something was amiss, because instead of posing at a distance to be admired before allowing me to greet him, he bounded over and rubbed against my legs. I picked him up and he didn't even protest, but snuggled in, purring. I stroked his soft white fur and felt a little better.

Then he decided that was enough of that, and squirmed to get down. I set him on the sofa, whereupon he jumped down and stalked off to the living room. I followed, wondering why I wasn't hearing Max working out the sticky parts of a new song. All I wanted was to fling myself into his arms and be comforted and encouraged to tell the whole outrageous story while he marveled at how brave I was. After all, wasn't that what husbands were for?

Starting to feel indignant about Max not being right there when I needed him, I went on to the kitchen, and stopped in surprise.

Max was sitting in one of the chairs at the kitchen table, holding a steak to his eye. It was a big steak. It looked like it could feed maybe three people. It also looked still frozen.

"Max!" I forgot my own fatigue and ran to him. "What happened to you?"

He regarded me from behind the steak. "I met one of your, er, fans, I think," he said wryly. "Who unfortunately saw me first."

"Let me see," I said, and took the steak from him. The area around his eye was puffy and red, soon to be seen in full Technicolor.

"I have a better bet for your eye."

I put the steak in the refrigerator on a plate, got out the icepack and the ice cube tray, put the ice in the icepack and handed it to him while he told me the story.

Some time after I had left, Max had gone outside and found Mr. Noguchi lying on the ground, near the garage.

"I started down there, of course," Max said, "to see what was the matter. But before I got to Mr. Noguchi, this big mug came hot-footing it around the corner and whacked me with something, not sure what it was. Maybe just his fist. I was concentrating on Mr. Noguchi, never saw it coming."

Attacked without warning, Max had staggered back into the side of the house, seeing stars. When his head cleared, he heard footsteps running away, but the man disappeared around the corner and Mr. Noguchi was still on the ground and needing attention, so Max went to him.

"How is he?" I asked.

"He got up without much help," Max said. "Just complained about his bad knee. He and Kit had gotten back from a shopping trip, and while she went into the house, he went to put the car away and apparently surprised this fellow lurking about the garage. And got knocked to the ground for his trouble. He said the guy rushed him, threw a shoulder into him and kicked him in the ribs when he fell."

I felt immediate anger at anyone hurting Mr. Noguchi, and also slightly ill, immediately connecting the intruder with the failure of the Duesie's brakes. Had he—or someone in cahoots with him—been the one who tampered with the brakes? And then been looking for other cars to sabotage? Perhaps just covering his bases? I hoped I wasn't being overdramatic. Sometimes things on cars could just fail. And people could be found trespassing for numerous other reasons, some of them harmless. Still, this would be quite a coincidence.

But first there was Mr. Noguchi.

I started for the door. "I'd better go see how he—"

Kit appeared in the doorway, in her off-duty dungarees and a gray-and-white striped shirt with the sleeves rolled up, a scarf holding her hair back, and fire in her eyes.

"Kit, how is Mr. Noguchi?" I asked.

"He's fine," Kit said. "He's lying down now; I told him to try and get some sleep. But if I find that guy who knocked him down, I'll take a baseball bat to him!"

She had several of them, and a mean swing. I made a mental note never to get on Kit's bad side.

"Do you have any idea who he was?" I asked Max.

"Not a bit," Max said, repositioning the icepack on his eye. "After we got Mr. Noguchi up and Kit was seeing to him at their place, I went out to the street to look, but he was gone. Must've had a car parked nearby. He didn't look like any of the neighbors I'd ever seen."

"Too bad he got away," I said, "because I think he might have had something to do with how my morning went."

"Nuts, I was supposed to pick you up!" Max suddenly exclaimed. "But I must've been outside when you called and wouldn't have heard. How did you get home from Raymond's?"

"Well, first," I said, "I never got to Raymond's."

Max and Kit both gave me quizzical looks.

"I'll tell you all about it," I said. "But let me get some water first."

I got the pitcher out of the refrigerator, and a glass, poured water, gulped half of it down, and wondered how to tell them what happened without being melodramatic.

I decided to just give it to them straight.

"So, first, the brakes failed on the Duesie," I began.

Max and Kit both turned alarmed looks on me and Max sprang out of his chair, the icepack tumbling to the floor. I could almost see thought balloons over their heads like in the comics: me in the massive car, hurtling into a canyon, smashing trees like kindling. I hurried on.

"But, as you can see, I'm fine," I said, taking Max's outstretched hands and giving them a squeeze. He moved closer and put his arms around me, as though even now I was in danger of being snatched from him. It was comforting. I quickly skimmed over the scarier parts of the ride, and got to what was,

136

in some ways, the more interesting part of the morning: the visit with Miss Merriwether.

Their alarm became mixed with something like wonder.

"She was in the first film I ever saw, when I was six," Max said, dreamily. "I thought she was the most beautiful thing I'd seen in my whole life."

He had such a faraway look in his eye that I had to chuckle. "Maybe we can arrange for you to meet her," I said. "She said to drop by anytime."

"Sure she did," he said. The rumors that placed her in town had mentioned armed sentries and large, vicious dogs guarding her privacy.

"She did!" I said. "I think she wants to know what really happened to Vernon too, if you ask me."

"You'll have to let that go sometime, don't you think?" Max said.

"Unless somehow what happened today is connected to what happened on the set and what happened to Vernon," I said.

He and Kit exchanged a look. I saw her face grow hard as she thought about someone hurting her father.

"I'll let Monty know about the car at Miss Merriwether's," she said. "And then stay with Dad, if you don't mind."

And she took herself off.

I turned to Max. "Miss Merriwether also told me something about Vernon," I said. "I don't know if it has anything to do with anything."

"Like?"

"Like … well, you know how we like making love," I said

Max frowned and rubbed his chin. "Hm, let me see if I remember …" he said, then switched to serious when I gave him a look. "Yes?"

"Well, apparently Vernon really liked it," I said. "I mean, really, really liked it. And often. More often than most men … I guess."

I felt my face redden just a bit. I hadn't had that much experience, and didn't want to misrepresent myself.

"It wasn't just that he was noisy with the girlfriend Mrs.

Botelho heard him with," I went on. "Also, he and Miss Merriwether had something going for a while."

"Well, well, Vernon," Max said. "With some people you just never know. And yet at work, you said he was … fastidious?"

"I think he was … controlled, usually," I said. "That's the feeling I got from him at the studio. And his house. Maybe he was so disciplined in most of his life, he had to let off steam somewhere else?"

"It sounds like he had a lot of steam," Max said.

"And then what Stanley said about her being on the set, and him yelling at her and them both leaving," I said. "And also from what Sam said. … I have to wonder about the girl Stanley saw him with, and that Sam mentioned," I said. "Sam said she looked pleased, like she'd had a little victory or something."

Max looked up.

"Some women might find it fun or a challenge to see how much control they have over a man," I said. "Maybe she wasn't even supposed to visit him on the set, but she did, so there was this clash between the part of his life that was so disciplined and this … wild part?"

"I could see that," Max said, and gave me a sly look. "I can imagine being psychologically enslaved by an irresistible dame."

I crossed my eyes at him.

"So there was lunchtime hanky-panky going on?" Max continued. "The girlfriend thinks it's fun to bewitch and bother him? And that threw him off, interrupted or distracted him in a big way, so he didn't notice something was not right with the gun? Maybe that was it?"

"It's something I can picture," I said, "after talking to Miss Merriwether, especially. This girlfriend coming to see him unexpectedly, which could have just been an innocent distraction, instead caused an accident where someone could have been killed …"

"So that seems like a more logical scenario than someone who had it in for Sam, or Ray … or you."

I nodded. "Vernon didn't have anything against any of us," I said. "None of us even knew him that well. Besides, he would
138

have known I wasn't aiming at anyone in particular. He wasn't so crazy as to take a chance that someone would be hit."

"So maybe it was the girl who wanted someone to shoot Raymond?" Max said. "And thought it would work because she wasn't familiar with how you do things with guns in the pictures?"

"But you would think, then, that she would be someone Raymond knew, or I knew," I said. "Except she wasn't anyone either Raymond or I knew. We would have encountered her at some point and recognized her. And Sam saw her, but he didn't know her, either."

"And she was also the one at the beach?"

"Given the timing, she must be," I said. "Unless we're talking about triplets. So she showed up uninvited, they had a roll in the hay—or on the sofa in his office—and he was bothered and distracted, the gun was mishandled, there was a shooting, and he was furious with her for it."

"And then what?" Max said. "So furious he tried to drown her?"

Max shifted the icepack again. We were both quiet for a bit.

Eventually he said, "And maybe succeeded? That doesn't sound like the guy. And then he also drowned himself? On purpose? Or by accident?"

"I don't know, I guess it could be any of those things," I said. "I haven't seen anything in the papers about another body being found."

"Sometimes they never are," Max said. "Or sometimes they turn up miles away."

I thought about seeing Vernon in the commissary with a woman, no one I'd ever seen before. What had she said? Something about guns, as though she found them scary. Maybe it wasn't even the same girl after all. Maybe my brain just wanted to make a pattern out of random items.

Max groaned. "This is becoming very hard on my head," he said, moving the pack again.

I was feeling pretty beat myself, too, by this time, both mentally and physically.

139

"I'm going to lie down," I said, and reached for Max's hand. "I think it would be a good idea if you did, too."

Neither of us had the energy for *double entendres*. We headed for the bedroom, and I was grateful for the pleasantly cool house. But my mind still kept playing with the paltry set of facts we had, arranging them this way and that to see if anything made sense.

Had the girl handled the gun? And why? Did she put the real bullets in the Colt? And why would she do that? Was she crazy? A wild thing? Maybe she was one of those fans of mine who thought it would be a good prank to make Frankie Franklin fire a gun with live rounds, and then was mortified when someone really got hurt? And if that was the case, maybe that's why Vernon was angry at her. Maybe she was distraught, herself, and went to fling herself into the sea? Maybe she was trying to end it all and he followed her, telling her what had happened was terrible, but that he would help her through it and it would all be all right ... only to have them both drown?

"Or maybe she saw what effect distracting him had, and she just thought she was in trouble, got hysterical, went into the ocean but didn't want to kill herself. And they just both got in over their heads?" I blew out my breath in frustration. "I don't know ..."

Max peered at me from under the icepack.

"I'd like to think about this more when my head isn't hurting," he said. "If it needs to be thought about at all. Which maybe it doesn't."

I nodded and gave him an apologetic smile. "I hope it doesn't."

I have never been one for puzzles, the kind where you solve a riddle, or crack a coded message. But this was different, and bigger. Something was out of order in my world and I needed to have it make sense.

Max closed his eyes—both of them, I assumed; I could only see the one that wasn't under the icepack—and said, "You're thinking this can't be as far as we get."

I shook my head, then shrugged. "But I don't know where we
140

go from here," I said.

"I have a friend who's a reporter on the *Call*," Max said. "I can ask him to let me know if they turn up the girl's body. Although we'd see the story anyway, eventually. Was Vernon important enough that the studio would pay someone off to not write about it if the girl turned up either dead or alive?"

"I doubt they're thinking of him at all," I said matter-of-factly. "He wasn't irreplaceable."

"As opposed to a Frankie Franklin, or a Clay West," he said.

"Right," I said.

In our room, Major Bowes jumped onto the bed, having sensed an impending nap and wanting to be a part of it. It was a rare occasion when Max and I were occupying a bed and all we did was sleep, but that's what we did, with Major Bowes curled up on the pillows above our heads. It was late when we woke up, foraged in the kitchen and found crackers and cheese, ate them, and went back to sleep.

By Sunday morning, Max's black eye was giving him a roguish, rascally look that I found irresistible, and it was a while before we actually started the day. Deciding to take it easy on ourselves, we spent an hour or so in the pool, and then retired to the office and the living room; me to memorize lines for next week's filming, him to write a new love song for a picture involving a boxer and some scrappy kids from his old neighborhood, called *Angel in the Ring*.

Max showed me how to make egg salad for lunch, and I assured him I could never do it as well as he could, even impaired as he was with that shiner.

At six o'clock, on the dot, we heard the back door open. Mr. and Mrs. Monty were back. Whenever they took their trips, always short, they would put their car away in the garage, leave their bags in their cottage and check in to let me know they were home. It was one of those routines that were, despite whatever else was going on in my life, comforting in their predictability.

"How was your brother?" I asked Monty, who looked happy to be home.

"Very well, thanks, Miss," he said. The chatterbox.

Meanwhile, Mrs. Monty saw Max's eye and began fussing over him. He looked to be enjoying it, at least at first. After a bit, though, during which he fended off her offer to cure it immediately with a home remedy involving potatoes, he told her about Mr. Noguchi, and she fluttered off to see to him instead.

Max and I filled Monty in on the eventful weekend. I was not surprised to see his jaw clench when I told him about the brakes—both for the danger I had been in, and to think someone would do that to such a fine car, if it was done on purpose—a position I had to agree with.

A little while later, everyone finally having adjusted to the fact that I had had a scare but was not hurt, and that Mr. Noguchi was none the worse for his encounter with the prowler, and that Max's face would recover from the punch, we resumed our usual routines at Casa de Frankie.

Mrs. Monty had one more thing on her mind, though. "Well," she said, fixing me with her bright, sympathetic gaze, "I think maybe it is a bad idea for me to leave at all.'

And then she handled the upset the way she handled everything—she washed her hands, put on her apron, and prepared to cook for us. She went to the refrigerator and pulled out the plate with the steak on it.

"*Merci* for thawing this," she said, sounding ever so slightly surprised that we would have thought of it. "Ze dinner shall proceed in minutes."

Max and I exchanged glances. Neither of us said anything.

Chapter Twenty

"You may go in now," Mr. Wiseman's secretary said. She was about a hundred years old, and thin as a stick, with a gaze that could paralyze a python at twenty paces. Or so Fortune's starlets all said. She did have a face like a pickle, but also a surprisingly sweet smile that she would deploy depending on how her boss was feeling about you at the moment. I saw it fairly often.

I wasn't seeing it now.

I stood up and smoothed my brown tweed flutter skirt before going past Miss Pickle (as I always thought of her—her real name was Agnes Colliers). I usually went for a sweet but serious look when meeting with Mr. Wiseman. Nice, muted colors, sensible shoes: two-toned, suede-and-leather heels today. Stocking seams straight. I only had a vague notion of why I'd been summoned, thinking it had something to do with not having ended up as Mrs. Knight of the Open Range by marrying Clay.

Miss Pickle swung open the huge, mahogany door and I went in, my feet sinking silently into the thick carpet.

Mr. Wiseman's office wasn't a white, mile-long affair like Louis B. Mayer's over at Metro, which was designed with the express purpose of intimidating all who entered. Mr. Wiseman was more subtle than that. With glowing, dark paneling and bookshelves full of books, tasteful bronze busts, deep armchairs, and heavy, expensive window treatments, his office was meant to make you think you had been ushered into the library of an English manor house, even though from the outside, the building looked like nothing more than a big, gray factory.

Mr. Wiseman was not nobility any more than the rest of us. He was a tough kid from Brooklyn who had dealt in scrap iron before buying his first theater and making his fortune producing pictures, diverting fantasies for the masses. We were in the business of make-believe. But his power over me, because of my contract, was quite uncomfortably real. Though I had an idea why he wanted to see me, I decided to let him do the work of bringing it up.

Mr. Wiseman smiled at me as I came in, rose from behind his desk, took my hand and kissed it, holding onto it just a little longer than necessary. He was a little taller than me, with a round bald head and heavy black eyebrows with sad brown eyes under them. He was actually, as studio heads went, not a bad guy. But like all the men who ran all the studios in town, he wanted to be in total control of his stars' behavior, onscreen and off. You had to follow a script, so to speak, pretty much all the time. It was just a way of protecting their investments.

"You look lovely, my dear," he said. "Married life must agree with you." Why did people always say that, like marriage was a dinner that either gave you a stomachache or didn't?

"Thank you," I said, standing because I hadn't been invited to sit. That's what you did in Mr. Wiseman's office.

So when he waved to one of the pair of tapestry-covered chairs flanking an elegant little cherrywood table, saying, "Sit. Please," I sat.

He took the other one, sitting forward on the edge. Not so bad, I thought. If I was going to get a big lecture, he would have gone back behind the desk. So he's probably just going to give me a small lecture, probably about the wedding. About how I hadn't followed the script for America's Kid Sister. About how I should have gone along with their plans and married Clay.

"We have put the word out that Clay West has retreated to his ranch to mend his broken heart after you impulsively eloped," Mr. Wiseman said. "And we've sent Ida Ivanovna to visit for a few days, to console him."

I blinked, impressed. He looked pleased with himself. Ida liked only girls, Clay liked only boys. In the fantasy that the studio was weaving, this would work well for both of them. I knew they'd be photographed in his pool, taking a walk under

144

his grape arbor, playing with the dogs, visiting the horses, while her "secretary" and Sam stayed in the background. Once the photographer left, the two couples would regroup into their preferred configurations and probably have a lovely time. Ida was an avid birdwatcher, like Sam, and she and Clay would probably get along well together because Clay got along with everybody.

I knew Mr. Wiseman didn't have to share all this with me. It had been arranged by Mr. Fixx. It was Fixx who paid cops and reporters to not do their jobs when it was in the studio's interest for them not to, he who paid bail and found doctors to treat conditions the studio did not want the public to know about, who sent flowers or new cars to wronged wives and performed all sorts of other tasks, as required.

Mr. Wiseman's telling me the cooked-up story about Clay and Ida (the studio's "dark Russian beauty" who really came from Des Moines and whose real name was Ivy Bryson) was his way of saying no hard feelings about my impromptu approach to getting married. He certainly didn't have to, didn't need to, fill me in on it.

So that was all he'd asked me to come in for. I started to relax a bit, expecting to be dismissed, when he spoke again.

"Now," he said, "what I wanted to talk to you about."

Uh-oh. I sat a little straighter. Like a schoolgirl paying attention.

"For the most part you have been exceptionally good for the studio," Mr. Wiseman said. "You haven't gotten into trouble that we've had to take care of (by which he meant shoplifting, or getting pregnant, or running over someone with my car), but we know you've been snooping."

I had no right to look surprised, but I was, a bit. I really hadn't thought I'd been being watched that closely.

"This is different than you dressing up as a cowgirl to hobnob with those reprobates around the Columbia Drugstore," he added.

I had to smile a little. Everyone knew the guys who wanted work as extras riding horses in pictures hung around the corner of Sunset and Gower where they could call Central Casting to see if there was work. My father had been one of them and many of them, including a big handsome fellow named Marion Morrison, had been friends of my father's, so they were almost like family. I liked to visit there sometimes and catch up with the gossip. I hadn't realized Mr. Wiseman necessarily knew about it, though.

"Of course I know about that," he said. "What do you think I pay Fixx for? And it's fine—I know many of them are your friends, and on the whole they are better for you to pal around with than most of the actors we employ, who are basically nothing but tomcats whose teeth have been straightened and whitened and who've been taught to talk."

He didn't need to tell me that, I thought. Why, just Gable—

"We are concerned, however, that you might be getting mixed up in something you don't want to get mixed up in." Mr. Wiseman always said "we" when he meant "I"—he called the shots at Fortune, but he had a need to make it look like everyone was involved.

"And we thought you might need something to do after *Prairie Princess,* but before the Josephine picture starts principal photography," he said. "Since you seem to have had too much time on your hands lately."

That took me aback. The time between would be hardly enough for a picture to be shot, unless I was only in a few scenes and why would they bother then? "What do you mean, exactly?"

"As I said, it has come to my attention that you have been playing girl reporter, or girl detective or something of the kind," Mr. Wiseman said. "And that is not the image of Frankie Franklin that we wish you to project. The image of Frankie is America's Kid Sister—wholesome, open, sweet, intelligent, without a care in the world."

Mr. Wiseman sat back, letting that sink in. "And do you know what else Americans want their kid sister to be?"

"Brave?" I asked.

"Sane," he said. "And you don't look sane creeping around a house in the middle of the afternoon like a meshugenah."

146

"I am not crazy," I protested. "I've only been—"

"Snooping," he said. "Showing up at a property master's house like a nosy Girl Scout, asking questions, hobnobbing with some bum on the beach ... it's not the level of ... decorum ... we expect from you."

He seemed to be pleased with himself again, him with his fifth-grade education coming up with a word like that. I didn't need to ask how he knew about either of those little adventures. And, when I thought for two seconds about it, I also knew that the version of me that the studio was selling did not include my driving around like any old girl and showing up in any old place. But I thought he should know one real thing about it.

"I'm curious about why Vernon died," I said simply.

"He was consumed by guilt for being careless," Mr. Wiseman said, as though, in his mind, that settled it. "I have seen this before. Though I have to say, people in this town usually get over it quickly. But the brakes on your car—rather, Raymond's car—"

"You knew about that, too," I said. Of course they did. When would I learn?

Mr. Wiseman just regarded me silently, then said, "We have heard from the mechanic. They were tampered with. A small cut made in the line that would have gradually made the brakes fail. We have not found out who did it yet, however."

I was impressed and must have looked it.

"Trust me," he said. "We're looking out for you."

"That's ... touching," I said. And it was, kind of.

His next pronouncement wasn't, however.

"That said," he said, "we're loaning you out to Universal. Your next picture will be on location at Mammoth Lakes. It's called *I Married the Invisible Man*."

I felt the color drain from my face, but otherwise tried to conceal my shock. Studios loaned actors out all the time, often as a way of punishing them for complaining about casting, refusing a role, or other behavior they wanted to discourage. It was often to lesser studios for lesser pictures. I had never before considered that it would happen to me, though. Which was stupid.

Sometimes this backfired on the studio, as it did just last year when Metro loaned out Clark to Columbia to make *It Happened One Night* with Claudette Colbert, directed by Frank Capra. The picture wasn't supposed to be much, but turned out to be a smash and the won five Academy Awards. That was an unusual situation.

"Gosh," I said. Neutral, I reminded myself. Stay neutral before he comes up with something worse.

Universal wasn't a bad studio, though not as high-minded as Fortune, and had made something of a specialty out of horror movies like *Murders in the Rue Morgue, The Mummy*, and the original *The Invisible Man*. I supposed I'd be learning what the part was about soon, but assumed that I'd be playing the "I" in the title role. Since Claude Rains' character had died in the original, I also supposed the script would have some clever way of still making it about the Invisible Man. To tell the truth, I wasn't exactly dying, myself, to know. The picture had been well received, but being cast in a sequel was not exactly a break for me. It felt like at least a slap on the wrist, as I'm sure it was supposed to.

"Also," he went on—apparently deciding that since I had taken that so well, he would revisit the earlier topic, "you really should have taken my advice about Clay and married him. He's a proper match for you, not this nebbish musician."

"Composer," I said. "He's a composer."

"You think I don't know that?" Mr. Wiseman said. "It may be something we can work with, make him into the perfect partner for Frankie Franklin. Maybe he can write a tune like 'Yankee Doodle Dandy.' You know, an American tune that can get people's feet tapping. Like Cohan."

I didn't say anything, and he was silent for a moment, then looked up, gave me a grin, and shrugged.

"I am just trying to do what is best for you," he said. "Sometimes you kids need to be protected from yourselves, see?"

I nodded, and said. "And when—"

"You'll rehearse and have fittings starting this Thursday. And the rest of the details will be worked out as usual," Mr. Wiseman said, looking relieved that I hadn't made a fuss. He stood up and so did I. "You understand, of course."

"I do."

"I mean about why I am forced to do this."

"So others don't get the idea they can do whatever they want."

He looked offended. "No, no, not to not do whatever they want," he said. "Not to do things that, in the long run, will be bad for them, bad for their careers—"

"And bad for Fortune Pictures," I finished. "I do understand, Mr. Wiseman, like I said."

"You might even have fun."

I looked at him and then held out my hand. "Good afternoon, Mr. Wiseman."

He took the hand and clasped it warmly, "No hard feelings, eh?"

I smiled brightly at him. What else was I going to do?

"Of course not, Mr. Wiseman. You're right, it will be fun. And I have no doubt you're making money on the deal."

"They're giving me five hundred a week more than we pay you, so, yes," he said.

Chapter Twenty-One

I shouldn't have been surprised that Mr. Wiseman knew all about my visits to Vernon's house. As I've noted—and I really should have paid attention to this myself—our personal business was studio business. They knew about, or even arranged, our trips to horse races, boxing matches, or the beach, our evenings of dinner and dancing. As they had tried to do with Clay and me, they also did their best to manage our love lives and marriages. It was like having a meddling auntie who was also your boss. I hadn't quite absorbed the implications when I signed my contract, and I had mostly counted it as a fair deal, for what I got out of it. Mostly.

Good for him, though, that he didn't mind me visiting with my friends the riding extras. They were like family. And in fact, I planned to visit them now.

At home, I took off my fashionable skirt, blouse and stockings and burrowed into the back of my walk-in closet. I pushed past dresses, coats, and shoes that cost what most people would earn in a year, and found the pair of boots that were my dad's last birthday present to me. They were black and brown leather, the uppers decorated with pretty white hearts, and I loved them. I quickly dressed in old, faded jeans and a soft, checked shirt, then tied a kerchief around my neck and pulled on my boots, feeling a surge of nostalgia.

I was due to leave for Mammoth Lakes on Sunday afternoon and I knew I should be thinking about that. But Mr. Wiseman's mentioning the riding extras had given me an idea. These men came from everywhere, went everywhere, knew everyone. If I couldn't run around finding things out, maybe they could help.

Wiseman wanted me to forget the whole thing, and I'm sure he wasn't the only one. Maybe others could let it go. But they weren't the ones who had shot Sam.

I drove down to Sunset and Gower, where I saw them outside the Columbia Drugstore: riders without horses, standing around talking or sitting on the bench outside, or leaning against parked cars, but all dressed in their cowboy clothes. I parked the Hudson by a palm tree across the street, waited for a red trolley to pass, and then went over to join them.

The drugstore windows still had the displays I had loved to look at as a kid: ointments, gadgets, elixirs, and cosmetics that at the time had seemed to be the trappings of adulthood to me. While my dad spun yarns with his friends, I would look at all this stuff and imagine what it was for.

The Columbia was the unofficial headquarters for riding extras, its main attraction being the phone the manager would let them use to make and receive calls from Central Casting. If the picture was a Western, all they had to do was show up and the studio would assign them a horse, a gun and gunbelt, and they were ready to chase stars like my friend Clay all over the countryside on location somewhere.

When I was thirteen or fourteen, I had been a sort of mascot, and my father had even let me work as an extra myself a couple of times, impersonating a shy, half-grown boy while the studio people barely looked at me to put my name on the roster. It helped that I'd always been called Frankie, and, as a skinny kid, if I played it just right, I could get my name listed as "Frank Jones" and soon be riding in front of the cameras and earning some extra pocket money.

This all stopped, though, when my father died, in 1930. By that time I'd had a screen test and was starting to get roles in pictures on my own. Good thing, too—the house in Beachwood Canyon needed maintenance and taxes paid, and my mother's paintings, though well reviewed by art critics, didn't bring in enough money to keep it all up. The ranch in Niles could support itself, just, even during these lean years. But Beachwood was my home, and it meant everything to me to keep it. So I was glad for how the career was working out. But sometimes I missed my friends.

I visited when I could, dressed, like I was now, to blend in. Mingling with the cowboys, I might not be mistaken for a boy like I used to be, but at least I wouldn't stick out too badly. Mr. Fixx's spies would probably already know I was there, but the general public at least would not notice.

At the moment that's all I cared about. I sauntered over and nodded at a big fellow in a black hat.

"Howdy, Frankie," he said quietly.

"Hi, Red," I said, moving a few steps closer in, becoming part of the group and feeling that I was among friends. Some I knew by name and greeted them briefly. "Joey, Dusty, Gordo, Shane. Hey, Slim, Myron." There was a muted ripple of voices greeting me, and a few looks of surprise from the ones that didn't know me, but recognized me, though they knew not to make a fuss. Some of them tipped their hats, and I nodded at them.

New fellows came and old ones went, but there were still some that I knew and some I'd gotten to know even after my contract and name change and all.

I couldn't help but think how different this was from seeing my fans outside a restaurant or at a premiere. Most of these fellows had known me since I was knee high to a grasshopper, as they would say. They had seen me riding my pony, and then horses, and more than once had seen me get unceremoniously flung to the ground by some grumpy cayuse on a set, only to get back into the saddle and keep riding. They were in no way in awe of me, but they did respect me and care about me. That was a hard thing to earn in this town. You couldn't buy it.

I, in turn, tried to look out for them as best I could. I would try to discreetly find out whose power had been turned off, whose kids were hungry, whose wife was sick or had just had a baby, and see that they got some help. Anonymously, if I could. These were proud families who preferred to make it by themselves, but they were hard hit these days, like everyone else. They knew it was me, most of the time, and knew that it was because I considered them friends, almost family. If it helped them hang on a while longer, or until they could get back on their feet, I was glad.

So I knew I could be straight with them.

"I'm looking for a girl, fellas," I said. A couple of them raised an eyebrow, likely fixing to crack wise, but I laughed at them and said, "Not like that, simmer down."

There were a few chuckles, and I heard the names of several actresses I knew whose fans would have been shocked to know they preferred girls. I didn't mind—anything went in this town and many of these women were friends of mine—but the public wasn't so open-minded. At the moment, though, I wanted to be serious.

"Listen, you all heard about Vernon Stone, I know," I said, and a couple of the cowpokes made as if to take off their hats in respect, as I went on.

"I'm curious to know more about how he died," I said.

"You think it was suspicious?" Red asked. "Heard it was an accidental drowning when he tried to save a gal."

I nodded. "That could be," I said. "But I just kind of want to know more."

"Because of the shooting?"

I nodded. I didn't go into how I felt responsible myself, and not just because I'd pulled the trigger. Briefly, I told them how I was looking for this girl named Ann or Annie because no one else was, and that if I found her, I might know what happened and be able to leave it behind, eventually.

"And the girl you're looking for?" Slim asked.

"She's most likely drowned, too," I said, "unless she got to shore without anyone noticing. I'm curious to know if she did, or at least who she was."

"And she's an Ann, Anna, Annie?" Myron asked.

"I think so," I said. "Yeah, I know, it's a common name. I'm pretty sure she was the girl with Vern when he died. She may have died, too. No one saw much that day. You know how people fool around on the beach, even in their street clothes."

I explained that I thought maybe this girl, if she hadn't died and did turn up, might have information about Vernon and what

153

he'd been thinking, at least. Not that she would talk if I found her. But it was worth a shot, I thought. If she'd looked for work as an extra, someone might have crossed paths with her.

Joey, a tall, blond cowboy from Nebraska, said, "Miss Frankie, my girl lives over at the Studio Club. She might know somethin'. I can ask for you."

"That would be swell, Joey," I said. The Studio Club was known for being the place where "nice" girls stayed, with a dress code and curfews and chaperones. Not that they couldn't get into mischief when away from there, but still, I thought it was sweet that Joey had a girl there. And with that many girls living together, friends and rivals, maybe someone knew something.

Joey's offer made me feel like I had accomplished something, and I stayed a while longer, gossiping—cowboys are inveterate gossips, don't let anyone tell you different—about people we all knew, recounting some stories about my father, which brought a tear to many an eye, and then made my way back to my car and through the city streets, up into the hills and home.

At the casa, I heard splashing and found Max doing laps in the pool, looking, as always, like it was a battle between him and the water. Watching him, with the sun on my shoulders and the smell of eucalyptus and chlorine in the air, I had a rush of feeling as I recalled seeing him for the first time, also in a pool. I think we both would have admitted the attraction had started out as purely physical, but now it was like we fit into each other's mind, body, and heart, as though we'd found the missing parts to ourselves, even if we hadn't known they were missing.

Marriages often didn't last long in this town, but I vowed this would be different, no matter how impulsively it had started. I guessed other people also vowed the same thing, including a lot who were now single again. You just never knew.

Max surfaced, shaking his head like a terrier to get the water out of his hair and eyes, took a look at me and smiled that angelic-devilish smile he had. I couldn't have not smiled back if I tried.

"Mr. Wiseman called you a nebbish," I said, watching him put his hands on the side of the pool and then, apparently, just
154

levitate out of it to stand in front of me, droplets running off him and his red swim trunks.

"I care what Wiseman thinks?" he said with a grin and a shrug, then took up a fluffy white towel from a pool chair. "He's probably just jealous that I got you and he didn't."

Toweled off enough to not get my clothes wet, he leaned in for a kiss. I kissed back. It was nice, kissing Max, with a little warm breeze rustling the leaves of the trees around the pool. I sighed happily and was about to propose we continue this in the house, when we heard a shout from the direction of the garage. We exchanged a glance, and I started for the sound. Max snagged his sandals and ran, passing me up.

As we came around the corner of the garage we saw Mr. Noguchi standing there, brandishing a rake, and looking resolute. A few more steps and we saw why. There was a man with his back to us, holding his hands out and moving his feet around, as though figuring out the best way to fight a rake-wielding gardener.

As we came into his view, Mr. Noguchi looked up. The man took that as his chance to make a break for it. He backed up, turned—and ran right into Max.

His mistake. Faster than I could follow, Max moved. He had told me about his high school wrestling days in Indiana, and had playfully showed me some of the holds he knew, just for fun, and that usually turned into another kind of wrestling.

But this was even different from that. Max deftly grabbed the intruder by an arm and his neck, and made some moves that, in a blur of muscled brown limbs, gave the impression he was tying the other man into a knot. There was a bit of flailing and grunting by our unwelcome guest, and then Max had him pinned to the ground and was sitting on him, almost casually, like he did this every day. Keeping an eye on the guy, Max said, "Cops."

I was already on my way to the garage where we had a telephone. I told the police we had found a prowler and they might be interested in coming to pick him up. Then I went outside to see how Mr. Noguchi was.

He had put the rake aside. Now he smiled and politely

brushed off my concerned inquiries about whether he was unhurt.

"Yes, this time," he said, "he didn't take me by surprise. You probably heard me yell at him."

The man tried to get up—he was a bit bigger than Max, but without Max's experience at throwing other people around, from what I could tell. When he moved, Max torqued his shoulder a tad, convincing him that keeping still was a better idea just now.

A couple of police cars arrived. The cops looked bemused at finding a man on the ground, another man clad only in swimming trunks holding him there, and me in my cowgirl duds, and then they did what cops do. The man was soon in the car and the officers were getting whatever information we could give them.

"You know this guy?" one of them asked me.

"Nope," I said, but went over to the car to make sure. He wouldn't meet my eyes until the officer said, "The lady wants a look at you, buddy."

He lifted his head and I realized that, no, I did know him. Had seen him before, anyway. He was an average-looking fellow with brown hair and a sad face, who showed up on the streets outside the studio sometimes, with a sign begging me to come back to him and our family because he thought we were married. I always just thought, oh, that guy again.

"I just wanted you to come home," he muttered. "We miss you."

The cop looked at me and I shook my head, feeling a slight pity for That Guy, but mostly wanting rid of him forever.

"Is that why you tampered with the brakes on my ex-husband's car?" I asked.

He scowled. "I thought it was yours. I just wanted, just wanted—" he darted a furtive glance at me "—to scare you a little."

"Well, congratulations," I said, "I was officially scared." He had clammed up and was not looking at me now.

The cop, writing, said, "Thanks, Miss Franklin. You got a confession out of him for us."

156

I stepped back from the police car and watched them drive off. I expected one or all of the cops were in the pay of the studio and that Mr. Wiseman would soon know all about this incident. I couldn't see that it would reflect badly on me, but I expected it would make him just as happy to have me safely on location for a while.

Chapter
Twenty-Two

The next day, I asked Monty to drive me to the Brown Derby on Vine, where I would see and be seen. The Derby was the perfect restaurant for it, and I wanted the studio to know that I knew how to play the game. I could be me, and I could also be the Movie Star about Town, letting photographers capture me doing extraordinary things like traveling from one place to another, getting in and out of a car, and eating. How does she do it, folks?

So I dressed in a smart spring suit with a belted jacket and a jaunty hat reminiscent of Robin Hood, threw a fur over my shoulders, and got into the Packard. We cruised down Wilshire, Monty in his uniform at the wheel, and me in the hush of the back seat.

The city streets were dressed up, too, with the jacaranda trees blooming in huge, fluffy clouds of blue flowers. A pair of girls who looked barely old enough to be out of high school saw me and started waving excitedly. I gave them a big smile and waved back.

There was more than one Brown Derby, but only the first one, on Wilshire, was actually a giant hat you could walk into. This one was built in the Spanish style, like so many buildings here, including my own house. There was a hat perched high above the red tile roof, though, in case the other two signs on the awning and the front of the building didn't make it clear enough. Inside the restaurant, curving, low-backed banquettes put us all on display, neat as eggs in a carton.

As we neared the Derby, I could see maybe fifty people waiting on the sidewalk, who began to gesture and turn toward us as we neared them. That was no surprise. There was always a crowd of fans waiting outside the Derby hoping for a glimpse of a star, and I was the next up for attention. Some of them were there just for me, because I had called my fan club president to let her know that I'd be there and in a mood to sign autographs. Monty let the Packard glide to a stop in front of the Derby, driving carefully as a few fans surrounded the car.

Office girls daring to take a longer lunch break, tourists, college men in sweaters, others in suits, all grinning big, nervous grins. Did I look like I was going to bite, I wondered?

After opening the car door for me and letting me out of the car, Monty stood back at attention like a Buckingham Palace guard. It had alarmed me at first, the crowds. But these folks were well-mannered. There were a few quiet squeals and giggles, and some discreet jumping up and down among them, every time I turned my head or spoke. They all thought they knew me. They all thought they loved me.

Sometimes I felt like yelling at all of them, "I'm not anything special! I'm just as mixed-up and idiotic as all of you!"

But instead I smiled and chatted with them in the sunshine, hearing about a million times how much they loved my pictures, asking them where they were from and where they went to school or work, and to be honest, I was enjoying it as much as they were. They weren't idiotic. They were just people who wanted a little magic in their lives. Sometimes we needed to be reminded that providing the magic was part of the job.

That was another thing I had learned from Joan. As she said about the fans: We owe them everything. She was like Queen Elizabeth in Shakespeare's time, knowing how to keep the love of the common folk. If they loved you, and went to your pictures, the studios couldn't ignore that. Joan was where I'd gotten the idea of letting fans know where I'd be, and then pretending to be surprised and delighted that they were there.

So for the next fifteen minutes I chatted, signed autographs, and posed for pictures with Betty from San Diego and Arnie from Seattle, and all the others. Then I told them I was expected inside, and went into the dim coolness of the restaurant. The door closed on their excited voices and I turned to the chief reason I'd come here: Raymond. He had called, wanting to see me.

I was looking forward to the Derby's famous Cobb salad more than I was looking forward to speaking to Ray, but he'd sounded in need of a meeting on the telephone, so I had felt I had to go.

He had assumed a pose of studied nonchalance, one arm on the back of the booth, and rose with a look of delighted surprise when he saw me—as though he really hadn't expected me at all. He looked good: normal, with a stylish blazer, pale blue shirt and ascot.

"Darling!" he said, guiding me to the banquette with a hand on the small of my back.

I saw movement a couple of tables over: Virginia Tuttle, in a square-shouldered, plum-colored suit and a plumed hat, interviewing a couple of actors from MGM. She raised a gloved hand to wave at me and I smiled, fluttering my fingers back at her. She nodded, making the plume bob like the crest of some exotic bird.

The image was so distinct—Virginia as cockatoo—that I had to turn away, stifling a laugh. She was probably going to write about how maybe I was having second thoughts about marrying Max, and maybe I was crying on my ex-husband's shoulder. So let her, I thought. At least I looked presentable. I shrugged out of the fur and laid it carefully on the banquette beside me.

"How are you, Raymond?" I asked. "You look well."

Considering that the last time I had seen him was when he showed up drunk as a skunk at my house, anything would have been an improvement.

"So do you," he said. "You look marvelous, in fact."

"Thank you," I said. "Sorry about the Duesie. I hope it's back in ship shape."

"Quite fine," Raymond said. "I'm just very happy that you're unharmed."

"Thanks, Ray."

His famous blue eyes searched my face for a moment. "I didn't deserve you," he said wistfully.

I had nothing to say to that, mainly because I agreed with

160

him. I was grateful that the waiter showed up just then with the menus. I scanned mine, pretending to be undecided about my order while salivating over the idea of chopped lettuce, bacon, tomatoes, hard-boiled eggs—all things I could actually eat. Half of.

"Well, what shall we have?" I said.

"Cocktails?" the waiter asked.

"I shall have a double dry martini," Raymond said, holding up his hand when I started to speak.

"Iced tea is fine for me," I said, and then, when the waiter left, added, "Are you sure that's wise?"

He smiled his brilliant smile at me, looking for a moment almost as handsome as he did in his black-and-white studio photos, and said, "It's my farewell cocktail."

"Oh, well that's different," I said, not even trying not to mute the sarcasm.

"You see," Raymond said, "I had a realization. I need to stop drinking."

"That so?" I said.

"Yes," he said, clasping his hands in front of him on the table. "When I came to your house that night, I hardly knew where I was. I remember thinking I still lived with you, for a moment." Ugh, I thought.

He laughed softly, wryly. "And when I woke up the next morning, I realized big chunks of my memory about that night were missing."

I nodded. I was familiar with his faulty recall of past debauchery.

"And I realize—if this doesn't sound too awfully ridiculous—that there were whole large chunks of my *life* I didn't remember," he said. "I walked around my house in nothing but my underwear for three days, looking at things, trying to recall where they came from."

"Where they came from?"

"Yes," he said. "To see if I remembered where I'd gotten this piece of furniture, that carpet ..."

"Some of them I bought." And left, gladly. Oh, how I had

wanted out.

"Yes, I tried to remember," he said, then looked at me in alarm. "And for many of them, I couldn't!"

"I'm glad you realize there's a problem," I said.

"Indeed," he said, nodding his head. The waiter came with the martini, and he let it sit in front of him.

I watched with interest. "Testing your willpower?" I asked.

He nodded, then picked up the drink slowly, and deliberately took the tiniest of sips.

Looking into the distance, he said, "There was a painting. By that Impressionist fellow, von Schnincken, von Schreiner —"

"Von Schneidau," I said. "Christian von Schneidau. You bought his painting of San Juan Capistrano, not long after you moved here."

"I did?" he said. "You see, I looked and looked at it, and could not remember buying it or being given it or winning it at poker—nothing."

"And you told me you wanted to commission a portrait of me by him," I reminded.

"I did?"

"Yes," I said. "But I didn't think it would be appropriate, since I was about to divorce you."

He nodded, and took another small sip of the martini.

"And that is my point." Indicating his glass, he said, "As I said, this is my last drink."

"I wish you luck," I said.

"I'll need it," he said. "Not only because drinking is bad for me, but because I need to stay on my toes … Frankie, I think someone really is trying to kill me."

I thought uneasily of the guy who had sabotaged the Duesie and what he had said. Of course Raymond knew.

"My mechanic told Gabby that the brake lines on the Duesie did not just fail. They were cut."

"Yes," I said. "That's been established. But you weren't driving it," I added, trying to ignore the sudden wave of alarm that came back to me as I involuntarily recalled the car's careening rush through the canyons. "The guy that did that was

162

sick, and he also thought it was my car."

"Unless he knew it was mine," Raymond said, "and didn't realize I would be … incapacitated and unable to drive that day. Perhaps he wanted to harm us both? And what if the shooting wasn't an accident? What if I did something to Vernon that I don't remember, something that would make him want to kill me?"

I shook my head. "That doesn't make sense—he would have known I wasn't even going to be aiming directly at you. If it was Vernon, it would have had to be an accident."

I didn't tell him that I thought Vernon had been so addled by his obsession with the mystery girl that he hadn't been as careful on the set as he should have been. I hadn't even satisfied myself, yet, that that had been the case, which was why I wanted to talk to the girlfriend, who might know.

"Besides," I said, "Vernon was … gone … by the time the thing with the Duesie happened. Even if he did have it in for you for some reason, he couldn't be doing it from beyond the grave. Or the urn."

Raymond looked a little unhappy. "At any rate," he said, "I'm getting out of town for a while. There's a small retreat up in Santa Barbara where I'm going for several weeks."

"To dry out," I said.

"Well, to get better. To take the cure," he said. "And to put myself in possibly safer climes, just in case someone here does have it in for me."

Dramatic as ever.

He raised his glass. "Cheers," he said, and he downed the martini in one gulp.

Chapter Twenty-Three

If you had to be loaned out to another studio, there were worse things than being loaned out for a picture whose location was Mammoth Lakes, with its majestic peaks, forests, and brilliant blue sky. At the end of spring, 1935, it was so beautiful, that it made me think of all the things I would rather be doing here than getting trussed up in a costume and having a camera pointed at me. Hiking sounded better. So did fishing. But, on the first morning here, I gave myself the lecture about how lucky I was, left my room in the rustic lodge, and went off to the set.

The director, a Hungarian-born *artiste* named Zoltan Nelson (changed from Nagy), was excited about setting the outdoor scenes against the beauty and drama of the Eastern Sierra. He greeted me with enthusiasm, and gave me a high-speed pep talk about how my acting had to be "as real as the mountains." His theory was that the real mountains around us would make it easier to believe that a man could become invisible. At least that's what I thought he was saying. Zoltan spoke so fast and his accent was so thick, it was hard to keep up. This was going to be an interesting couple of weeks.

The Invisible Man in the first picture, played by Claude Rains, had died at the end. To get around that, the scenarists had made this story about the original scientist's grandfather, and set it during the California Gold Rush.

In our story, the prospector Hezekiah Griffin had been given the secrets to invisibility as a young man by a mysterious Chinese railroad worker, but his notes were lost before his descendant could find them. Hezekiah was played by an insufferable actor named John Barratt. I got to play the dance-hall girl who marries him. Lucky me.

Zoltan was the kind of director who didn't say much if you were doing a scene right. Sometimes that meant we moved on quickly, and sometimes it meant we shot a scene over and over, without any extra direction to give us a clue what we should do differently. Today, at least, we moved quickly through the shot list. Barratt and I had great chemistry in front of the cameras. I felt as though we each knew what the other was going to do by mind-reading, almost. It was uncanny. Off-screen, the chemistry evaporated like smoke and we barely acknowledged each other, which was fine with me.

Now in the makeup chair, I shifted under the smock covering my costume, and tried to find a comfortable way to breathe in my corset.

I paged through my copy of the script, thinking it was as though I had traveled back in time a few decades from the 1870s of *Prairie Princess*. Next I was going to do the Josephine picture. I made a mental note to demand a modern scenario for my next picture. Something in which the clothes had zippers.

"Frankie!" came a voice I hadn't heard in two years.

A small, round figure with an aurora of blond, fluffy hair popped up from my left: Sophie Nightingale, barely a year older than me, had been my first makeup artist. It had been some time since I'd seen her, so this was a welcome surprise.

"Sophie!" I said. "I thought you'd left the business to marry Tom."

"I did, kiddo," Sophie said, with a grin, sidling over to give me a hug. "But it was so boooooring. After the first six months, fixing his eggs and bacon just right nearly drove me nuts. Tommy said all the light had gone out of my eyes. And also, he got laid off. So he couldn't complain if I wanted to be a working girl again."

"Well, I'm glad you're back."

"You and me both."

She got to work on my face with her pots of creams and powders, giving me a porcelain finish and bedroom eyes, 1850s-style, or at least a 1935 idea of a Gold Rush floozy. I carried on the conversation looking down while she did my eyebrows and up while she applied eyeliner and mascara to my lower lids.

"You've got to look semi-ladylike," she said, delicately applying false lashes. "And for sure you'll smell better than most people did back then."

Fixing one of my eyebrows, she said, "I was sorry to hear about that business on *Prairie Princess*, and what happened to Vern Stone later. That was a real shame."

"Did you know him well?" I said.

"No, but he seemed like a nice guy," Sophie said. "I heard he'd started out as an actor before he got into props. And he drowned, right? What a way to go. Bad luck, huh?"

"Or suicide," I said. "I guess we may never know."

Sophie looked up from her pots and brushes. "It wasn't an accident?"

"No one seems to know that either," I said. "Except maybe the girl who was with him."

"There was a girl?"

"Yep."

Sophie gave a wry grin. "Isn't there always," she said.

"I haven't found anyone who knows what happened to her, whether she died, too, or what," I said. Probably wouldn't do to add anything about the inquiries I'd made, considering my apparently budding reputation as a busybody and snoop.

She finished my makeup and removed the smock. "There you go, beautiful as usual. Barratt will probably complain that no one will be looking at him."

I thanked Sophie, checked myself in the mirror, and then got up to report to the set where, decked out in a low-cut gown with striped skirt, garters and high-heeled boots, I would sit for long periods of time in a canvas chair, going over the lines yet again, knitting or gossiping, and then being summoned in front of the cameras to emote my heart out.

But then I remembered that my old friend might actually know something that could lead to the elusive Ann or Annie … it had been a few weeks now since I'd asked anyone about her, and the topic was starting to feel almost like an old hobby I was keeping up with out of habit.

"Sophie," I said, "you know all the best seamstresses and fashion houses in town, right?"

"Pretty much," Sophie agreed. Makeup was her department but fashion was something of a mania with her. And she knew all the tailors and seamstresses.

"If I were to give you an item, could you identify who made it?" I asked Sophie.

"A lot of the time," she said. "Even if there's not a name in the piece, I might recognize some signature thing they do. Like Teresa uses this lace she gets from somewhere in France—where, she won't reveal, but it's exquisite. Molly puts a line of tiny Xs in royal blue thread at the hem. Yolanda always sews in a little bee somewhere."

I twitched like a cat that's finally seen a mouse dart out of the hole it had been watching.

"Well, what do you know," I said, almost to myself. Then to Sophie, "That's exactly what this piece has on it. It's a camisole, dark green, dark red roses, and a little bee."

"And you acquired this piece without knowing who made it?" Sophie asked. "It was a present? Somebody leave it at your house?"

What was I going to do? Tell her the truth? That I'd swiped it from under Vernon's bed?

"Oh, Raymond—you remember, the ex-husband?" I said with an eye roll. "He gave it to me, but of course when I wanted to buy more from the same place he couldn't remember where he'd gotten it—or even that he'd given it to me. I just know my lingerie lady, Miss Parrott, didn't make it."

Sophie laughed, satisfied with that answer, and we gossiped a bit about the people we both knew—who had been seeing whom, who was on the outs with the studio, who had said something stupid to Virginia Tuttle or one of the other columnists—in other words, the usual—until a production assistant came to collect me.

My mind was on two tracks as the day progressed. I chatted

167

with the crew, sat in my folding chair and knitted, got in front of the hot lights and said lines like, "But he was here just a minute ago!" and even did a bit of singing and dancing in the saloon.

The original chemistry between me and Barratt the Insufferable broke down after a few days, but I refused to be rattled by my costar's constant flubbing of his lines, and the swearing that followed, and the glaring at me afterward, like it was my fault.

It all slid off me, because I was thinking more about how to approach this Yolanda that Sophie had mentioned. Sophie had given me directions to Yolanda's small studio on Sunset, but it had gradually dawned on me that getting the name of a client out of her might take some doing, or not even be possible.

That night at the lodge, I called home. Max answered and we said quite a lot of lovey-dovey things that would have had me rolling my eyes and looking for the exits if I'd overheard someone else saying them, but which gave me a warm feeling of contentment, all the same. I liked knowing he would be there when I returned and that the welcome-home reunion would be well worth the wait.

Pleasantries with Max out of the way, I asked if he could find Monty for me. Then I asked Monty if he could go to the Columbia and look for Joey. I didn't know if Joey had a working phone at home—if the drugstore phone was the only one he had access to, I didn't want him spending his hard-earned pennies calling. I also didn't know if Joey had had time to talk to his girl, let alone for her to have told him anything useful, but when and if he did and she did, I didn't want to make it a hardship for him to let me know.

The riding extras all knew Monty, and respected him for his experiences in the Great War, something he shared with many of their fathers or brothers. Unlike some of them, he had made it back alive, and I had seen them treat him as though he was the stand-in for someone they had lost.

So he would exchange his chauffeur's livery for something more suitable to hobnobbing with the boys, and would quietly let Joey know that he'd be checking in now and then over the week
168

or so while I was on location.

We felt far from Hollywood up here. But we had brought it with us—we were it. As I walked down the halls of the lodge where we were staying, I was aware of the curious, shy looks stolen by maids and waiters as I passed by. They didn't want to be seen seeing me, I knew, and I was happy to pretend I didn't see them unless I needed something.

It was strange, but it was my life.

Chapter Twenty-Four

Major Bowes wasn't speaking to me. This happened every time I went away for more than a few days and it was happening now, as I returned from being married to the Invisible Miner.

After any absence he deemed too long, I had the impression that, instead of pining for me, he decided I was gone for good and that he would now have to begin the annoying process of advertising for new help. In cases like this, my reappearance hardly cheered him up.

As I went through the courtyard I found him absorbed in stalking a butterfly near the pond, and his glance at me was brief and distracted, as if to say, "Excuse me, have we been introduced? Do you have an appointment?"

"What," I said, "no warm welcome for the one who puts the tuna on the table?"

He blinked and went back to the butterfly. I said "hmph" and went into the house.

I was barely home and already had a commitment for the next day: an interview with a women's magazine, about Thanksgiving. Though it was far from the holidays, and a Saturday. Though I didn't, technically, cook, as I'd asked Kit to explain to them. Though I didn't, technically, even eat. They didn't care. The crazy schedule was starting up again.

Max was already home, sitting at the piano, surrounded by crumpled sheet music. When he saw me, he took the pencil out of his mouth and gave a wolf-whistle.

"What is this vision I see before me?" he said, getting up and coming to me, hands out as though to receive a gift. I had to admit, he looked pretty good to me, too.

Quite a bit later, he said, "The magazine editor called, said she'd be here at nine. Do you want me to clear out?"

"Nine?" I groaned. "I should go to bed right now." It wasn't even dark yet.

"You're in bed," he reminded me.

"Sleeping," I said.

I supposed it was good for the image of America's Kid Sister to let the fans see what were, supposedly, my plans for a lavish Thanksgiving dinner for friends and family. In a slight concession to the truth, the story would be that my own faithful and talented chef was helping me learn how to be that envied, husband-pleasing creature, a good cook. Luckily, Mrs. Monty was willing to play along.

The only not-made-up thing about it was that Thanksgiving was the one day of the year I let myself enjoy food without worrying about my waistline. I just made sure to starve more over the following weekend.

The studio sent Alice from wardrobe and Lulu from makeup and Teddy from hairdressing to get me, and Max, ready for the magazine's photographer. We donned tweeds and wool as though Hollywood in the fall got much colder than its usual sixty degrees—and tried not to sweat too much as we posed with the turkey Mrs. Monty had been roasting since early that morning. She hadn't complained. It was a chance to show off.

People would gather at my home, so the story would go, and be treated to a menu of turkey and dressing, candied sweet potatoes, asparagus, orange beets, pureed spinach, cranberry jelly, and pumpkin pie.

Ah yes, the pie. The magazine editor suggested that Max and I be photographed making the pie. So Mrs. Monty set me up in my kitchen where I could pose at the counter with flour and a rolling pin and a pastry board, wearing a frilly apron and pretending to roll out a pie crust. I appreciated her for not laughing out loud as she stepped back to observe the shoot.

"Have Mr. Franklin—"

"Mr. Gold," I said.

"Right. Mr. Gold," the photographer said, motioning to Max

who was now wearing neat pleated slacks, a perfectly tailored shirt, and a bemused look. "Come over here and peer over her shoulder, and admire what she's doing."

Max got behind me and peered. And goosed me playfully. I jumped and the photographer's flash flashed. At least that photo captured a real moment. I was quite happy to be looking forward to our first Thanksgiving together. Other than that, I thought, doffing the apron and leaving Mrs. Monty to finish the actual pie, this town was never more fake than when it ran spreads in the magazines and newspapers that purported to give readers an intimate look at how we "really lived."

In real life, we would have a wonderful meal featuring many French dishes, as Mrs. Monty surrounded the all-American turkey with her own specialties. Served with champagne. My mouth watered just at the thought of her pureed chestnut soup, her savory *pain perdu*—her version of bread dressing—and the French apple pie for dessert. I wouldn't be fastening my waistbands for several days, and it would be worth it.

The holidays also meant Raymond would be returning from taking the cure, just before Christmas, and I imagined we'd have to encounter him sometime during the course of things. To be quite honest, aside from knowing he was more or less okay, and wishing him well in a sort of distant way, I really didn't care if I ever saw him again. But as long as he and I lived, though we were no longer bound by wedding vows, I would feel as though I had to be there to help him pick up the pieces when he fell apart. The same as I would for any friend. It was hard for me to give up on people. That was probably stupid.

With the photographer gone, I kissed Max good-bye and left him pestering Mrs. Monty for her secrets to the perfect pie crust.

"You must remember to chill it," she said patiently. "If you don't chill ze crust, it will fall apart when you try to roll it."

Who knew, I thought, as I left them to it in the kitchen.

Then I changed into a slim, green dress with a white collar—chic but understated, the Star on Her Day Off—and drove myself downtown to the lingerie shop Sophie had told me about.

It was a small and tidy place with pale pink satin curtains and
172

a sign on the front that said "Yolanda's Creations" in curly script. Shapely mannequins wearing nightgowns, corsets, and other underpinnings populated the shop windows. I peered in for a closer look and even behind the glass could see workmanship as refined as that on the camisole.

A bell tinkled when I opened the door and went inside. Behind a glass counter, I found a large man—large meaning about the size and shape of a polar bear, if you can picture a polar bear wearing a rather nice black suit—minding the place. He was nearly completely bald, and had a neat black mustache. His eyebrows went up when he saw me, and he smiled under the little mustache. It was a nice smile.

"Miss Franklin," he said. "We are honored. What can I do for you?"

"Thank you," I said, looking around appreciatively at the displays featuring more mannequins wearing frothy confections in silk, lace, and satin. "This is a lovely shop. I was referred by a friend, and I was hoping to meet Yolanda, if she's in."

He smiled and spread his hands as though on stage. "Why, I am Yolanda," he said. "Yolanda is me."

"Oh!" I said. "Oh! I don't believe I've ever met a gentleman named —"

He gave a soft laugh, nodding. "I should explain," he said. "I was not the original Yolanda. The original Yolanda was my lovely wife."

He turned and indicated a photo in an ornate frame on the wall behind the counter. It featured a much younger, slimmer version of himself and a full-figured, dark-haired woman with a warm smile posing in front of a row of bathing beauties wearing, I guessed, Yolanda's creations, rather than swimsuits. She was holding a very small, black poodle.

"You see," he said, "my wife, the original Yolanda, died three years ago. I miss her more than words can say. But, I can tell you, we shared everything, and she taught me her secrets. Continuing her work is my way of keeping her close, you might say. With every stitch, I feel that I am drawing her to me. And, you see, I have even taken her name."

"I do see," I said. "Ladies don't feel a bit—odd—having you make their lingerie?"

"Not when it is the finest to be had," he replied.

"And so your name is …"

He smiled. "Everyone just calls me Mr. Yolanda."

"Ah," I said. "I understand."

Figuring there was no time like the present, I reached into my handbag and pulled out the tissue-wrapped camisole, holding it out to him. "I have a rather unusual request, regarding this."

Mr. Yolanda took the garment in his big hands and turned it this way and that, inspecting it with expert interest, handling the fine silk delicately.

"Ah, yes, I remember this. But I didn't make it for you, as I recall. You have not graced me as a patron here. Yet."

He smiled almost coquettishly.

"No, not yet," I said, smiling back—winningly, I hoped. "You see, there was a party …"

He nodded.

"And, well, it was a rather large and … spirited … party," I said, then paused, allowing time for his imagination to fill in the details. When he only waited politely for me to go on, I said, "And there were a number of people coming and going, some bringing friends. I didn't actually know everyone who showed up. You do know how these parties can be."

"So I've heard," he said, with a twinkle. "I don't attend them myself but my clients have told me."

"And, well, after the party, the next morning, I found this," I said, gesturing to the garment before him. "And I would like to return it to the owner. I have nothing to go on except that her name is possibly Ann, or Annie. Something like that."

"Allow me," he said, producing a fresh, unwrinkled sheet of tissue paper from somewhere under the counter and preparing to transfer the camisole to it. "I keep extensive notes; although I know you were not the client, it would be a small matter to look her up and return it to her."

"Oh! No—no, I couldn't ask you to do that," I said hastily. "Deliver it, I mean. You see, this was found in the guest room,
174

the morning after the party … if you know what I mean. So I hope you understand that I would like to return it to the owner as discreetly as possible. My assistant can return it with a personal note from me, striking the right, well, tone."

"I'm sorry, Miss Franklin, but I can't reveal the name of a customer. I couldn't share that with you any more than I would tell someone else—who could be a gossip columnist or, who knows who—that I made items for you."

I let my face show ladylike disappointment, and sighed, then reached and took the camisole back, trying not to look like I was snatching it out of his hands. "Perhaps the owner will miss it and get in touch with me herself," I said.

"As you wish," he said.

We smiled at each other pleasantly for a bit after this stalemate, and then I said, "Do you know, I admire your work very much. Would it be possible to persuade you to make up some things for me? A nightgown and a peignoir, perhaps? And I have recently formed a real liking for tap pants."

"Of course," he said, his eyes alight at the prospect of this turning into a profitable visit for him after all. "Let me just set you up with an appointment."

Chapter Twenty-Five

ored. Bored. And I'd knitted where I should have
purled. Sitting in my folding canvas chair, legs crossed
under my saloon-girl skirt, I examined the stitches in the
white wool sweater I was working on and wondered if I
should take them out back to the mistake, or just move on
and hope whoever I gave it to wouldn't notice.

I expect I wasn't as bored as my stand-in, a young woman my
exact size and coloring, who patiently took my place while the
lights were adjusted and shots discussed. By the time everything
was ready, I would be fresh for the scene.

Fresh but bored. Another day of sitting around knitting,
reading, gossiping, and only occasionally, it seemed, being
trotted out to do my bit.

Finally Zoltan was satisfied and I was in front of the cameras,
sitting at a card table in my floozy costume. We were back down
from the mountains and on a Culver City set, so I could go home
and sleep in my own bed. We'd come to the scene in which the
prospector, having gained the Secret of Invisibility from the
mysterious Chinese railroad worker, was now going to use that
power to expose a cheat at poker.

I was dealing, the lights glaring at me, the microphone
hovering, the camera moving in close. I planned to barely move.
That's the thing about acting for a camera—often, it's about
not doing anything much at all. The actors who came from
Broadway, like Raymond, had to learn to go smaller because it
wasn't like the theater, where you needed to project your voice
to the rear balcony. You didn't need to make grand, sweeping
gestures. You had to trust the camera to catch you thinking.

When the camera moved in, my job was to convey my

desperate worry about my true love, the Invisible Miner, and the danger he would be in when the evil card-sharp discovered him.

And I was thinking, but not about that. I was thinking of everything I'd learned about Vernon and his mystery girl, Annie, and trying to organize what I knew and didn't know.

What did I know? I knew Vernon was dead. I knew he had drowned and that someone, probably this Annie, had been with him. And that she was, at the very least, missing. At the most: drowned, too. A strong swimmer may not have gotten into trouble, but Vernon was not a strong swimmer. And who knew about the girl?

If she could swim well, had he chased her into the water, gotten in out of his depth, and then she tried to rescue him? Had she tried to save him, but failed? Failing to save him, had she drowned, herself? Swum ashore somewhere else? Maybe she had survived and was lying low, afraid she would be blamed for his death because she couldn't rescue him. Unless he had tried to save her and failed, and they both drowned, which seemed the most obvious answer.

I knew now that the studio didn't like me asking people questions about this. And why was that? Because it didn't fit into the "Frankie story" they had created about me. Vernon, to them, was close to a nobody. I couldn't be too obviously concerned about someone like that. The fans would wonder if I had loved Vernon, this nobody, instead of Max. Who, they were to believe, had stolen me away from Clay. That would complicate my story. Fans didn't like complicated.

"Action," came the order from the first assistant director.

I said my lines, something about what kind of poker it was and which cards were wild, while looking concerned about the Invisible Miner, still turning over my own questions in my mind.

The men around the table said their lines, and played their cards. The first take ended with one of them saying, "I fold."

Then we did it six more times. You wouldn't believe how many ways there are to say, "I fold."

By take sixteen, I wasn't any closer to figuring things out than I had been before take one. Sophie stepped in to fix my lipstick and powder me before take seventeen, the hairdresser made some minuscule adjustments to my wig, which was itching me, and we shot it three more times before Zoltan was happy.

A little later, knowing I wouldn't be needed for a bit, I walked out of the saloon set and into the street, to see a cluster of riding extras standing around with their horses and talking. I knew most of them, and smiled a greeting, but kept my distance. Ronnie from wardrobe would be cross if I let the horses slobber on me.

Still, one of them separated from the group and I recognized Joey's tall, gangly frame and sweet smile.

"Hi, Miss Frankie," he said, handing the reins of his horse to another extra and coming over. He took his hat off. "I talked to my girl at the Studio Club."

"That's wonderful," I said. "Was she able to tell you anything?"

"Yes," he said, looking happy to have something to offer. "There was an Annie who lived there who sounds like the girl you were wondering about. Black curly hair, kind of skinny, and working as an extra for a while."

I nodded. It could be her. "Anything else?"

"Well, she was kind of wild," he said. "Not really the kind of girl, if you know what I mean, who would stay at the Studio Club. Not like my girl, Jessie."

His pride in this Jessie was sweet to see.

"Anyway, she went out a lot, to parties at the Garden and so forth," he said.

The Garden of Allah, again: nonstop merriment amid the bungalows and villas in the tropical gardens. People setting each other's welcome mats on fire, playing piano loudly at all hours of the night ...

"She'd do things like jump in the pool with all her clothes on—you know how they do there," he said. "And she liked to show off by diving for stuff—bracelets, cigarette cases—at the bottom. And once, she dived in and came up with—well, with nothing on."

She certainly wasn't the first one to think of this trick, but it was a detail I hadn't yet learned about the mystery girl. And it

178

indicated she was pretty comfortable in the water, at least in a pool. Of course, even a good swimmer can drown.

I'd swum in the Garden pool, too, though I hadn't ever done it in anything but a bathing suit that, against all odds, stayed on.

"But then she met somebody in the property department and he was sweet on her, and, well …" he trailed off, blushing madly, and then continued just above a whisper, "… and she moved in with him."

I nodded, smiling to show I wasn't shocked. Far from it. For me, it confirmed that this was the girl both Stanley and Sam had seen at the studio. She was also the likely owner of the camisole, I thought, though I couldn't dismiss the possibility that the item might have belonged to a previous girlfriend. I supposed it could have just been there because Vernon didn't look under his bed much, naughty magazines notwithstanding. But if it did belong to this girl, this Annie, why hadn't she ever gone back to Vernon's to reclaim it, or other things she might have left there?

"So she never showed up again at the Studio Club?" I said.

Joey shook his head. I thanked him and waved at the assistant who'd come to find me, and let myself be walked back to the set.

***

A few weeks later I had a fitting for which Mr. Yolanda came to the house, bringing the pieces he'd designed and almost finished for me, along with a traveling kit of pins and needles, thread and measuring tape.

The nightgown was a pretty confection of pink silk with white ribbons. I liked the way it fell over my body, and I turned in front of the mirror, admiring how it swirled and clung to just the right degree. I also liked the peignoir, in the same lovely fabric, that went over it. I had expected them to be perfect, and they were. The tiny signature honeybees were sewn neatly into them, of course, in hidden spots, like secrets.

Max came in and gazed approvingly for a long moment, then took a deep breath, grinned, and made an abrupt exit.

"These are just right," I told Mr. Yolanda. "My husband can

hardly control himself."

We chatted about the other items I ordered, and I thought I might just ask him to keep making things for me. The lady on Pico didn't have to know. Also, perhaps if I continued to be a client, it would encourage him to let more details slip about his other client. He had seemed adamantly discreet, but maybe if I kept working on him …

"You know, I am still curious about the owner of that green camisole," I said, tying the belt on my robe and sitting at my dressing table as Mr. Yolanda packed up his bag. "If you ever feel you can reveal her identity to me."

"Yes," he said. "And I must apologize again for—"

"No, no," I said. "Please don't. I am well aware that your clients place a high value on discretion. I certainly do—it's one of the reasons I decided to order from you myself."

"Yes," he said. "I am so glad you understand."

"I do," I said. "And I'm confident that I can find her without your having to divulge anything you shouldn't."

He smiled politely at this.

"And I actually have found out a bit about who she might be, by other means," I said, smiling to show I was not desperate to have it from him. "I know she lived at the Studio Club for a while, and I had hoped to return the camisole to her there, but she's moved. And I know that her name is Annie."

I laughed, lightly. "It's almost fun," I said, "like a game of some sort, actually."

Mr. Yolanda went still for a moment. I could see him thinking.

"Well, Miss Franklin," he said, at last. "Although I can't speak about her address or other personal details, I do think the least I can do is to let you know if your information is correct."

"Is what I've mentioned incorrect?" I asked.

"Yes," Mr. Yolanda replied. "Her name. It's not Annie."

Chapter
Twenty-Six

Sam was recovered enough to costar with me in
Martinique's Rose, where I played the dark-haired
Empress Josephine as a romantic heroine opposite a veteran
character actor as Napoleon. It had been an easy shoot, with
Arthur in a good mood and the crew working happily and
very hard, and the picture was a success.

"Should I go brunette, not just in a wig?" I asked Max after
the premiere. He gave a start and looked at me with something
like alarm, and I laughed. I felt compelled to add, comfortingly,
"I'd still be the same person. And also, I'm not serious. I just
wanted to see what you would say."

He looked out the window of the Packard as we left the
grand Chinese Theater behind us and cruised down Hollywood
Boulevard. Monty, driving silently, gave no sign he had heard
anything we were saying.

"It's interesting seeing you up there on the screen as different
people," Max finally said, after giving it some thought. "But I
like knowing I get to come home with the same old Frankie."

I laughed. "I'm glad you like the same old Frankie," I said,
nestling against him. "I'm fond of the same old Max, too."

Sam and Clay had attended the premiere, too, Sam paired
with the lovely Iva Ivanovna, the dark Russian beauty from
Iowa who had been sent to Clay's ranch to console him after I
had run away to marry Max. She and Sam had actually become
good friends, and Sam, whose performance as Jean-Pierre had
been greeted with rave reviews, was enjoying the whole thing
immensely.

Clay had been seen about town with every starlet you could
name, having a genuinely good time with all of them, because

he was Clay and wonderful. Tonight he was accompanied by an adorable young RKO contract player named Lucille Ball, who seemed to be keeping him laughing.

Fall seemed to speed by, it actually rained a bit, and the nighttime temperature plunged all the way into the fifties. The weeks before Christmas also brought a round of parties where we all drank with professional seriousness. The magazines ran ads for our upcoming pictures, comparing them to Christmas gifts, and the studios sent out holiday-themed photos. I posed on a ladder in shorts and espadrilles, looking like I was trying to hang ornaments on a palm tree. It looked as silly as it sounds.

We received Christmas cards by the sackful, as well as some Western Union holiday telegrams, and we displayed the prettiest on wide, red ribbons hanging next to the fireplace. My own cards featured one of my mother's watercolor sketches—a sprig of holly—and a wish for happy holidays and a peaceful New Year.

As usual, the snowless streets of Los Angeles were turned into a fantasy winter wonderland, with lights, tinsel, silver bells, stars, boughs of evergreen, reindeer, elves, and more, all doing their best to make us forget it was not going to snow here, ever.

"Well, here we are again," I said to Clay as we waved to the crowds lining Hollywood Boulevard for the Santa Claus Lane Parade.

We were both on horseback and enjoying ourselves. Clay looked every inch the cowboy star in his white ten-gallon hat, fringed shirt, white pants and boots, riding the prancing stand-in for his movie horse, Tornado—who was too valuable to be allowed out on the streets. Original Tornado was black with a white star. Tornado Two was also black, with a white star provided by the makeup department—just in case some sharp-eyed kid out there might notice he wasn't the same horse. He was also a ham, mincing along, tossing his head, snorting happily, loving the crowds.

We were in the middle of a riot of lights, music, fancy cars, other stars—and, of course, Santa Claus—all of it meant to stir up the holiday spirit in an event originally staged to get folks out and shopping. A lot of them in 1935 were doing very little shopping, but they came out to see us parade down the street all the same.

"You look terrific, honey," Clay said as my silver-dappled mare did a quick dancing sidestep, tossing her head, not terribly happy with the crowd and the lights and the bands. She was a pretty thing the studio had found for me, and someone—it might have been me—had decided a few weeks before that I would ride her sidesaddle. Wearing a red velvet habit trimmed in white fur.

"I'm roasting in this," I complained, pulling my collar open and trying to cool off. My right leg, bent in front of me over my horse's withers, was starting to chafe, and the mare was sure that the fake reindeer on the flatbed truck passing by were coming to get her. I welcomed the distraction of patting her neck reassuringly and talking comforting nonsense to her. She snorted and crabbed sideways again but eventually decided not to bolt for the hills.

Hot, itchy velvet riding habits aside, I liked the parade. It was a tradition that had begun in 1928, just before the Crash. I had started appearing in it when my name got to be known, and it had come to feel essential to the holiday season. It was part of the job. But it was still fun, with the lights and the crowds and horses and bands and floats. It wasn't a Currier & Ives New England Christmas, but it wasn't bad.

"Are you going to be at Arthur's on Saturday?" I asked Clay, while waving my white-gloved hand at the crowd.

"You bet," Clay said. "Though Sam thinks he should stay away."

I made a sound of dismay.

"Arthur doesn't mind," Clay said, "but Sam, you know …"

Reviews of *Martinique's Rose* had all approved of Sam's performance as Napoleon's smooth courtier, who was maybe a villain—or maybe not. And if he wanted a career, Sam was realizing, he was going to have to play the game. That included not being seen in public too much with Clay.

"How about you?" I asked. "What do you think?"

Clay took off his big hat and waved it at the crowd, smiling his famous smile. People cheered, and little kids, some dressed in cowboy clothes, jumped up and down.

"He deserves his chance."

"Ray's going to be there," I said. We had stopped for a moment so a band up ahead could play "O Come All Ye Faithful" all the way through in one spot. The dappled mare tossed her head and played with the roller in her bit, making a ratchety noise.

"He's back from taking the cure?"

"Apparently," I said. "He called, and sounded good. He said he has a surprise."

Clay made a noise that sounded a lot like a snort. "As I recall, honey, you have not always cottoned to Ray's surprises."

"You're telling me," I said.

The band moved on, and so did we.

The next Saturday, dressed in our holiday best, Max and I were deposited by Monty at Arthur's house on Roxbury Drive. The whole place was aglow with thousands of lights, making me wonder if there were any left for sale in the city. Live Christmas trees, draped with tinsel and ornaments, lined the estate's major pathways, which had sprouted temporary street signs: Holly Avenue, Reindeer Way, Jingle Bell Road.

Musicians and groups of singers unfurled one carol after another from strategic locations around the grounds and the grand house, and many of us, unable to resist performing, joined in. So did some of the three dozen very small people, dressed as Santa's elves, whom Arthur had hired to serve canapes.

"Ah, there she is," the director called as he spotted us. He was holding forth, as usual, telling stories, with a crowd around him. He complimented me on my slithery red dress and I complimented him back on his aloha shirt, which was covered with a repeating pattern of Santa Clauses. With his jolly round face, he looked like one more of them.

"You must try my new cocktail!" Arthur exclaimed. "Vodka, cranberry juice, orange juice, and a secret ingredient I refuse to reveal."

He gestured to a girl serving sunset-colored drinks. She was regular-sized but still dressed as an elf, right down to curled-toe shoes with jingle bells on the toes. She tinkled over to us with her tray and her big I'm-waiting-to-be-discovered smile and we each took a glass.

"I call it 'Santa's Reward,'" Arthur said, raising his own drink. "Happy holidays!"

We made our way to the dance floor next to the pool, where silver and gold spheres bobbed about on the surface of the water. Max was a good dancer, and we spent a lot of time out there, making the most of his not having to be the one providing the music.

We had just finished a rumba during which Max did his best George Raft impression, and were headed for the punchbowl when I heard a voice behind me.

"Darling!"

Raymond. I tried to feel charitable; it was Christmas time after all. I'd gotten used to not having to worry about Raymond Sinclare while he'd been off drying out, and knew I'd see him here. The least I could do was talk to him.

"You look ravishing!" Raymond said as I turned around, deploying my own best happy-to-see you smile and noticing there was a young woman with him.

Ray took me by the shoulders and kissed me once on each cheek. No scent of anything alcoholic on his breath: that was a good sign. He looked well, too: no puffiness in the face, and he'd lost weight. Maybe the studio would actually let him in front of the cameras again.

He greeted Max with a handshake, and then turned smoothly to include his companion in our circle.

"Frankie, Max," he said. "I'd like to introduce Evangeline Oakes."

She was not Raymond's usual blonde or brunette starlet type, but an ivory-skinned redhead with a yellow silk rose in her hair, which was cut in a feathery, short bob. Her slim figure was swathed in an eccentric costume of filmy layers of golds and greens, which made her look like a nymph temporarily escaped from her enchanted woodland.

"I'm so pleased to meet you," she said. "Raymond has told

me ever so much about both of you."

I smiled politely.

"I met Evangeline when she was volunteering at the retreat. She and I hit it off right from the start," Raymond said. "I've never been so comfortable with anyone in my life; the way we were talking, it was as though we'd known each other for years."

She looked up at Raymond with adoring eyes, and I thought, well, one thing hasn't changed about him. Flies to honey. She looked—what was the word?—ethereal. And also—I don't know what told me this—rich.

Ray seemed oddly calmer than I'd seen him in years, and, as we talked, catching up, I noticed that for once he actually seemed interested in other people, not needing to be the subject of every sentence.

"Evangeline's family has a ranch in Santa Barbara," Raymond was saying. "We're invited there for the weekend of Valentine's Day. A country weekend with a mob of visitors, I expect. I'm ever so excited to see it. And you will have to come, too."

"Me?" I said, startled out of my bemused observation that they were already starting to talk like each other … ever so much.

"Yes, you and Max," Raymond said. "You're the closest thing I have to family anymore."

How sad for him, I thought, but essentially true. Except for the older sister who lived somewhere back East, most of his circle could be classified only as drinking buddies, whose friendship was based on a mutual love of a good bender.

I was glad Ray had had enough presence of mind to realize he needed to do something about his drinking. And as he talked more about Evangeline and her family in Santa Barbara, it struck me that, whether he knew it or not, he was executing the same plan Miss Merriwether had: find someone with more resources than you yourself have, and charm them into marrying you. I hoped Evangeline would still love him as much as she seemed to now, when she realized that's what he had done.

All through the party, I never saw Raymond with a drink in

his hand any stronger than club soda with a slice of lime. His companion was drinking the same, whether in support of his being on the wagon or because she herself was a teetotaler, I didn't know. But I supposed, if there was an invitation to this ranch in the offing, I would find out. Either way, I was glad he seemed to be staying on the wagon.

"Well, maybe we will come, if we're invited," I said with a smile. If we were all Ray had to show for family, now that he was trying to stay away from the drinking buddies, I could hardly turn him down.

Away from the crowd, Max looked at me. "Do we have to?" he said with a comically exaggerated whine. "I don't do well in the country. What if I need to hail a cab?"

I laughed and patted his arm. "Maybe there's a pool. I find it strange that you like to swim in outdoor pools, and you'll walk on the beach, but you don't, in general, actually enjoy the great outdoors."

He shrugged. "It's part of my mystique," he said.

It was true. He even found Beachwood Canyon a bit rustic for his tastes, despite the growing number of houses lining the hills, and the huge, Hollywoodland sign declaring the presence of humans and their desire to dominate nature. The cries of red-tailed hawks unsettled him, and he was always looking for rattlesnakes in the garden. And yet he swam outdoors and generally had an enviable tan.

Raymond came through the crowd, alone this time, with a ginger ale in hand.

"Isn't she lovely? So unspoiled and unlike the women in this town," he said dreamily.

"Thanks, Ray," I said pointedly. I guess by most measures I could be considered spoiled by now, so I didn't put on any more of an offended act than that. "You met her at the retreat?"

"Yes," Raymond said. "It was the damnedest thing. She was bringing books around to read and I had just been thinking that I missed reading Wordsworth, and here she came with a book of his poetry!"

"Naturally I fell upon it like a starving man," he said. "And when I couldn't find the poem I was looking for, I quoted it to her. Something about, 'We can make our lives sublime,/And, departing, leave behind us/Footprints in the sands of time.' And wouldn't you know it, that was not a Wordsworth poem? It was Longfellow! And she knew it by heart. Her favorite. I've never thought of things as meant to be, but it's like this really was meant to be."

"Well, I'm very happy for you," I said.

"And did you notice I remembered lines of poetry?" he said. "Even my memory is starting to come back. I remember conversations with friends, pages of plays I did, women I thought I loved …"

I didn't mention the drunken visit to my house where he had gone on about that. I just said, "And it looks like you have found someone to love again."

"Yes! And isn't it grand," he said. Then he lowered his voice. "You know, her family is terribly well-off. Not that I knew that when she first arrived at the retreat. She didn't want me to know. And I would, in turn, have hidden who I was, if I could have. It would have been perfect if we had just been able to come to each other as man and woman, without all the complications of my job."

"And all the complications about your drinking," I said. "Because, well, there you were."

"Yes, that is true," Raymond said. "Although at first she said she thought it was for exhaustion. I promised her, though, that I would stay off the stuff, and that having met her, for the first time I thought that it might be a real possibility that I can stay sober. Can you imagine?"

I grinned wryly. "I used to try to," I said.

"I know. I'm sorry, darling," he said. "But I really feel as though I've turned over a new leaf—a whole new forest!"

I recognized the signs of a Ray enthusiasm. He would try to quit drinking from time to time, usually right after I'd caught him in another affair. It never took. For his sake, and for his new friend's, and with his stay at the retreat, I hoped it would stick, this time.

"I've a feeling she will be very good for me," he said. "She's refined and educated but also, well —" he looked around slyly "—quite passionate, if you know what I mean."

"Well, that's—great, Ray," I said. "But should you really be telling your ex-wife that sort of thing?"

He smiled the smile of a man who thinks he has found the answers. "It's the new me. The honest me. I learned a lot at the retreat. I learned I should just say what I really think, out loud."

"Well, that sounds good, Ray."

"And something else," he said. "I want to share it with you first. I've asked Evangeline to marry me, and she said yes!"

I made more appropriate sounds, and was not surprised. I had already seen the signs.

"So the trip to her family's ranch—we've just started planning it and we're so excited—will be for an engagement party!" Ray did look excited, and happy. I smiled to show I was happy for him. "There's a private chapel that her parents are building, and that's where we'll be married. As close to a little English country church as you can get."

He was touchingly eager.

"So please say you'll come," he said. "Valentine's Day is on a Friday and will start off the weekend. It will be perfect."

I felt a bit disappointed—though we hadn't even discussed it, I had thought maybe Max and I could get away by ourselves that weekend. Oh, well. This was a special time for Ray, I told myself, and if he wanted me to be there to see him off on the beginnings of a new life, I should go.

Maybe he would get married, retire to the country and finally be sober and at peace, I thought. The least I could do was help him get there. If she could make him think of something besides himself, I wished them both well.

Chapter
Twenty-Seven

"So her name is not Annie," Max said thoughtfully from behind the wheel of the Speedster. We were headed up the Pacific Coast Highway to Santa Barbara, zipping past green fields, quaint farmhouses, and tall jagged cliffs on one side, and the vast, sapphire blue ocean on the other, with one of those bright and clear California winter skies above.

It was Valentine's Day, and we had the top down because it was such a beautiful day. In the couple of months since I'd last spoken to Mr. Yolanda, no other information about the mystery girl had surfaced. I hadn't been summoned to Mr. Wiseman's office again, and he had not shown his displeasure with my activities by loaning me out again, but that was only because I had hit a dead end trying to find answers to a question no one wanted me to ask in the first place.

"Apparently it is not Annie or anything like Annie," I said. "Unless Mr. Yolanda's code of discretion for his clients includes lying for them, in which case her name *is* Annie, and he's trying to do her a favor by throwing me off the scent."

"Why would he care?" Max said, downshifting as we came upon a farm truck. We followed along behind for a bit while he waited for a clear stretch to pass. That was something I liked about Max—he drove a car as expertly and effortlessly as he played the piano, and though he liked to go fast, he was cool as a cucumber when he drove, and, unlike me, didn't swear with impatience when the fates threw a farm truck in front of him.

"That's the thing," I said. "As long as he wasn't the one I found out about her from, he shouldn't care. And he doesn't know the real reason I want to know who she is. He just thinks I want to return her camisole."

"And from what Joey's girl said, they knew her as Annie at the Studio Club," Max said. "But Mr. Yolanda doesn't."

"Yeah." I thought for a moment. "I did consider the idea that the camisole could have belonged to a completely different girl, one not named Annie. Mrs. Botelho said there were several, after his wife left him."

"So where does that leave us?"

"Well … on the road to getting rid of Raymond, at least," I said. "Er, I mean toasting his engagement."

"Getting rid of him?" Max said with a chuckle.

I sighed. "Just in the sense that he's marrying into a family where they're not after his money, because they have boatloads, and the girl apparently adores him, so his future is assured, and …"

"And he becomes someone else's problem, rather than yours," Max finished for me.

"You said it," I said.

"You would have," he said.

"Yes." I gazed out at the ocean for a bit. The blue of the water was broken up by great dark tangled patches of giant kelp, which grew from the bottom to the surface, where it fanned out to make sprawling, floating mats.

"I've been looking after him long enough, don't you think?" I said.

"Plenty long enough, if you ask me," Max said. "I mean, I know you were married. And I know loyalty is important to you."

"It is the Code of the West," I said, doing my impression of Clay. "Be there for a friend when he needs you."

"Even if that friend ran around on you when you were married?"

"Well, he never beat me," I said.

"I'm sure he didn't," Max said with a chuckle. "The way I can tell is that he is still alive."

The car swept around a couple of wide turns, and he added, "I, on the other hand, have my own ideas about physical contact

191

with you," he said, "which I would like, with your permission, to demonstrate when we get to the place where we're going."

He managed to leer at me without actually looking at me, and I felt that little spark again, much like I did the first time I saw him emerge from the pool at Arthur's party. I hoped it never went away.

We soon came to a stretch of neat rail fences enclosing green pastures on the ocean side of the Pacific Coast Highway. The grass would dry and turn golden as winter gave way to spring and summer, but at the moment it was a nice deep green under the blue sky.

"I think this is their place," I said. "Their pastures, anyway."

Following Raymond's directions, we turned off onto another road that would eventually lead to the ocean and soon came to the drive, its entrance marked by a pair of solid-looking adobe pillars, each topped with red tiles like a tiny roof. A brass sign set into the front of one of them said OAKES RANCH.

The drive went through rolling pastures and up and down a few rises, then straightened out to give a view of a grand Spanish colonial house whose wings stretched out in all directions from a two-story section in the middle. It looked like a grander version of one of the old California missions.

The drive, made entirely of red brick, went in a circle around a small garden of cactus with a statue of Saint Francis in the middle, a real dove joining the carved-stone one on his outstretched hand.

As we pulled up in front of the house, three men dressed in white shirts and pants, with red sashes, appeared out of nowhere to take our bags. Quick, quiet and efficient, they then melted into the shadows of the flower-filled patios and overhangs of the huge edifice.

Max gave the car keys to another servant who seemed to be waiting to see to the car, and we looked around.

"Some dump," he said. "Where'd they say he made his dough?"

"Raymond said he has a beverage business," I said. "Like Sparkletts, I guess. Also wine and beer and stuff, after

Prohibition."

"That's a lot of seltzer water," Max observed, taking in the surroundings.

At the top of the tiled stairs, Raymond and Evangeline appeared, looking almost royal, Evangeline in a filmy white dress with little green flowers on it and a floppy green bow at the neckline, and Raymond in a tweed suit, as though he had just returned from shotgunning a couple hundred defenseless birds out of the sky. I thought of the dove on Saint Francis's hand.

They started down the stairs to greet us, but before we could get to the ceremonial greetings, from behind them burst a red-haired sprite who seemed to be all arms and legs going in every direction at once, wearing a dress but looking like she'd be more at home in dungarees and a sweater.

"It's you!" came a childish voice. "It really is you!"

I braced myself, having the impression she was going to launch herself off the top step into my arms, but instead she did a coltish sort of scramble down the steps and skidded to a stop in front of me, blue eyes wide and red curls still bouncing.

"This is my sister Edie," said Evangeline, a laugh in her voice, as she and Raymond descended the stairs. "She's ten."

"I'm Edie!" the sprite announced as though her sister hadn't said anything. "And you're Frankie Franklin. It's really you!"

I had to laugh, her manner was so disarming. "Yes, it's really me," I said, with a smile that this time I didn't have to force.

"I loved when you were the princess who's really poor in *Kings and Lions,*" she said, grabbing my hand and shaking it vigorously. "But my favorite is *Father's Circus.*"

"Why, thank you," I said.

"When you popped up behind the bad guy and said, so quietly, 'And just where were you planning to hide that elephant?' I laughed so hard!" Edie said.

I had to say, she did a pretty good impression of me. "You're so brave, so smart—"

I held up my hand. "Now, now, I'm not so brave or smart as all that," I said. "Those are characters I play in the pictures."

"I know that," Edie said, calming down a bit. She was still

193

holding my hand in her cool little one. I didn't mind. "But you'd have to be just a little of those things to play them, wouldn't you?"

She didn't wait for a response, but dropped my hand and said, "C'mon! I know where your room is!" and dashed off into the house.

Raymond and Evangeline looked bemused. I gave them a shrug and a smile, and started off after Edie, who promised to be much more fun than anyone else we were to meet here. The others followed.

The kid led us down the house's gleaming, shadowy halls, sometimes stopping to point out sights along the way with commentary such as, "My papa has a grizzly bear—it's in there." Stuffed, I presumed.

The house was built around an interior courtyard with a fountain, as grand inside as it had looked outside. With arches, whitewashed walls, iron sconces and tile floors, flowers spilling out of terracotta pots everywhere, it was like an overblown version of my own home. I had a brief twinge, wishing Max and I were there now instead of here, delightful children notwithstanding.

Evangeline walked along with her hand hooked in Raymond's elbow as though sewn there. She looked as happy to be around him today as she had at Christmas. Don't mess up this one, Ray, I thought to myself as we stopped at the end of the hall to our room.

"We're so glad you could come," Evangeline said. "Tea is in the library. Please join us when you've settled in."

Our bags were already neatly placed in the room, which had been thoughtfully arranged for a guest's every comfort. Max sat on the eiderdown-covered bed, bounced tentatively, pronounced it sufficiently silent, and we went off to tea.

We found the other guests and Evangeline's parents, Charles and Elizabeth Oakes, in the library, a vast space with heavy, dark ceiling beams, patterned rugs, and bookshelves that had more decorative objects on them than books: small statues, photos, small boxes of silver, carved wood, or covered in seashells.

194

Elizabeth Oakes looked like a paler version of her elder daughter, thin and wraithlike in a mauve dress, with a heavy gold cross on a chain around her neck. She shook my hand and gave Max a long look before shaking his, as though deciding whether to risk it. Her smile was late in coming and seemed forced.

I felt a surge of anger starting, but was interrupted by Charles Oakes enclosing my hand in his large one.

"Miss Franklin," he said, grabbing my hand in a rather too strong grip. "Aren't you the pretty little thing?"

He looked at me with something more than open appreciation, and as though he didn't realize I could see him looking—as though I were on the screen and not right in front of him. The look almost seemed acquisitive, as though, I thought uncomfortably, he was picturing how I'd look on display. Maybe he wanted to put me next to the grizzly bear.

"And you must be Mr. Gold," he said, shaking hands with Max. He didn't seem to have any of his wife's qualms about Max. "The one who wrote that song about, what was it, the moon should swoon, something like that?"

"Something like that," Max said pleasantly. "It's called 'Let's Not Hide from the Moon,' actually."

"That's right," Oakes said. "From that show about the gangster's girl who loves the cop."

"That's the one," Max said. "Thank you."

"I want you to play it for us later," he said. "We've got a nice piano here. That one wanted it but she never kept up with the lessons."

He had gestured in Evangeline's direction when he said it, with an oddly dismissive tone. I didn't think I would have liked my father talking about me like that. But, families were all different.

Later, in our room, Mrs. Oakes' strange, nearly rude treatment of Max came back to me, and I stood in front of the dressing table mirror brushing my hair with more force than was strictly necessary.

"What was wrong with her, anyway?" I said.

"She doesn't like that I'm visiting," Max said with a shrug.

"That was mild, believe me."

"She doesn't even know you," I said. "How could she—oh."

I tended to forget what life was like outside—and sometimes inside—the business we were in. I had not been raised in any particular religion and found it odd that some people used it as an excuse to hate.

Elizabeth Oakes apparently was one of these. So many of us had professional names different from the ones we were born with. But people like her … they were the reason so many actors changed their names to something that sounded English or French, rather than Jewish. Emanuel Goldenberg became Edward G. Robinson. Mendel Berlinger became Milton Berle. Even the first cowboy star, Maxwell Henry Aronson, had changed his name, to Bronco Billy Anderson.

It might have seemed strange that this was the way things worked in an industry controlled by powerful Jewish men, but, though they were proud of their heritage and beliefs, they were also well aware that vast swaths of the country still thought Jews had horns or other such nonsense, and that this could hurt business.

I stopped brushing and realized I had frozen on the outside as anger bubbled up inside. When Max spoke to me, his words seemed to come through a fog of it.

He put a hand on mine. "Hey," he said. "You're about to break that brush. Or your hair." He took it out of my hand and laid it on the dressing table.

"It happens sometimes," he said. "I'm—well, not used to it, but I've learned there's not much I can do about it. And it's nothing compared to what's happening in Europe right now."

I had to agree. There was so much wrong in the world. "Oh, Max," I said. "I just don't want anyone to do anything … anything at all … to hurt you. I want you to be happy."

He gave me the angelic-devilish grin and leaned into me. "I have a suggestion for something we could do that would make me very, very happy," he said.

And we were almost late for dinner.

196

Chapter
Twenty-Eight

There were twelve for Friday's dinner, and I was glad that we hadn't missed cocktails. Despite Max's talent for making me forget the world in a most enjoyable way, soon afterward I was tense again, anticipating more chill from Mrs. Oakes and not trusting myself to take it quietly. I didn't like to admit it, but alcohol could help.

"Don't give her a second thought, sport," Max had said as he tied his tie. "I've had weekends start off worse at summer camp. Now let's go see if the Beverage King can mix a decent drink."

I was at the dressing table again, applying rouge, inspecting both cheeks critically. After spending so much of my life sitting in chairs and having makeup and hairdressing have their way with me, it was good practice to do it myself sometimes.

Not that I couldn't have called for a lady's maid from the Oakes's staff to do practically anything I wanted done. I'd never seen a house with so many servants running around. Maids of various degrees, a household manager, footmen, hall boys or whatever they were called ... there was a man or woman (or boy or girl) to attend to any and all needs, apparently.

As far as wardrobe, my main challenge was to choose outfits that would live up to my hosts' idea of Frankie Franklin, movie star—and yet not upstage young Evangeline. The result for tonight was a black bias-cut Vionnet gown with a filmy short cape over the shoulders.

Max wore a dark suit with a subdued tie. It was easier for men.

In the library, we found Mrs. Oakes enthroned once again in a big brocade armchair, still wearing her gold cross and a high-necked, rather old-fashioned gown in another indeterminate color. Evangeline was talking quietly with her mother, and Raymond was over by one of the library shelves, looking with apparent interest at some framed photos. Interspersed with the photos were sports trophies—tennis, golf, swimming, horse shows.

Mr. Oakes was presiding over cocktails.

"Name your poison," he said with the kind of bluff jollity you find in a certain type of salesman. "I don't indulge, myself, but I can mix anything you like."

I had seen a bottle of Campari, and asked for a Negroni.

"Coming right up for the lovely lady," he said, smiling under his walrusy mustache.

Filling the cocktail shaker, he said, "Did you ever hear where this drink came from?"

I started to answer yes, actually, I did, but he continued to talk over me, relating a long story that had little to do with the one I knew to be true. The inventor of the cocktail, the Florentine Count Camillo Negroni, had had a number of adventures in America, including being a cowboy, and had been a friend of my father's. That may have been one reason, when I got to be old enough, I decided to try his drink. It was love at first sip. The Negroni, with its combination of sweet vermouth, bitter Campari and strong gin, had turned out to be my idea of the perfect cocktail.

Max asked for the same, and Mr. Oakes made some remark about how touching that we liked the same drink, while he mixed it.

"Max Gold, hm?" Oakes said, obviously turning over some remark in his mind, something that made him chuckle. "Doesn't that mean 'the most money'?"

"I suppose it could," Max said mildly.

"Pretty appropriate, eh?" Oakes said, now laughing at his own joke. "Eh? Pretty appropriate."

Max smiled blandly at him. As we moved away from our host, I took a sip and whispered to Max, "Not as good as yours."

Evangeline and Ray finished the conversation they'd been having with Mrs. Oakes and came over to us, bringing two couples with them who wanted to meet me.

We talked about the pictures for a bit, finding that both couples, though impressed to meet a well-known movie face, also seemed to regard us as not quite in their class. I didn't mind; they were nice enough.

Ray seemed tense, though. Understandable when meeting your beloved's family, I supposed, especially one whose wealth and calm didn't quite hide subtle undercurrents of unhappiness.

"Tell that funny story about the time you had to work with two lions on *Oasis*," I urged Raymond, to take his mind off whatever was bothering him. "You know, there was a friendly one and a mean one, and the director had the trainer switch them on you as a joke in that one scene?"

It was a story Ray was good at telling, and he looked relieved to have been reminded of it. He launched into the well-rehearsed tale with gusto, and his listeners laughed at all the right spots. I sipped my bittersweet drink, only half-listening, marking time until we could go in to dinner. Max was looking longingly toward the door, no doubt thinking about the music room down the hall, where he would rather be.

Evangeline had chosen yet another floaty outfit, layers of chiffon with roses. I complimented her on it. Her father barely seemed to notice her, and, in fact, only appeared to be waiting, while Raymond gave his all to the lion story, for a chance to turn the conversation back to himself. I was edging away, pretending interest in a nearby painting, as I heard our host start a story about hunting lions in Africa.

It was a relief when young Edie joined us for dinner, her sunniness almost immediately clearing the social storm clouds away. She seemed to be the one person that everyone present enjoyed, and I was happy she was seated next to me—even if her questions bordered on the impertinent.

"Can I call you Frankie?" she asked, blue eyes bright. "That's such a pretty dress. Do you think we could be friends?"

I couldn't help but smile. "Yes," I said. "Thank you. And yes, of course. I think you would be a very good friend."

She beamed. "Why aren't you eating all your soup? Don't

you like it? Cream of artichoke soup is my favorite," she said.

I had eaten about half of the soup, my usual strategy. If I only ever ate half of what was put in front of me, it would help me to keep from growing seam-splitting hips. Not that a ten-year-old should have to worry about such things.

"Well," I said, "you see, I have to save room for the other dishes."

"I won't eat all of mine either, then!" she declared, with a mischievous look.

Mrs. Oakes gave us an icy glance, which I ignored.

"Edie," I said, "when I was your age, I ate everything on my plate. And on everyone else's plates, too, if they'd let me."

"Really?" she asked.

"Yes!" I assured her. "When you're ten, you're growing, and you need the benefits of all the food your parents provide for you."

Maybe I was laying it on a bit thick. But it did seem to make Mrs. Oakes subside. She turned her attention away from us, and it reminded me, oddly, of an alligator sliding off a riverbank and back into the bayou. A mama alligator.

Edie kept up with the questions, mostly to me, through the fish course and the venison—shot by Mr. Oakes on this very ranch, we were told—and the vegetables, and finally, at long last, the sherbet for dessert, made with lemons from the Oakes orchard, we were informed.

Though Charles Oakes didn't drink, he did become expansive as dinner progressed, telling story after story, still mostly having to do with his own various business successes or hunting trips. He seemed rather fixed on everything he did or owned being the best, or the first, or the biggest.

I was glad to have been occupied with Edie, and was working up an excuse about a headache and needing to go to bed, irritated that this was how our Valentine's Day was going, when Charles Oakes invited us all into the music room.

"Max here, he's going to play for us," Mr. Oakes announced. "Start with that tune, the one about the moon and so on."

Max and I exchanged a look and he gave an infinitesimal

shrug. As I took his arm for the trek to the other room, he whispered to me, "'Dance, monkey.'"

And so Max sat at the grand piano, looking for all the world like this was his own idea, and played. His own tunes, some Gershwin, some Porter, some Carmichael, and the ragtime songs he loved. I could see him warming to it, and thought that was good, even though I knew Mr. Oakes hadn't considered Max's feelings for a second, when ordering him to play.

With Max thus occupied, I scanned the group arrayed on the heavy, expensive furniture. Raymond, I noticed, had seemed preoccupied all evening, and had kept surreptitiously glancing at me. I had the feeling he wanted to talk, and on my way back from a trip to the powder room, there he was, waiting for me in a hallway a bit away from the music room. We could still hear Max playing, a lullaby-like Satie piece that sounded like his signal that the session was winding down.

"Darling, I must talk to you," Raymond said in a low voice, glancing back toward where the other guests were. "It's all right—I said I needed to go back to my room for cigarettes."

"What is it, Ray?" I said, matching his volume, and then took a good look at him. "Why, you look like you've seen a ghost."

He looked at me anxiously. "That's the thing, darling: I think maybe I have. Well, not a ghost exactly, but—"

He edged over, beckoning me, until we were next to a small table in the hall. On it were a large vase of hothouse flowers, an ebony statue of two gazelles, and a photo of the Oakes family in a heavy silver frame.

Ray picked up the photo and handed it to me.

"Who do you see in this picture?" he asked.

I looked. "Evangeline, and Edie, maybe six years old, and—is this another sister? A cousin?"

Even in a black-and-white photo, you could tell the third girl had red hair like the other two. And that there was a definite family resemblance.

"Frankie, I think I know this girl," Ray said. "Or … knew. I think she came to town to try and be in pictures, and I think I, well, I—"

I looked at the photo again, and put it down on the table. "She was one of the women." I was surprised that the thought still bothered me, and found myself saying archly, "Not the one I found you with in our bed."

"I think she is one of the … girls that I … oh, God, for a while there I was such a cad!" he exclaimed. "I'm almost positive it's her."

"Well, what about it, Ray?" I said, trying for reasonable. "Plenty of people marry the sisters or brothers or cousins of a former flame."

"But Evangeline doesn't know!" he said. "I feel that she should know. Or maybe she really shouldn't. Oh, I don't know … We're supposed to announce our engagement tomorrow night!"

He paced a few steps down the hall and then back to me while I waited.

"But maybe she does know," Ray said. "Maybe that's why Ellie isn't here. She knows, and Ellie stayed away. Maybe there's bad blood between them?"

"Her name was Ellie?" I said. "And you're sure this is her? Was her last name Oakes?" I remember thinking once that there were only a few faces that went with red hair, and I was always seeing redheads that reminded me of other redheads. He could be mistaken. It would be simpler if he remembered her name. If she hadn't changed it.

"No, it was … was … Atwood," he said. "Ellen Atwood." He looked briefly happy that his memory had served that well. But then the restless worry came back.

"But I don't know if she changed the name, or the studio did. I don't remember anything else about her. You see, that's my problem. If it's not her, I'll look like the devil's own fool for mentioning it to Evangeline."

"And if it is?"

"Then I'll feel like I kissed and told," he said. "That wouldn't be gentlemanly of me."

"You've picked a fine time to decide to be a gentleman," I said, unable to stop myself.

202

"But, darling," he said. "You know, I just fear that—well, I just don't know that I can go through with the wedding if it's not all out in the open. And if it is in the open, she might not want to marry me."

"That's why you were looking at the family photos in the library," I said. "You seemed to be quite interested in them."

"Yes, but I didn't get a chance to look at them all," he said. "And the ones I did see didn't have Ellie—if that is Ellie—in them. If I saw more than just this one, I might be more sure."

"So go look later," I said.

"It's hard … Evangeline sticks to me like lint," he said.

I sighed and said, "We need to get back to the others. We'll be missed."

"You go in first," he said, then put a hand on my arm. "But I needed to talk to you."

"Why?" I said. Although I knew.

A searching look on the famous face. A look of helpless admiration.

"Because, darling," he said, "you're the one who always knows what to do."

Chapter
Twenty-Nine

It had been a tiring evening, going through the motions of a dinner party with none of the enjoyment one gets when in the company of actual friends. I could not bring myself to make small talk with Mrs. Oakes, who could barely hide that she was unhappy to have Max as a guest.

Mr. Oakes had moved on from talking about himself to talking about how smart Edie was, and how she would grow up to have a mind like a man's, which he seemed to think was a great thing. The few times I had tried to lead the conversation to the happy couple, or tell interesting stories about the movie business, his responses were mostly bad jokes regarding how Evangeline would now be Raymond's problem. Her too-bright smile was painful to see.

And then there was Raymond and the inconvenient timing of his memory coming back. I thought there was a good chance the memory he did have was faulty, and that the girl in the pictures quite likely wasn't the one he remembered as Ellie.

"He says I always know what to do," I said to Max back in our room.

"So what are you going to do?" He had his suit jacket off and was hanging it up in the heavy armoire.

"Search me," I replied. "It has occurred to me that I could do nothing. Let Raymond figure things out on his own for once."

Max nodded. "That's an option." He yawned and flexed his fingers. "While you decide if you need to ride to his rescue yet again, I'm going to take a bath. My shoulders feel like I've just played ten innings in the World Series."

I smiled, kissed him. "I did think of one thing—"

"Of course you did." He gave an indulgent laugh, sat down

on an armchair and started taking off his shoes.

"I would like to go back to the library and see if there are any other photos of the Oakeses that include the girl he thinks he knew," I said. Then, I thought, I could at least point him at them and perhaps occupy Evangeline while he got a better look.

Mystery girls, I was thinking, as I descended the carpeted staircase and went down the hall to the library. I doubted I'd be any better at helping Ray with this than I was in finding out who Vernon's mystery girl was. It was getting late, and there were no maids in sight, nor footmen or whatever all those other servants were. The big house was quiet and dark except for a light every so often on the hallway wall.

I never had found out anything more about the elusive Ann, Annie, or not-Annie. I wondered if I ever would. No other bodies had ever turned up along the coast. So she had also either drowned, or somehow gotten away, and never gave a report to the police on Vernon's drowning. Maybe she'd gone back to Ohio or Texas or wherever she'd come from.

So many ways to fill in the blanks if you only had part of a story. You could take a scrap of information and imagine hundreds of details to go with it. And maybe one of them would be close to the truth. Maybe that was why people became detectives—they feel a need to gather up all those scraps of story and stitch them together so they make sense. Maybe I should ask Detective Jameson about it, I thought.

One of the double doors into the library was open. Two mica-shaded lamps glowed on the desk. I switched on the floor lamp that stood near the shelf with the photos.

The girl Raymond had shown me was in three of the eight photographs I could find on the shelves. Sharper-featured than Evangeline. Striking. The photos all seemed to be from about the same time, about three or four years ago, judging by the hair, fashions, and Edie's age. A happy group of sisters, at least for the camera.

I heard the library door close behind me, and turned to see Mr. Oakes. "Ah, Miss Franklin," he said. "Were you looking for me?"

"Why—no," I replied. He had startled me, and I didn't like it. "I was just … looking for something to read. I hope you don't mind."

"Not at all," he said, with a smile. I didn't particularly like his smile, either. Or the closed door. "I just thought—hoped—you were here because you had found out I often work late in the library at night."

He approached and stood a little too near.

"I had no idea," I said, backing up a step. Some people—men, usually—also had no idea when they were standing too close.

He smiled under the mustache and stepped back, himself. His smile looked like a learned behavior, something to gain an advantage, but not connected to genuine joy or affection.

"Right now, for instance," he said, going to the desk, "I'm looking over some notes from the workmen about the new chapel."

"Ah," I said.

"It's costing an arm and a leg, but I'll tell you something," he said, "Mrs. Oakes wanted it, and if it's not finished like she wants, I'll never hear the end of it."

That was admirable, I guess, that he wanted to keep his wife happy. My opinion of him rose maybe half a degree.

He went on. "Have you ever been to the mission in town?"

I had, when Raymond and I came here to get married. But I didn't think this was the time to bring that up. I didn't even know if he had been told that Raymond and I had been married, that we had once been more than just two of Fortune's players.

So I just said, "Yes, once, a long time ago."

"Elizabeth wanted the chapel to look like the Santa Barbara mission," he said, looking down at the notes, which sat atop architect's sketches.

I didn't care to get too near, but I could see the drawings did indeed look like a mission, one of the twenty-one the Spanish had built up and down the California coast in the eighteenth century. I murmured something just to show I'd heard.

"I said I wouldn't pay for two bell towers, though, and told the architect to see what he could do with one," Mr. Oakes was saying. He looked up. "Why don't you come over here and give me your opinion?"

You tend to learn, especially in my business, when an invitation to one thing is really an invitation to something else.

"Oh, I'm not much on visual design," I said lightly, moving away and toward the door. "I really was just looking for something to read. Having trouble getting to sleep. This looks good."

I had plucked a book from the shelf at random. It was *Blandings Castle* by P.G. Wodehouse. I made a bit of a show of being excited to have found it here.

"Yes, I love Wodehouse. Just the thing to read myself to sleep."

You always hear about big men who can move swiftly despite their bulk. Mr. Oakes turned out to be one of those. In the time it took for me to look down at a page of Wodehouse's lighthearted prose, he had risen from the desk, covered the few paces between us, and was now in front of me, even taking a step forward as I backed up against the bookshelves. I caught the smell of his hair pomade, which I found objectionable. His expression was no longer blandly friendly but something else I recognized.

"You're trying to tell me you weren't looking at me all evening? That you didn't come in here wanting something besides a book?" he said. "I know how you actresses are."

I was suddenly aware that no one was around, and that he was rather large. And extremely unattractive. Oddly, maybe foolishly, I felt little fear, and only wondered what the repercussions would be if I had to hurt Raymond's future father-in-law.

"No, actually, I was just paying attention to my host in an attempt to be a well-behaved guest," I said, standing my ground, giving him a chance to be well-behaved himself.

He smiled his unpleasant smile.

"Right. And you're telling me that handsome Jew husband of yours doesn't do right by you, that you have to read yourself to sleep?"

I could almost physically feel the satisfaction I would

get from decking him. Rising anger, I found, was also doing something funny to my vision.

My father had told me he had experienced this once, when another little boy tried to steal his marbles. He only remembered the boy trying to grab the marbles, then quite literally seeing red, and then nothing else until he felt people pulling him off the thief. He had been sitting on the other kid's chest and pounding his head into the ground.

Oakes was now openly leering at me. His small feral eyes, set in saggy flesh, reminded me of the eyes of a wild boar I had accidentally cornered once, on a camping trip with my dad and Clay. It had charged, and Clay, coming up behind me, had shot it dead.

Clay wasn't here now, but that did not matter. If I had been a cat, my tail would have been whiplashing a warning. Oakes was much larger than I, by maybe eighty pounds and six or so inches. But it never occurred to me that I couldn't inflict serious harm on him. I was pretty strong from years of pushing horses around, and from the physical conditioning required for my work. I had also to learn fighting techniques for several pictures. In that context, of course, you never connected when you threw a punch. But I had no doubt I could connect now if I had to.

I forced my breathing to slow, and looked straight into his eyes.

Like all bullies, he expected people to fear him. And when he didn't see fear in me, a flicker of confusion crossed his face.

I was still holding the Wodehouse book in front of me, I realized, and now I smiled, putting as much sweetness into it as I dared, throwing him off. I turned in the cramped space he was allowing me, placed the book on a table, and then looked down demurely, my hands stealing to my décolletage.

Oakes made an approving noise. I expect he thought I was going to produce something having to do with family planning—and why wouldn't he, with the dim view he took of actresses' morals, not to mention self-control?

As I often did, I had my penknife tucked into my bra, one of the ones with a tiny pocket. My hand touched the antler handle.

The knife was the kind you could snap open with one hand, and I had a brief urge to open it and poke the small blade right up under his jaw, to bury it in his flesh. That would have been satisfying, feeling the knife go in, the stubble under his chin—

Somehow a cooler part of my brain made me resist the urge to mayhem, however, and my fingers moved from the knife to a weapon much less likely to land me in jail: a tube of Max Factor's Super Indelible Lipstick in my favorite color, Crimson.

I heard his breathing quicken. Ugh.

Taking advantage of that brief moment when a man's desire makes him pause to anticipate conquest, I brought the lipstick up—and quickly scribbled some nice Max Factor Crimson lines all over his face, ending with a line down his already florid nose. His eyes widened, and crossed, and almost bulged. I suppressed the urge to laugh.

Now I saw that he was shaking, but I wasn't.

Keeping my voice low and just above a whisper, forcing him to pay attention, I said, "Listen to me, you disgusting old lecher. I am going to pretend none of this just happened, for your daughter's and Raymond's sakes. And, if you're smarter than you look, you will forget it, too."

I gave that a moment to sink in, and then jutted my chin at his face. "You might want to take care of that before your wife sees it."

Now he had backed away a step and was sort of sputtering, and scrubbing at his mug with a white handkerchief as I slid out from between him and the bookcase and walked, with studied nonchalance, to the door.

As I got there, he finally found his voice, and it was tight with anger. "You will regret this, Miss Franklin."

I turned and gave him one raised eyebrow.

"I doubt that," I said. "And you can call me Mrs. Gold."

Chapter Thirty

I couldn't go back to our room. Though Oakes was even creepier than Raymond's character Dupree in *Prairie Princess*, I hadn't been shaking when confronting him. But now I was, with anger and that enveloping fury you get when you really want to punch someone in the nose or jab them with your knife but have to settle for decorating their face with lipstick instead.

And ugh, I thought: Now I'll have to take a tissue to my Max Factor Super Indelible and remove any layer that came in contact with Oakes's odious face before I use it again.

Needing to walk, I went down a couple of tile-floored corridors, past stucco arches and sconces with electric lights in them, my footsteps echoing off the hard surfaces and my shadow dancing on the wall. I met no one—I supposed they didn't keep the throngs of servants on duty around the clock: one of the few positive impressions I had so far of Evangeline's family.

How could Evangeline be so cheery, I wondered? Edie was still young, with the energy and optimism of a child. But I could picture Evangeline as a dreamy girl who, ignored or disliked for some reason by her father, most likely had retreated into a rosy world of her own, with her volunteer work and whatever else she occupied herself with.

And then there was the other girl, the one Ray thought was Ellie, with whom he'd had an affair. If she was, maybe she was socially adept enough to realize she should stay away from this gathering, not cause a scene. I wondered if she had tried to talk Evangeline out of marrying Ray, after her own experience with him. I even wondered, briefly, if the mysterious Ellie might also be the mysterious Annie.

Thinking about this, and still simmering with frustration at not having been able to rearrange Oakes' face, I went out a door and through the garden, down a path lined with oleanders. Eventually, through a break in the hedge, I could see a bell tower, pale against the dark sky. This must be the private chapel that Oakes had pretended he wanted to know my opinion of. How many other buildings on the place would look like a small version of a Spanish mission with a fifty- or sixty-foot bell tower?

Mrs. Oakes was, I guessed, a devout Catholic who, thanks to her wealth, could indulge a whim like a private chapel, built to look any way she wanted it to. The bell tower was evidently still being worked on. There was scaffolding on the two sides I could see. The moon was bright, nearly full, and the building glowed like ivory in the dark.

Though this was California, it was still winter, and I was cold in my thin dress. That was helping to dissipate the hot anger I still felt, but I wasn't ready to face Max yet. He would know something was amiss, and although I would have to tell him what happened with Oakes, I didn't want to do it right now. I had seen him nearly tie a guy into knots in Mr. Noguchi's defense. I had no trouble imagining what he would do in mine. I reminded myself that nothing had, in the end, happened. But I didn't think, somehow, that Max would see it that way.

I went up to the chapel and found that its heavy wooden door was unlocked. Curiosity alone made me go through it. The interior, dark and quiet, looked to be already completed, with pews of polished wood flanking a short aisle leading up to an altar in front of the crucified Christ. Candles in wall sconces gave off a flickering light and a faint honeylike scent.

Just as I was wondering why they were lighted, I heard footsteps. and shrank back into the shadows by the door. I wondered who could be coming in here this late—maybe a workman retrieving a forgotten tool?

The footsteps were too light for a man, though, and soon I saw it was Mrs. Oakes, all in black, including a black veil, like an old Spanish widow. She didn't go all the way up to the small altar at the front, but over to the side, where there was an alcove with a statue of the Virgin Mary in her blue cloak, hands spread in welcome, ready to comfort.

Elizabeth Oakes knelt on the padded knee rest in front of the statue, clasped her hands and bowed her head, briefly, then looked up again, took a match from nearby, and lit several candles. Not one for religion myself, I had no idea how long this would go on, and prepared myself to settle in for a while, while trying not to sneeze. Which, of course, immediately made my nose start itching.

After perhaps ten or fifteen minutes, though, which felt like an hour, the black-clad figure rose from the bench and turned around, looking right at the alcove where I was, if I were to be honest, hiding.

"It's all right. I know you're there, whoever you are," she said.

Cool customer, I thought. I stepped out of the shadows, saying, "I'm sorry, I didn't want to interrupt you, but wasn't quite sure how to, er, announce myself."

"Please don't worry," she said. "This place of worship is here for anyone—" she stopped herself, then amended "—anyone of faith—to come and pray." She just couldn't leave Max out of this, I thought.

I saw that she had lit five candles. They now flickered behind her under Mary's benign gaze: two for herself and Mr. Oakes, I guessed, and three more, for their daughters. At least that's what I assumed. Did one light a candle for oneself?

Mrs. Oakes glanced back briefly when she saw me looking.

"You know, it takes constant prayer to keep a family safe," Mrs. Oakes said softly.

I thought about all the people I wanted to keep safe: Max, my mother, Mr. and Mrs. Monty, Kit and Mr. Noguchi, Clay and Sam, my friends the riding extras. Even Raymond. I wondered if taking up the practice would really keep a horse from stumbling, prevent car brakes from failing, stop someone from replacing blanks with real bullets in a gun? I wondered if it was even possible to say enough prayers to keep everyone you loved safe.

I didn't pray, I told her, but I did like to think there was something bigger than us out there that might hear us if we asked for guidance.

She looked at me for a moment, her face framed by the black veil. She looked very pale, and sad. Finally she said, "Have you ever lost a child, Miss Franklin?"

"No," I said.

"Do you have children?"

"Not so far," I said.

"If you do, you will start praying," she said. "I should have been praying before. Before Eleanor … well, before we lost our eldest. Now I pray for the safety of Evangeline and Edie."

"I'm sorry for your loss," I said. It sounded inadequate, like it had any other time I'd said it. Eleanor, I thought. Ellie. Lost?

"It's not enough, I know," she said, as though acknowledging, not my expression of sympathy, but her own attempts to protect her family with prayer. "So I do what I can in other ways. You know Edie is not going riding with you all tomorrow?"

I had almost forgotten the outing scheduled for the next morning. I realized I would have been expecting the girl to come with us, probably on the finest of ponies, unless she wasn't interested. Some little girls weren't interested in ponies, I had heard. Though I'd never met one.

"She wanted to ride, like Eleanor and Evangeline," Mrs. Oakes said. "But there's no need for her to do anything so risky. She's young enough that I can influence her. She's properly convinced they're dangerous."

I wondered if Eleanor had died in a riding accident. But I didn't think this was a time to ask.

"Evangeline, though," she said, as though to herself. "She always had a mind of her own. Not happy at her boarding school, adopting stray animals, not happy with her college, running off to work for a magazine, coming back with her hair short as a boy's, getting all sorts of crazy ideas."

"I think she's quite lovely," I said. Complimenting people's children usually disposes them to be nice to you, and I wasn't above it.

"I will say that she has changed a bit since meeting Raymond," Mrs. Oakes said. "She seems to have a focus, a purpose, now."

I made a that's-nice sound, all the while thinking that Raymond was more likely to be a highly annoying, time-consuming project rather than a focus.

She leaned against the nearest pew. "You know, Miss Franklin," she said, "you don't seem as … flighty … as other actresses I've known."

"Thanks, I guess," I said. "I got into the business sort of by accident."

She didn't find this of interest. "I've seen some of your pictures," she said. Not adding that she liked them, didn't like them. Instead she said, "Do you consider them suitable for children?"

That took me aback. The Hays Office had been in the business of censoring motion pictures to keep all sorts of things off the screen, including nudity and bad language. It dated back to before the first time I had stepped in front of a camera.

"Most of them, I guess," I said.

"I consider them all unsuitable," she said abruptly.

I tried not to be offended at that.

"Not just yours. The pictures in general," Mrs. Oakes said. "They lure young people to the theaters and fill their heads with ridiculous ideas. They stop listening to their parents, and some of them think they can go to Hollywood and be 'discovered.' But all that's waiting for them there is betrayal. And a road to hell."

Mrs. Oakes's voice had a hollow sound. Not only did she seem like a wraith in her own house and chapel, she sounded like one. And now the wraith was going to give me a lecture about the moral depravity of Tinseltown. Which I didn't need.

"I don't mean to insult you, Miss Franklin," she said. "I know what it's like because I was one of those young people, years ago. I learned that the casting couch was no myth. And I thought it really would lead to a contract. But it was only for six months. At the end of that time, the studio threw me away like a soiled hankie."

214

There was a distinct creepiness to this whole scene, the both of us in our black dresses, in a place of worship, talking about the seamier aspects of the motion picture business. Despite that, I felt sympathy for her. I knew what those girls went through, and knew I was lucky to have escaped it.

"And then I met Mr. Oakes," she said. "I guess you could say he saved me. He needed a secretary who made a good appearance but was also smart, and discreet."

I tried to picture Charles Oakes being interested in saving anyone. Couldn't.

"Before long, we were married," she said. "And our children came along, Eleanor, Evangeline, Edie."

I nodded, wondering how soon I could excuse myself. I wanted to go and think. Eleanor must be Ellie; I was almost sure of it. And she had died somehow, somewhere. Had it been in the ocean at Santa Monica? No, that would be far too much of a coincidence, Ray falling in love with the sister of the girl who was with Vern when he died, a girl who possibly had something to do with the shooting on the set, somehow.

"And now there are only two," she said. "So you see, I have devoted my life to the Church. I realize now I wasn't sufficiently devout, and God saw fit to take one of my children from me. So I protect the other two with my life, and my prayers."

She looked around at the saints and candles and stained-glass windows.

"I promised God that if he kept Evangeline and Edie safe, I would build a chapel in His honor," she said. "When it's light, you will see it in all its glory. It's almost finished. The workmen are correcting some flaws in the plastering."

She smiled at me. "We'll show it off tomorrow. You know, Evangeline wants the wedding to be held here."

Which couldn't come too soon, I thought, for me. I was ready to have the Oakes family out of my life, and Raymond away from Hollywood and its threats, real or imagined.

Mrs. Oakes had wound down, finally, and I left her returning to kneel in front of the Virgin, two mothers who had lost children.

Walking back through the garden, I thought about the lost Eleanor. She looked so full of life in the photos. Like all young people did. What had Mrs. Oakes said? Something about "being discovered"? Well, that fit. She did show a spark. And she had gone to Hollywood, met Raymond, had an affair …. Ray couldn't possibly know what had happened to her, I thought. He had just tonight recognized her in the photos. I doubted it would be much comfort to him to know she was dead.

Chapter Thirty-One

At least they employed people in these strapped times. Servants were circulating all over the sunny breakfast room. More guests than last night, in addition to the Oakeses, Raymond, Max and me, were assembling for breakfast. Outside the French doors was a covered gallery with arches through which you could see one of the courtyard fountains, currently bubbling away for all it was worth. Birds were chirping in some red-flowered vines that grew against the walls.

If the house itself was a fantasy on the theme of a Spanish rancho, breakfast was straight out of a Wodehouse country weekend. A sideboard bore an array of silver-covered chafing dishes with eggs, sausages, fried tomatoes, and potatoes.

We were going riding after breakfast. Or at least some of us were. Max decidedly wasn't.

"I'm from Indianapolis," he had said earlier, kissing me on the nose as I knotted the tie on my ratcatcher shirt. "I ride streetcars."

Pulling blank sheet music pages from a briefcase, he said, "I'll be perfectly occupied here. They don't seem to mind my using the piano. I've been needing to work on some of these songs for the Stock Exchange movie—"

"I still think no one is ready for the stock market with songs—"

"Nevertheless, I'm getting paid for these songs, so write them I must," he said. "I have great hopes for the lyricist managing to put 'dash,' 'crash' and 'smash' into one of them. I get paid whether or not the picture's a dog."

He stopped, holding the sheet music, and took a moment to

look me up and down as I buttoned my fitted jacket. "So—that's what the well-dressed equestrienne is wearing these days?" he said, admiringly.

"Yes," I said, twirling to show off the whole ensemble, which included jodhpurs that flared out next to the thigh and then hugged my legs down to my short boots. "Just like Ginger in *Top Hat*. Well, except she had on a stock tie. This is slightly less formal."

"Ah," Max said, the way people do to indicate they understand when they don't understand but don't really want you to go into it. The intricacies and rules of equestrian wear, fascinating as I found them, were not burning questions for Max.

"At least you'll have breakfast with us," I said, raising an eyebrow.

"That I will," he said.

Now we were lifting silver lids from dishes and sniffing appreciatively while guests and servants circulated about, filling plates, pouring coffee, talking animatedly.

I scanned the room. A few people seemed to be neighbors, some young men and women who I guessed were friends of Evangeline's from school or somewhere, and an Argentinian polo player I recognized.

And then, with delight, I spotted someone else I recognized: a slim figure with upright posture, white hair in a low chignon.

"Miss Merriwether!" I exclaimed, feeling uncommonly happy that she was there. The last time she had seen me, I had just escaped death in Raymond's Duesenberg only by crashing into her serene garden and mowing down a small tree.

She looked at home here, dressed for riding in breeches and tall black boots. She turned, saw me, and gave me a genuine smile.

"Miss Franklin—Frankie!" she said, coming over to me. We kissed on both cheeks and she said, "Don't you look a treat?"

"What are you doing here?" I asked.

"I was invited by our friend Raymond Sinclare," she said. "And I have a place just down the road and was going to be in town anyway, so I thought, why not? I would like to toast someone making an honest man of him."

She leaned in. "Besides, I heard you were here and I've been interested to know how you're getting on," she said.

"Oh," I replied. "Well—just fine. But you mean—"

"Yes," she said. "Any closer to answers about Vernon?"

I shook my head. "It's all dead ends," I said.

"There are some mysteries that will always remain mysteries," she said. "This is starting to look like one of them."

She helped herself to some scrambled eggs.

"Is that excessive car of Raymond's back on the road?"

I chuckled. "Yes," I said. "He drove it here, in fact. You probably know that the brakes failing was not an accident."

She nodded. "I did hear that. A fan?"

"Yes, apparently," I said. "One of mine—if you can call someone a fan if they want to cause you harm. He seemed to think it was my car."

She looked grim. "It's one of the disadvantages of fame—just one," she said. "Some fans love you so much … it's as if they want to destroy you if they can't have you."

She looked over at Max, pouring two cups of coffee: one for me, one for him. "At least," she said, "you have that remarkably attractive husband of yours to look out for you."

"Join us at our table?" I asked.

She gave me a warm smile. "I don't think so, my dear. I have my eye on Señor Beltran." With a nod of her head, she indicated the polo player. Tall, muscular, ridiculously handsome, tolerable grasp of English—I could see her point.

After breakfast we gathered under the majestic oak trees around the stable, waiting for grooms to bring the horses out. Raymond was dressed for riding as well, looking smashing as always in his tailored jacket, breeches, and tall, shiny brown boots. But under his tan, he was pale as a ghost. I really wished he had begged off, with whatever excuse he could come up with.

Poor Raymond. He was no Duke Wayne. For all the knights and cowboys he'd played on film, Ray had never learned to ride well and didn't really like horses. In fact, he was rather afraid of them. The director always had to cut away just before his character mounted and rode off, or they'd have to put him on a mechanical horse and have men rock it up and down, with the moving landscape projected behind him. This always looked so fake to me that I wished directors wouldn't even do it. But there were no mechanical horses here. I hoped they'd at least have a calm and gentle mount for him.

I gave him an encouraging smile. "Very nice turnout, Ray," I said.

"Thank you," he said, almost absently.

"Ah, there you are!" Evangeline smiled gaily at Ray. She was turned out perfectly herself, in a beautifully cut plaid hacking jacket, much like the one I was wearing.

"I'm so looking forward to the ride," she said, eyes shining. "I can't wait to see Raymond ride, in person. I think I fell in love with him ten years ago, when I saw *Cowboy from Boston*."

Ah yes, that picture. The one where Raymond played the hero who impressed his sweetheart's Wyoming relatives by riding the meanest bronc on the whole ranch. The publicity photos made it look like Raymond had far more affection for the equine race than was actually the case.

"That so?" I said.

Raymond was smiling his on-camera smile which convinced most people, but not me. In fact, I thought he looked a little like he was about to go to the dentist to have a particularly hard-to-reach tooth pulled.

I had to say, the Oakes Ranch horses were fine ones. I admired them as a squadron of grooms got them ready, each horse perfectly turned out and wearing a saddle and bridle that would cost some hard-working people several months' salary.

"I thought we'd ride out along the bluffs and then take the trail down and have a nice gallop on the beach," Evangeline said brightly, looking at Raymond as though for approval. "And I have a surprise for you!"

"I'm sure it'll be fine, Ray," I said, bright as a camp counselor, as Evangeline skipped away to attend to her other guests.

I suppose if I were of a meaner nature, I would have enjoyed his discomfiture. But I knew that his fear was real, and that fear transmitted itself to the horse you were on. No matter how gentle a nag they found for him, his tension would transmit itself to his horse, which could lead to dangerous misbehavior.

"Ah, there she is, my beauty!" Miss Merriwether exclaimed when a groom handed her the reins to a deerlike, golden bay Arabian mare. She caressed the gleaming, arched neck and smoothed the black mane. "You'll be a lovely girl for me, won't you? Here's a bribe, just in case."

She winked at me and produced a peppermint candy from a pocket. The mare's pink tongue flicked out and the candy disappeared. A groom gave Miss Merriwether a leg up. She landed lightly in the saddle and gathered the reins, looking very happy.

The riders were matched up with their mounts, one by one. I was talking the finer points of neck shots with the polo player and wondering where Raymond's horse was, when I saw Evangeline emerge from the shadows of the stables, leading a chestnut mare.

The sight of the horse stopped me in mid-sentence. She was a stunner.

At least sixteen hands, the chestnut was put together beautifully and had that noble seeing-into-the-future expression some horses have, called "the look of eagles." I always figured it wasn't anything any more special than the way movie faces caught the light—but still, she had it. And she moved, on long, clean legs, with the grace and restless power of an Amazon queen.

She was also as fidgety as any racehorse going to the post. As Evangeline led her toward us on a short rein, the mare danced and jigged, snorting. Veins showed on the thin skin of her neck, arched now against the restraint, and she was already breaking a sweat. Her steel-shod hooves beat a jagged rhythm on the ground.

"She looks ready to go," I said mildly.

Evangeline smiled at me. With her red hair and the mare's chestnut coat, they made a striking pair. "She's definitely a star," she said, beaming. "A star for a star."

And she walked over to Raymond, and held out the reins.

I wondered if anyone else saw it as obviously as I did. All color had drained from Raymond's chiseled face, and he looked less like he was going to the dentist and more like he was headed for the gallows. He was not going to last a minute on this horse.

The mare sidled nervously, and tossed her head. She looked eager to be off, and I wondered how long it had been since she'd been exercised.

Raymond was tense and trying not to show it, but I could see his chest rising and falling too rapidly. He was going to look an utter fool in front of his fiancée in a moment. I was glad her parents had stayed in the house, lingering over breakfast. Evangeline still held out the reins, her face starting to show concern, and some confusion.

"Ray?" she said, indicating the reins.

I had to do something. That is to say, America's Kid Sister had to do something. I excused myself from the polo player, who, like me, had been gazing admiringly at the mare. Like he wanted her for himself. Which had given me an idea.

Striding purposefully over to Evangeline, I said, louder than was absolutely necessary, "Golly, that is the nicest horse I have seen in some time."

I gave Raymond my most impish grin and turned back to Evangeline, mustering every bit of entitlement I could manage.

"Now, Evangeline," I said to her, in a tone of mock admonishment, as though teasing a very good friend, "I know you actually meant this beauty for me!"

And I held my hand out for the reins.

Evangeline looked at me like I'd suddenly grown two heads, while Ray had the tentatively hopeful expression of a man who's just heard the governor might be calling to stay his execution.

The mare snorted again and shook her head. Pretending I had not noticed or did not care that Evangeline had chosen her for Raymond, I now turned to him and even batted my eyelashes a little.

"Oh, Raymond, you big sweetheart, surely you don't mind?"

222

I said. "She's so magnificent, and I may never have the chance again!"

And I gave Evangeline the most brilliant, self-involved, oblivious smile I could manage. "After all, you did say 'a star for a star.'"

A brief look—maybe irritation, maybe uncertainty—flitted across Evangeline's face before she composed herself to smile back at me sweetly, saying, "She's our best horse. I picked her out for Raymond."

For a moment our gazes locked.

"But *I* want to ride her," I insisted, almost laughing, like an indulged child who has never not gotten her own way.

There was a moment of silence in which Evangeline gave me a stare of remarkable steeliness.

I met her look, my own smile fading and my expression hardening into something else. I felt people gawking at us, but that meant nothing to me. Wasn't I paid quite well to let people gawk at me? I let my voice throb, even allowed it to sound a bit unhinged.

"I said: I. Want. To. Ride. That One."

I considered stamping my little foot, but decided that would be too much.

Evangeline's lips compressed briefly. She clearly was also used to getting her own way. But I was a guest, someone she didn't know, someone who might possibly be uncouth or insane enough to start an actual fight. I could see her wavering.

Raymond finally took the cue and joined the scene. He bestowed on me a look of affectionate indulgence, and announced, "You're absolutely right, my dear." I was relieved to have been demoted from "darling," at least around his fiancée.

"Much as I was looking forward to it," he went on, "I'm afraid I cannot deny Miss Frankie Franklin anything she desires. Who could?"

Then he addressed our little audience, letting them in on the joke that America's Kid Sister was a bigger spoiled brat than anyone had suspected, all her positive publicity notwithstanding.

"Miss Franklin is a much, much bigger star than I," he said,

223

smiling broadly. "And of course it is she who must ride this fine animal!"

Evangeline, eyes narrowed, looked like she was about to breathe fire—and then, all at once, decided not to push it. She laughed gaily.

"Why, of course you may ride her! There will be plenty of chances for Raymond to, later."

She handed me the reins, and I took them with a gracious smile, happy now, ignoring her eyes, which were looking daggers at me. Then I turned to the mare, speaking softly and stroking the gleaming neck. Her coat felt like satin.

A groom about sixty years old came over to me, took the reins and put them over her head, and cupped his hands to give me a leg up. As I settled into the saddle, he looked up at me, a serious look on his kind, weathered face, and said, "You be careful now, Miss Franklin."

I thanked him, as the mare gave a slight rear and tugged at the reins, as though to test me. I kept her in place with hands and legs.

Raymond, meanwhile, had mounted the pretty, stolid palomino gelding that had been meant for me, and joined the first riders who were heading out of the stable yard. He looked as relieved as I've ever seen a man look.

"I'd like to walk her just around here for a few minutes," I called to him and Evangeline, "to get used to her and let her calm down away from the other horses."

Evangeline, mounted on a stylish, white-stockinged Thoroughbred, shrugged, and turned toward the others. They were heading across the nearby pasture toward an open gate that led to the trail we'd be taking.

As the others left and I tried to get a feel for my excited and sensitive mount, I noticed Miss Merriwether was still sitting there on her horse, looking amused.

She called to the others, "I'll stay back with Miss Franklin. We'll catch up to you in a bit." And to me, she said, "Quite a performance, Your Highness. I see why the studio keeps you around."

224

I gave her a wry grin and let the mare walk around for a bit. She seemed to calm down, or at least be willing to get from point A to point B by walking instead of dancing sideways. I pulled my velvet cap down on my head and nodded to the groom.

"I think she'll be fine," I said. "By the way, what's her name?"

"Rocket," he said.

Chapter Thirty-Two

We turned our horses toward the trail. The others were already perhaps an eighth of a mile away, and by now I didn't care if we didn't catch up to them.

"Spirited," I said, patting Rocket's neck and fussing over her mane, smoothing it so it was all on the same side of her neck, as she jigged and snorted.

"Maybe she's in heat," Miss Merriwether said. "That would make me act like a bitch sometimes."

I laughed and tried to keep Rocket walking beside the Arab, whose presence seemed to be somewhat calming for her. The rest of the group kept their lead over us, but it didn't seem to bother Miss Merriwether any more than it did me. We crossed the pasture and followed the trail along the fence line, Rocket walking fast, snorting and tossing her head, but seeming to accept the fact that I knew what I was doing.

The trail along the bluffs had a grand view, with a few wispy clouds painting a pale blue sky over the dark blue ocean, and the breeze was briny, and fresh. Ahead, the other riders looked like miniatures.

"My goodness," Miss Merriwether said, looking out to sea. "Keeps things in perspective, doesn't it?"

I considered that as we rode along, high above the beach. The Oakes' pastures extended all the way to the bluffs and beach. Below, I could see where the trail down to the sand joined a dirt road that led to a short pier, and a picturesque adobe structure about the size of a small garage.

"Part of the original Spanish rancho?" I asked.

"Not hardly," Miss Merriwether said with a short laugh. "Charles Oakes had it built himself, oh, maybe fifteen years ago.

That's what my neighbors in town have told me, anyway."

I counted backward and made other calculations. "Near the beginning of Prohibition?"

She nodded. "I doubt he bought this place just for its charm and so his daughters could ride horses," she said.

Of course, I thought. "Raymond had said he was in the beverage business," I said.

Specifically, I realized now, that meant the kind of beverages that were illegal from 1920 until near the end of 1933. Charles Oakes had been a bootlegger. Of course he had.

"Yes, well, he continues to be in the beverage business, as you know," Miss Merriwether said, "only now it's the legal importing of liquor—whisky from Scotland, gin from England, wine from France and Italy for the Sacrament and the table … And he makes sure to support a variety of good causes: Catholic charities, orphanages … which has the advantage of making everyone's memories very short."

So the shed was where he'd stored the illegal booze brought in by boat from Mexico and even Canada. It was a squat, solid-looking building with a heavy oak door.

"Just a law-abiding storage shed now?" I said.

"I suppose."

As we continued the ride, I noticed a new tension in Rocket. Instead of walking, she moved forward with jigging, uncomfortable steps. I tried to stay relaxed and to telegraph calmness to her, but it only got worse, and she began to add a little hop every few strides.

The trail met the dirt road, and Miss Merriwether suggested a canter, to take the edge off. It couldn't hurt, I thought. I nudged Rocket with my heel but instead of a canter she unleashed a huge buck, like a rodeo bronc, and I nearly came off. I grabbed a handful of mane as she took a smaller jump, and I knew another big one was coming.

Instead of trying to stay in the saddle while she thought of new moves, I took my feet out of the stirrup irons and leaped off, landing next to her. The mare snorted, threw her head up and backed away to the end of the reins, eyes rolling at me.

Accusingly, I couldn't help but think. I stepped toward her and she flinched away.

The other riders were now out of sight, somewhere off in the distance in the shadows of oak trees lining the trail. I exchanged glances with Miss Merriwether.

"Something's hurting her," I said.

Letting the mare stay as far away from me as she liked while I still held the reins, I talked softly to her until she calmed down somewhat. When I felt I could approach her again, I carefully unbuckled the girth and lifted the saddle. She hadn't been limping, so it couldn't have been her legs bothering her. It had to be something else.

Reins looped over my arm, I looked under the saddle. I couldn't see anything, but as I ran my hand under the pad, something sharp poked me, and I said, "Ow!"

I yanked the saddle off and flung it to the ground. Between the saddle and pad, I found a short length of an alarmingly thorned plant. A couple of the sharp points had worked their way through the pad as we rode, until it came in contact with the already-restive mare's back. Poor Rocket, I thought. She had tried to behave. Even with this thing poking her. It would have happened more quickly with Raymond, as his greater weight would have pushed the thorns through sooner.

I held it up for Miss Merriwether to see. She dismounted gracefully and held out her hand.

"*Euphorbia milii*," she said. "The crown-of-thorns plant. Of course she'd have that in her garden."

At my quizzical look, she said, "You haven't gotten to know Mrs. Oakes yet," she said. "She's a—how shall I put it—fervent Catholic. The kind who listens to Father Coughlin, er, religiously."

"Actually," I said, "I did get that impression already. We spoke last night in the chapel."

"So you can imagine why she'd grow one of these. Some people think it was the plant that provided Jesus's crown of thorns. Hence the name."

"But how did it get into a saddle pad?" I said.

"Not by itself, clearly."

"Poor old thing," I said to the mare, who had calmed down considerably, now that the thorn wasn't poking her. "I think I'll just walk her back to the stable, to give her time to forgive me," I said.

"I think it's only about a mile," Miss Merriwether said. "I'll walk with you."

The thorn in my pocket, I put the now-harmless pad and saddle back on Rocket, and fastened the girth loosely.

It was, actually, a fine day to be walking along past oak trees, the ocean at our backs and a soft breeze blowing. I wished I could enjoy it.

"So who do you think did this?" I said at last. "Someone who doesn't want Evangeline and Ray to be married? Like her parents, maybe?"

"One young fellow I was talking to last night, Jack Mayberry, did have an eye for her himself, he was telling me," Miss Merriwether said as we walked. "But he doesn't seem that bright. Unless he's just bright enough to try something like this but not think it through."

"A groom?" I said.

She shook her head. "Their grooms seem to treat the horses well. I can't see it."

"Mrs. Oakes?"

"You never know," she said. "Do you think they know you and Raymond had been married?"

I stopped walking. The chestnut mare bumped me with her head. Stroking her velvety nose, I said, "It's not exactly a secret, but I had wondered about that before. If they knew, their faith wouldn't even allow them to get married, would it? If he was a divorced person?"

"Not without something like a decree from the Diocese, as I understand it," she said. "It's also possible the Oakeses, despite trying to put the best face on things, just disapprove of Raymond in general. You know—show people."

"We're scum for sure," I said.

"Many believe this," she agreed amiably.

"Even former bootleggers."

"Reformed sinners are the worst prudes," Miss Merriwether observed.

We walked along for a while, leading our horses. This seemed to agree with the chestnut mare, who had calmed down considerably and now walked easily beside me.

"So maybe someone in her family was trying to make Raymond look like an idiot in front of Evangeline—or even to harm him. Maybe cause her to change her mind. What if the thorn had gone through the saddle pad and Rocket had started bucking at the top of those bluffs?"

Ray wouldn't have been able to stay on, I was sure of that. But even if he had, the thought of a panicked horse near the edge of those cliffs made me shiver. Just getting too close to the edge, the weight of a horse could, in some spots, be enough to break a chunk loose, and after that—it was a long way down to the beach.

"One thing to consider," said Miss Merriwether. "People like the Oakeses don't usually do this sort of thing for themselves."

I did consider that.

The other riders were also just returning to the stables when we got back. There were concerned looks as I handed Rocket off to the old groom and went over to Evangeline. I decided to just be direct.

I took the thorn out of my pocket and held it up. "This was under the saddle and poking her," I said calmly. "After she nearly threw me, I thought it best to walk her back."

"What?!" Evangeline's eyes widened. Her face reddened. "May I have that, please?"

I let her take the thorn, and she strode quickly off toward the stable. I had to wonder if she suspected a groom. I looked over at Jack Mayberry, who was either concerned or smirking, or maybe the poor guy's face was just made that way, I couldn't tell.

Miss Merriwether and I looked at each other. Miss Merriwether's eyebrows went up as we both heard Evangeline's voice carrying from the depths of the stable, berating a groom for being so careless.

230

"Gosh," I said.

Eventually Evangeline returned, still looking angry. "No one will admit to anything," she said. "I'll have a talk with my father about it. I'm just glad you're not injured, Frankie."

"You're too kind," I said.

Chapter
Thirty-Three

Later, as we dressed for dinner, I told Max what happened, trying to be as matter-of-fact as possible. After the incident with the Duesenberg, I didn't want to cause him more worry.

"You could have been hurt pretty bad," he said.

"I've been thrown before." I said it with a shrug. I never liked it, and it could be serious, but every rider knew it would happen eventually.

"Or Raymond could have been."

"Or Rocket."

"Rocket?"

"The mare. The horse I was riding."

"Ah," Max said. He put his pipe back in his mouth and looked out the window, then looked back at me. "How many years have we been here, again?"

"It's only another day," I said.

He looked out the window again, and sighed heavily.

We dressed for dinner, I in a white satin gown Charlie had designed for me. As we got ready to go, I picked up the blue Chinese silk shawl that I never traveled without. Max had changed into pleated trousers, spectator shoes and a pale blue cashmere sweater over an impeccable white shirt.

"We are very coordinated," I said. "I'm eager to get this over with, too, you know."

Tying his bowtie, he gave me a grin.

"Feel like you're giving away a problematic son?"

"Something like that," I said.

The usual mobs of servants were about as we arrived in the library again for drinks, and there were more friends in addition to those from the morning, and, I supposed, more of the Oakes family. The long dining room looked grand, with flower arrangements down the center of the table, and thousands of dollars' worth of sterling silver and crystal.

Even the quite wealthy, I noticed, seemed to be excited to find faces they recognized from the movie screen in their midst, and Raymond was in his element telling stories.

I took perverse pleasure in noticing that Charles Oakes appeared to be trying to stay as far away from me as possible. Not even looking at me, if he could help it. Of course I had no interest in paying him any attention—which was made only slightly difficult by this being an engagement party where he was the father of the bride.

There was the usual dinner small talk ("Are you one of the Boston Franklins?" "Er, no. The Pennsylvania, Iowa and rodeo circuit Hickenloopers. Actually.") And then it was time for toasts.

Evangeline, pale and smiling, sat next to Ray, who wore the traditional look of bemusement appropriate to the soon-to-be-wed gentleman as Charles Oakes raised his glass. And delivered one of the odder toasts I had ever heard.

"As many of you know," he said. "I had expected to be holding this sort of celebration for our eldest daughter first. Our Eleanor." His smile at Evangeline was fixed, and not pleasant. "But, that was not to be. Very good work, my dear."

A few guests exchanged looks of concern and confusion. Some, like me, were going for the neutral poker face. I had no idea what he was talking about, unless he somehow blamed Evangeline for Eleanor's death.

"I would call Raymond here a very lucky man," Mr. Oakes went on. Now he smiled like a man who thinks he's about to say something incredibly funny. "However, I would argue that I am luckier by far." He gave his daughter a thoroughly unpleasant smile. "I am lucky because I found someone to take this one off my hands."

There were some muffled gasps, and people exchanged glances, trying to divine what was amusing about that while Oakes laughed at his own joke. A couple of people did laugh short, uncomfortable laughs.

Evangeline's face had gone masklike. Mrs. Oakes's gaze was fixed on the damask tablecloth as she moved her glass around and around in circles. The servants looked afraid to move.

Oakes surveyed the crowd, realized his humor was not going over well, and laughed in a way meant to get everyone to join him.

"Come on now, I mean to say this is a joyous occasion!" he exclaimed. "And to demonstrate just how happy I am about this turn of events, I want to announce I have bought a house for them in San Francisco!"

I saw Evangeline give a start. She hadn't known. Raymond carried them through with a stage professional's aplomb, pretending to be nothing but surprised and delighted, but I suspected he hadn't known, either. There was some talk about the damp, cold summers in San Francisco, and the revolutionary new bridge being built across the Golden Gate, the strait that led from the Pacific Ocean into San Francisco Bay, as well as the few other things those assembled knew about the city.

As far as I was aware, Raymond knew no one in San Francisco, and had never expressed an interest in living there. It probably sounded like Siberia to him. He and Evangeline must both have seen it as a banishment.

It was nearly eleven by the time the other toasts and the dinner had run themselves out. I was glad the evening was almost over, but I still had something I needed to do.

Back in our room, I told Max I was going down to the stables. I dressed in trousers and a sweater, and after going down a couple of the wrong hallways finally located the kitchen, where it seemed twenty or thirty people were busy with pots and pans and dishes and silver and tablecloths, cleaning things, putting things away.

Most of them stopped and looked up, a murmur going through the small group, when I appeared in the doorway. Damn. I forgot, sometimes, that I dragged this fame thing around with me, and that for some people, seeing me was a special occasion. But I had never felt so ordinary.

234

"I'm really sorry to bother you," I said to an older woman who seemed to be a manager if not the chef. "I wonder if I might find an apple or a carrot or two here?"

All of the above were fetched, a young kitchen girl actually polishing the apple on a clean towel as she brought it to me, and they seemed to think it charming that Frankie Franklin wanted to visit a horse.

I thanked them for the treats and went to the stables, maybe a ten-minute walk from the house.

The place was quiet, with just a few lights on, and the only sounds were those of large animals settling in for the night, some drinking water or already asleep. On the door of each stall was a white card with the horse's name and neatly lettered notes about feeding, training, and veterinary care. There was a blackboard with notes about a hay delivery and the vet's and farrier's telephone numbers, in the same hand. On the wall hung a commercially printed sign that said: "ABSOLUTELY NO SMOKING IN THE BARN." It felt homey, well managed, safe.

I heard unhurried footsteps, and saw the old groom who had helped me onto Rocket, walking along and checking each stall.

"One last round, before I turn in myself," he said when we got close enough for conversation. "I expect you're looking for this young lady."

He showed me to Rocket's stall, where she was on her feet, dozing. Her eyes opened when we stopped there. Her ears flicked forward.

"Sorry about today," I said to her.

"She'll do all right, Miss Franklin," the groom said.

"I'm glad." I offered my hand. "Call me Frankie, please."

"And you can call me Doc." We shook.

I asked if I could give her a treat.

"The carrots, yes," he said. "Let's save that apple for tomorrow."

Rocket came to her stall door and gently took the end of the proffered carrot between her teeth. While she bit down, I broke it off so she could eat a piece at a time. We did that a couple of times with both carrots.

I wondered what Evangeline had said to Doc about what had happened this morning, but couldn't think how to bring it up. So I asked him about the mare, instead.

"She's a retired racehorse, just eight," he said. "Miss Eleanor saw her at the track, Santa Anita, when she was a three-year-old. She was fast but seemed to be too smart to run just because someone told her to. Miss Eleanor talked the owner into selling. That was a few years ago."

"So she was Eleanor's horse?"

Doc nodded.

"The one who died?"

"She was—" he broke off and shook his head. "I shouldn't be talking out of turn and that's just what I'm doing. Doc sees a lot but don't say a lot. And I done said too much already."

"It's all right," I said.

When in doubt, talk about the horse.

"Well, she's a grand mare," I said. "I'm glad she's all right."

"Too smart for her own good," Doc said. "See the padlock here on her stall? She figured out how to open the regular latch. One night she let some of the other horses out, too."

"Really," I said, impressed. "I've only heard of ponies being that bright."

"She's that bright," he said.

"I can believe that. She also seemed a little high before the ride."

"She hadn't been ridden in a week," he said. "Miss Evangeline said she'd take her out every day but every day something else came up. Guess she's got a lot on her mind. But you don't leave a horse like this in a stall for a week and not ride her. She's like to blow up under you. Thorn or no thorn."

It was my opening. "And you don't know how it got there?" I asked.

"Miss Evangeline said the new stable-boy, Archie, did it as a prank to show off for the other boys, make Mr. Raymond look bad. He's been fired. Gone already. I was not consulted. Though I am the head groom."

Well, they certainly moved fast, I thought.

"I'm glad Rocket is all right," I said. "But is it wise to have a lock on the stall door? I mean, what if there's a fire?"

He nodded. "We're real careful about that, but you're right," he said. "That was my worry, too. I'm putting her in the lower pasture tomorrow morning. She'll have some room to move around, not get herself into trouble for having nothing to do."

Miss Merriwether had left after dinner. I missed her. I wished I had asked her more about the Oakes family, and told her about my encounters with the two parents.

"There's a lot of sorrow in this family," I said to Max when I got back to our room.

"In most families, when you look close enough," said Max, putting down the book he was reading in bed. "We all think our own families are nuts, too—but I think it's just that most families are."

"Maybe humans just aren't meant to live together in close proximity," I said.

I was changing into my silk nightgown, and he watched, appreciatively. "I like being in close proximity to you," he said, wagging his eyebrows at me. "In fact, the closer the better."

"Did you know you sounded just like Groucho when you said that?" I said.

"I will consider that a compliment," he said, tapping the ash off an imaginary cigar. "Pretty soon I hope to have a full complement of compliments."

I laughed and put my arms around his neck. "I'll see what I can do."

He had jollied me out of my mood, and I looked forward to a good night's rest. And it would have been except for the splintered, unsettling dream I had, in which Raymond was sailing away from me on a boat, to San Francisco, and then he was in the water, drowning. I was standing on the shore, not able to swim for some reason, but calling to Evangeline to go save him. But she, standing on the shore, did nothing but yell so that I had to cover my ears.

Chapter Thirty-Four

I awoke with a whole-body start, resentful of a dream that had me worrying about Raymond, with Max nowhere in sight. The winter dawn hadn't quite come yet, but I didn't want to go back to sleep for fear of encountering the same dream.

Lying there, I saw the room slowly brighten, then got up and dressed, thinking all the while. Evangeline: I needed to talk to her, and soon. I also wanted coffee, and though it was too early to gather for breakfast, I thought I might be able to charm the kitchen staff out of a cup.

It turned out I could, and I took my porcelain cup back through the halls. Along the way I found young Edie sitting on a cushioned window seat, her carrot-top hair in braids, reading a magazine.

As I neared, she looked up and held up the magazine cover for me to see. It was *Modern Screen*.

"This is you," she said, "on the cover."

It was indeed, my mug, taken from a studio photo but painted by an artist. It still reflected the result of the best efforts of the studio's hair, makeup and wardrobe people. They had made my skin pale perfection, eyebrows drawn in thin, precise arcs, eyelashes ridiculously long. I was smiling my America's Kid Sister smile: starry-eyed, optimistic, ready to try anything. Sometimes I could hardly stand myself.

"Yes, that's me," I said.

"You're so pretty," she said, gazing at the cover.

"No," I said. "Look at me."

She looked. I'd put on makeup, but not that seriously, and I'd done my own hair, which by sheer luck had decided to fall into a softly curling bob on its own when brushed. My guess was that I looked like thousands of other presentable blond women in their mid-twenties who took reasonable care of themselves.

She smiled. "You have a pimple."

I touched my chin. "I do indeed. And when I have one of these, there are people where I work who all come running like it was a five-alarm fire, and put makeup on me so it will never show up on screen."

"My sister was beautiful."

Was. She didn't mean Evangeline. Who I needed to talk to.

"I'm so sorry," I said.

"Would you like to see her picture?" Edie said. "Mother and Father took most of them down when she died, but they're still in her room."

I wasn't sure I needed to see more pictures of poor lost Eleanor, possibly the girl known to Raymond as Ellie Atwood, but I liked Edie. I didn't think about kids much, and the ones in my business were usually pains in the neck. But Edie was sweet, and when I was around her I found myself wondering what unexpected thing she'd say next. So I went along with her down the halls to a wing of bedrooms.

She stopped at one of the many lookalike doors.

"Come on," she said. "They're all busy getting dressed for breakfast, and we can go in."

She opened the door. I was sure beyond a doubt that I was not welcome there, but Edie seemed determined that I should see it.

Eleanor's room looked like it hadn't been touched in several years, although it was clean, like the maids had at least dusted regularly. On a bureau and next to it on the floor were photos and paintings, as though some had been removed from walls elsewhere in the house and put here to be out of sight. Some showed the Oakes family with three daughters, looking happy, and some were just of Eleanor. She looked much like Evangeline, a blue-eyed redhead, but, as in the other photos, more striking.

"She was nicer than Evangeline," Edie said, picking up one of the photos. "She wanted to be in the pictures, like you."

We both looked at the photo she held.

"She was supposed to be going to school at UCLA," Edie said. "But I don't think she went, ever. There was a big row the night Evangeline drove her down there, and after that we didn't hear anything much from her."

"That must have been awful," I said, thinking, that's what Oakes meant by Evangeline's very good work. She had taken her sister to Hollywood.

Edie nodded. "I was so little, no one thought I noticed how mad everyone was, but it was awful," she said. "And then after Ellie died, well—Evangeline really changed."

"How?"

"She got meaner to me," Edie said, picking up a picture and looking at it sadly. "After a while, she left, too, for a job, she said. But I don't think that was it. I think she just started hating us all and wanted to go away."

I thought about that for a moment.

"Evangeline says I steal things from her," Edie said with a look of hurt resentment. "She's said I stole her shoes, and a hair ribbon, and even some of her clothes. Some stupid undershirt or something. Can you believe it?"

"Who would do that?" I said, in a tone to show I was on her side.

"Yeah, who," Edie said, flipping the pages of the magazine but not seeing them. "Her feet are way bigger than mine anyway. She has shoes made specially for her, in Italy."

"And ... her shoes are missing now?" I said.

"No, she found those. But some of her clothes she took with her," Edie said. "She said I was hiding them. I told her I don't want her dumb old clothes."

"What did she say to that?"

"She pulled my hair." Edie said it as though this was not a surprising thing, and I felt a stir of anger on her behalf, and wished I'd been there.

It would have been hard to picture Evangeline being this mean, if I hadn't seen the spark of it when I told her I wanted to ride Rocket, and then her treatment of the groom afterward. I hoped Raymond was ready for that temper, if he hadn't already seen it. If he returned to his old ways of drinking and running around, I didn't think she would put up with it for a moment. Certainly she wouldn't for as long as I had, I thought, and more power to her.

And that didn't begin to cover the possibility that she knew Raymond had had an affair with her sister, which I was now almost certain he had. I would need to tell him about this, and also to break the news that the poor girl had died. He would be shocked and sad about that, but he needed to know. And before I told him, I needed to talk to Evangeline, and tried to think what questions to ask that would give me the information I wanted without making Ray look too much of a cad.

I was also fairly sure Evangeline hadn't known about Eleanor's romance with Ray. Eleanor would probably have been embarrassed about a relationship with a man who, though wildly handsome and famous, also was prone to drunken rants and blackouts. I could picture her, like so many struggling young actresses, sharing with her family good news of roles she'd gotten, but keeping to herself the more unflattering or sordid aspects of life in show business.

We were supposed to leave right after breakfast, but first I was looking for an opportunity to speak with Evangeline, and Raymond, separately. Breakfast was again served hunt-country style, with dish upon dish on the sideboards, replaced the moment they were down to a few pieces of bacon or spoonfuls of eggs. Maids circulated to serve coffee and tea and juice to anyone who was seated.

I had already changed into a traveling costume of dark brown wool trousers, toast-colored light wool tunic and a long silk cord sash around my waist, all in browns and beiges. It had a sort of medieval feel that I had liked. And it was comfortable.

"That's a lovely outfit," a woman guest said. "You're so independent. Trousers!" She was rather stout but I thought she'd also be more comfortable in them, too. She looked at her husband, who was about the same beam and draft as she was, as though for approval. He ignored her.

"Thank you," I said. "You should try them sometime."

We chatted a little about fashion, but I kept an eye out for Evangeline, and eventually spotted her across the room with Raymond. In a chic sweater and skirt in a shade of blue that set off her red hair, she looked like she was already dressing the role of young society matron. She was even playing at hostessing, bringing over a silver pot of coffee and pouring for Max and me.

Any hard feelings she might have had over my claiming Rocket for myself seemed to have evaporated. Now she seemed to want to chat, in maddening detail, about her inability to decide just what kind of wedding cake she wanted, and what kind of gown she was having designed, and what the flowers should be, while I tried to think of a way to talk to her privately and ask the questions I really wanted to ask, though I didn't know if she could or would provide them.

After pouring second cups for us both, though, she provided the opportunity herself.

"Frankie," she said, "before you go, I want to show you and Max some of my favorite spots around town here, since you've never been before. I hope you'll visit again before the wedding, and then you'll know some of the best places to visit on your own. Raymond's even letting us use his car. It's a beauty, isn't it?"

I gave Max a look. Though he wanted to leave as much as I did, and I hadn't clued him in on wanting to get her alone for a chat, I knew he'd catch on.

"Is Raymond coming, too?" I asked.

"No, he and Daddy were supposed to be discussing something boring about money and things," she said, making a face. "Daddy was joking about a dowry. And then we're all going to the chapel and discuss wedding ceremony details. I wish you could stay for that."

I made some kind of noise meant to mean that I did, too.

The Duesenberg was brought up from the garage, looking as imposing and impeccable as ever. Its brakes now in fine working order, it purred along as Evangeline drove, with me in the front and Max in the back seat.

242

I stifled a yawn and rubbed my temples, feeling the beginnings of a headache. The stress of the weekend was getting to me, I thought.

"I'm glad you agreed to come along," Evangeline said brightly over her shoulder so Max could also hear. "Since you're Ray's friends, before you left, I wanted to show you one place that's especially important to him and me."

I glanced at Max and rolled my eyes, but discreetly. I really could not care less, I thought, a bit callously, about her favorite places. At this point I only wanted to ask her my questions, and be on the road home, maybe take a nap in the car and sleep off this whole weird weekend.

The road climbed until it was on the cliffs above the beach, and she pulled off to the side, where there was a spectacular view. It looked like a good place to come and think, I thought.

After a while of gazing out to sea, Evangeline spoke.

"This is where it happened," she said. Her voice sounded far away.

"Where what happened?" I asked, stifling another yawn and thinking I really should feign more interest, and wishing that my head didn't hurt.

"Where Eleanor died."

That gave me a little jolt, and I looked back at Max, who was gazing off into the distance. Apparently he was as eager to be gone as I was. But that got his attention.

"Oh," I said. "I hadn't known— "

"You hadn't known she died? I didn't think so," Evangeline said. "But I thought it was important for you to know. As Raymond's friends."

She looked out to sea. "You see, she was coming home, driving her car just along here. And she went over."

I thought of the drop for the second time in as many days. This one was not far from where we had ridden, atop jagged cliffs soaring above the beach. A car going over them would probably have crashed into several outcroppings of rock before landing on the beach and very likely catching fire. Though I knew Eleanor had died, I had not known how. I had a brief, flashing memory of my own near disaster, not far from my own house, in this very car. I was already feeling ill; this made it worse.

"I'm so sorry," I said, my tongue feeling thick. I shouldn't be this sleepy, I thought. It seemed an especially inappropriate reaction to hearing about a family tragedy.

"The papers said it was an accident," she continued. "It wasn't."

Evangeline now was not looking at us, but somewhere off toward the haze on the horizon over the Pacific, talking as though to herself.

"No, my sister had telephoned me the night before," she said. "She had fallen in love— I knew that. But I hadn't known who with. Or that there was a child."

She paused, and I heard her take a shuddering sigh. "She told him about it and do you know what he said? He said, 'It can't possibly be mine. Can't you just take care of it?'"

"That's awful," I said, and even to me my voice sounded indistinct, muffled.

But at the same time, one thing was becoming clearer. I put my hand out, and laid it on her arm. Evangeline looked at me. Her gaze was cold.

"She said she would be better off dead," Evangeline said. "And that was what she was going to do about it. I told her to come home and that we would talk about it."

She was quiet a moment, then said, "There weren't even any skid marks. She wasn't braking when the car went over."

"Evangeline," I said, having to concentrate hard on each syllable to get it out. "Who was she in love with?"

"Why, you know, of course," she said, expressionless. "Raymond."

Of course. My brain, in a fog like I had never experienced before, hadn't made the obvious connection. Of course it hadn't been just any random fellow; it had been Ray. Who had not remembered any of this, not remembered telling her to go away when she told him she was pregnant. Who behaved like the worst kind of cad. The kind of man you would want to see dead.

244

"Evangeline," I said again, struggling now to form the words. "You. You are … Annie."

I was feeling weaker and weaker. I just wanted to sleep, and finally the realization worked its way into my increasingly befuddled brain that the way I was feeling was no accident.

"Yes," I heard Evangeline say, sounding as though one of us was in the bottom of a well. I could hear the ocean on the beach below. Or maybe it was just my own blood rushing in my ears.

"I am Annie. Or that, at least, is how poor Vernon knew me."

I tried to keep my eyes open, thought I should ask Max … Max … ask him …

"I am sorry about Vernon," she said, her voice trembling. "And that other fellow, the one you shot. I didn't mean for you to miss Raymond."

Miss Raymond, I thought muzzily, drunkenly … how could I miss him when he hadn't gone away?

"If you hadn't missed Raymond," she said, "he'd be dead and I could have just come home with no one the wiser."

Oh.

"Raymond," I said with effort. "You did want me to shoot Raymond."

But she had been too unfamiliar with how things are done in the pictures. And so I'd shot poor Sam instead.

"It's important that you know these things," Evangeline said. "I want you to understand why I have to do what I'm going to do, and why I did everything before. I'm not a villain. I won't be punished for this, not in a just world. But I want you to die at least understanding why I have to."

And just before I lost consciousness, I heard her say, "I want you to understand that this time I will not be stopped from killing Raymond."

Chapter Thirty-Five

It was dark, and my face was pressed uncomfortably into soft leather that I sluggishly realized was the Duesenberg's front seat upholstery. It was dark, wherever we were, and ... what else? I took stock, fuzzily, able to think about just one, simple thing at a time. There was a steady thrum and vibration. The engine was running. So Evangeline hadn't somehow run the car over the cliff with us in it, in some form of poetic justice and vengeance. For the second time in a few months, I had reason to be grateful I wasn't lying dead in the Duesie, at the bottom of a cliff.

I had no idea how long I'd been unconscious. In the pictures, including one or two of mine, people were always being slipped mickeys in their drinks: something to knock them out, often a sleeping aid known as Veronal. But I didn't know much about how they worked. Or I hadn't, before.

Now I discovered that when the stuff starts to wear off—if you're lucky enough to have just gotten a dose that would knock you out temporarily and not kill you—you're not immediately restored to original working order. I was awake now, but felt ill and fatigued. I tried to think. My doped brain protested. *No*, it said. *Tired. Just sleep ... think later ...*

I fought it. *Think now*, I ordered myself ... Let's see, there was something, something important. What was it? Oh, yes: The Duesie's big engine. It was running. Purring along in all its exquisitely engineered precision. And it was dark. But not because it was night. No, we were inside somewhere ... a garage, it seemed. A small building, anyway. A small building that the Duesenberg's massive engine was industriously filling with fumes.

How ironic would that be, I thought dully, to wake up from being drugged just in time to die from carbon monoxide poisoning. That thought was followed, oh, so slowly, with another one: *Turn off the engine.*

I pushed myself up, groped clumsily for the ignition, and turned it off. That seemed to be a major achievement. I was tempted to rest on my laurels.

Dully, another thought drifted up … there was something else … Max! Where was he? Cold panic clutched my heart, and I felt for the back of the front seat and hauled myself up to look over it. He was there, slumped, unconscious, but breathing.

"Max!" I cried. His eyelids fluttered but the rest of him didn't move.

I dragged myself out of the front seat and groped my way to the back door, opened it, and crawled in beside him, just wanting to feel his warmth, reassure myself he was alive. I put my hand on his cheek, feeling the stubble I always teased him about, and called his name. He had to be okay, I thought desperately. He just had to.

I could feel him fighting his way to consciousness. He groaned. I took that as a sign he was coming to, told myself that was something, and looked around to figure out where we were.

It was still daylight; that much was clear from the pale outline of light around a door. So Evangeline—or someone working with her—had backed us in and left us here to die.

Coughing, I got out and felt my way over to the door. It was two doors, actually: heavy, wooden, and latched from the outside. Moving over, I found the walls. Adobe, I thought. I went along the wall, and tripped over something. A wooden pallet, the kind you might set storage containers on—storage containers like barrels. Or cases of contraband gin, during Prohibition. I closed my eyes, and could hear, faintly, the sound of waves lapping on a beach not far from where we were.

Max started to stir. I heard a groan and a few muttered curses. I went to the door and he regarded me with a look that made me wonder if he was seeing two of me.

"Max," I said, "I think I know where we are."

He said, "Mrrrf?"

"It's a shed on the ranch—one Oakes used as a bootlegger."

Max made an indistinct sound and rubbed his face vigorously with both hands, then ruffled them through his hair, as though trying to wake up his brain, get it to work.

"And I think Raymond is in danger," I added when he seemed to be able to take in information.

"Need to get outta here," Max mumbled.

"I can't argue with that," I said.

I ran back to the door and pushed. Locked from the outside, of course. But I would have felt like an idiot if I hadn't tried.

And it came back to me. She had told us what she was going to do, and where Raymond was, if she had been telling the truth. The only thing was, I didn't know how she was going to do it. I only knew we had to get out of here, and fast. And then find Raymond. I told Max all this, as well as I could manage.

Now Max was sitting up, weaving in the back seat like a punch-drunk fighter. He rolled the window down. "Raymond? Dead? Raymond is dead?"

"Not yet," I said, tensely. "But she thinks it's his fault her sister died. Her sister Eleanor. Were you awake for that? Max, Evangeline is Annie!"

"It's all so clear now," he said thickly, reaching and rolling the other window down. He got out of the back seat, and seemed pretty steady, seemed to be shaking off the effects of the drugs a bit better than I was, and I felt a surge of hope. We would get out of this together.

Now he was rolling down the driver's side window and the one opposite.

"What are you doing?" I asked, running up to the driver's window.

"Escaping, I hope," he said, starting the car up again. The Duesie's engine roared back to life. "And making it less likely we'll be covered in broken glass."

He looked ahead, at the solid wooden door, and then back at me.

"Get as far away as you can," he said.

248

I looked sadly at the big, beautiful car. The polished bumper whose curves always reminded me of giant silver lips. The grille and the pristine headlights. The glass falcon head mascot. Raymond's pride and joy. Well, I thought, none of that would matter if he was dead.

"Oh, poor car," I said, and retreated to a far corner of the shed.

Max glanced at me to make sure I was out of the way, then put the car into reverse, and backed it up as far as he could. The shed was about two car-lengths long, not far enough to get going very fast, but, possibly, just long enough.

"Here goes nothin'," he said. And floored it.

The engine roared, the tires dug into the dirt and the huge car leaped forward. The bumper, and then the headlights and grille, hit the heavy door with a jarring crunch and the sound of shattering glass. Wood and metal groaned and squealed, immovable object and irresistible force struggling against each other.

I put my fingers in my ears as Max jammed the car into reverse and backed up again for another assault. Once again the huge vehicle sprang forward, less lioness and more like a buffalo with a battering-ram head. More sounds of tortured metal, splintering wood, tires spinning on the dirt floor. Dust and exhaust fumes filled the air. We would either get out or die quicker, I thought, ears covered, eyes squeezed shut.

In the end, the doors were no match for the Duesenberg's weight and sheer, brute power. A last, bashing impact burst the radiator, sending hot water everywhere. Wood, nails, and hinges screeched, the doors sagged outward, and we saw daylight.

Max backed the steaming car up again and we ran to the shed doors. They had given way just enough for one semi-starved blonde and one trim, former wrestler to squeeze through.

I went first, splinters catching at my tunic and trousers, and burst outside, stumbling a bit, gulping the fresh sea air into my lungs. I heard a squirrel chatter up in a pine tree, and looked up. But all I saw was a turkey vulture soaring leisurely overhead, its wings separating at the tips like long fingers, looking for carrion.

Not yet, buddy, I thought.

Max got himself out of the shed and we staggered toward each other and held on tight, the way you do when you think you might have lost someone forever.

Gradually, the thought surfaced that we might not be alone. Still holding him, I looked over his shoulder a bit wildly, expecting to see a goon with a gun, at the very least. I think he was doing the same thing over my shoulder.

But there was no one. No one at all. No Oakeses. No accomplices. Nobody. Whatever was happening was happening at the house, almost a mile away, I thought. I wondered how long we had been here, and if Evangeline had had time to walk to the house, or if someone had picked her up.

These minor details were overwhelmed by the certainty that Raymond's life was in danger, had been in danger all these weeks and months while I stupidly tried to find out only how Vernon had died. Raymond's fear that the shooting might not have been an accident no longer seemed to be so irrational. It hadn't been. And the Duesie's cut brake lines: the guy we had caught said he had done it to scare me, but why wouldn't he have lied about that, if someone had paid him to lie? Maybe Raymond was the target there, too.

I broke away from Max and looked around, wondering if we should just take off running to the house. Nearly a mile. The world's fastest runners could cover that in a little over four minutes. I didn't think I could come anywhere near that, even when feeling my best, and I was far from that now. Neither of us could. The Duesie, crippled and trapped in the shed, would be of no use.

Trying to come up with any idea at all before I just started running, I leaned my aching head against the boards of the pasture fence next to the shed. No matter what I decided to do now, I would, almost certainly, be too late. Tears pricked at the back of my eyes.

And then I heard a soft nicker.

Sauntering up to the fence, with every sign a horse can give that she was pleased to see me, was Rocket. The sun gleamed
250

off her chestnut coat and sleek back, and her red forelock hung winsomely over one eye. So this was the lower pasture Doc had mentioned moving her to. She looked relaxed, quite at home.

"Hey, pretty girl," I said almost absentmindedly. It was second nature to climb up on the fence and scratch her behind the ear under the strap of her halter, though this wasn't really the time for that.

Except ...

I looked up the road, then looked back at Rocket. And got an idea.

Ducking through the rails of the fence, I patted her neck, and untied the silk cord around my waist. Rocket regarded this approach with interest, and then butted me with her head, looking for treats, probably.

"Sorry, baby, I don't have anything for you right now," I said, working with the cord, attaching it to the halter ring to make reins, of a sort.

Rocket's ears swiveled back and forth at me, clearly wondering what I was doing.

"It's sugar lumps forever if you'll get me there on time," I said.

She had tried to do her best for me even when being poked by a thorn. I hoped now, without even a proper bridle, she would do what I needed her to. I had to try.

Grabbing a good hank of her mane, I vaulted to her back. She was a tallish mare, but I had learned to scramble onto full-size horses as a kid. The skill came back to me.

Rocket tossed her head as I tested the reins, and I felt her collect herself under me as though saying, "Okay, where to?"

"Good girl," I said, stroking her neck. And then I called, "Max! Open the gate!"

Max had been leaning forward, hands on knees, like a man with a bad hangover. He nodded gamely, though, and trotted to the gate. And swore.

"There's a padlock on it," he called.

I hadn't noticed. I swore, too. Of course. Doc had said she was talented at opening latches.

My heart sank, and I fought off the feeling of despair. But Rocket, shifting under me, seemed to be eyeing the fence, and all at once it was crystal clear what we needed to do. There was one way out of the pasture, and that was to jump.

I had no doubt Rocket could do it. She was a Thoroughbred, and had the ability, I was sure. Horses who can jump out of pastures usually don't, if only because the food and the humans who provide it are inside the fences. It doesn't mean they can't.

The fence was maybe four-and-a-half or five feet high. Though I was no show-jumper, especially not without a saddle, I'd hopped horses over smaller obstacles, fallen trees and the like. I was maybe seventy-nine percent sure I could stay on, if she didn't refuse. I had to chance it.

Either this was the fastest way to get to Raymond and help him—or the stupidest idea I ever had. It could, I realized, end with me on the ground with nothing to show for it but a concussion, maybe a broken collarbone. And that wasn't even the worst that could happen. Rocket could get hurt, too.

But I didn't have a choice. Shaking off a small wave of apprehension, I used the silk cord, knees, and weight to turn the mare away from the fence and felt elation as she responded. She took up a floating trot, and then the familiar, three-beat cadence of a canter, her strides as balanced and even as a rocking horse. We made a big circle, one-two-three, one-two-three.

And then I felt something else. The power of a horse is immense compared to a human's. It can be almost frightening— is frightening, to people like Raymond. We harness it and use it, not always with their enthusiastic cooperation. But somehow, if we treat them right, something happens and they give us that power voluntarily, some would even say joyfully. And that's when you feel like the two of you could leap over the moon, or conquer kingdoms.

I felt it now. Cantering in a circle, flicking her sharp ears back and forth, snorting almost playfully, Rocket gave me her power. Without a saddle, I was sliding a little on her sleek back, but I felt secure. I felt the warmth and the springy strength of her big body, her muscles working, her boldness. We were partners. She would do whatever I asked. She told me she would.

Chapter
Thirty-Six

The world came down to me and the chestnut mare, as we completed one last circle, warming up her muscles. I pointed her at the fence.

Throw your heart over, my dad used to say. *The horse will follow.* I looked at the fence, imagined throwing my heart, my soul, over it, and I felt her attention go there.

"That's my girl," I said, and gave her a squeeze with my legs.

We were only a few strides away. Rocket's ears swiveled back once, twice, and then both pricked forward, and stayed there as she looked, judging where to take off on the soft ground, how much spring to put into it. She was reading it, taking its measure.

I saw Max's horrified face beyond the gate. His expression said, "You're crazy."

"It's all right!" I called as Rocket bounded toward the fence, tossing her head and nearly tearing the reins out of my hands in her eagerness. "Move over!"

Three strides away, then two, then one. I threw my heart over the fence, and the mare gathered herself and sprang, making me gasp at the sheer strength of her.

We seemed to hang in the air forever as Rocket sailed over the fence, leaving plenty of room below. She came nowhere near touching the top board, and landed without a stumble, though the impact slammed my crotch into her withers. That would be a bruise tomorrow, I thought, wincing, as I gathered up the reins. The mare snorted, ready to go anywhere now, and as fast as I wanted. I felt her, ready to run.

When we turned toward the house, she took off like she was breaking from the starting gate at Churchill Downs. Winding my hands into her silky mane, I just hoped I would be able to stop her when we got there. Then I concentrated on hanging on.

Rocket ran with a Thoroughbred's huge, ground-eating bounds. All I could hear were her hoofbeats, her snorting breaths with each stride, and my heart pounding in my ears. We would be there in no time.

Trees and fences flashed by, Rocket galloping easily, me clinging like a burr. The road met the paved drive and I kept her to the mowed strip of grass on the side, her hooves kicking up clods of dirt behind us. I didn't give a damn if we tore up the Oakes family's nice lawns. I saw no reason to risk her legs pounding on the pavement.

Over a rise, there were the back gardens and part of the house, crowds of servants going about various tasks. If any crimes were being committed in the house, they were either completely unaware of it, or better actors than anyone I knew.

Now the ones nearest me, working in the vegetable garden, hidden from the house by a hedge, looked up. I wanted to laugh, almost, at their wide-eyed amazement. They looked as though they'd found themselves unexpectedly in a Frankie Franklin movie and wondered where the camera was.

Rocket and I sped past them, and just ahead I saw a uniformed man next to a delivery truck. That was good, someone not on the staff—who knew who was in on this, I thought. I sat back and pulled on the reins, praying for her to stop, and she did, snorting and prancing in place. The deliveryman, a youngish guy wearing a cloth cap, recognized me.

"By God, it's Frankie Franklin!" he cried. "I love your movies!"

"Thanks," I said, "but I'm in a hurry. Do you know that shed they have, that's down by the water?"

He nodded, slack-jawed. I aimed the full-wattage Frankie Franklin smile on him. "Wonderful! There's a man down there who needs a lift back up here. Can you do that for me?"

"Yes, Miss Franklin!" he said, and got into the truck.

Two maids had come out of the house. I rode right up to them. This time when Rocket stopped, she threw in a little half-rear, forelegs off the ground, and snorted, and the younger maid squealed and scrambled backward. I addressed the other.

"You there!" I said. "Listen carefully. I need you to call the police. Do you understand?"

She nodded, looking doubtful.

"Just have the police come here," I said. "Call them, now! Also, do you know where Miss Evangeline is?"

The older maid pointed toward the back of the house, in the direction of the chapel, and then spoke carefully, as though addressing a crazy woman.

"They're … they're looking at the chapel," she said. "For the wedding."

"Thanks!" Rocket took off again. *I'm too late, I'm too late,* I thought. But even as I thought that, I thrilled to how responsive she was, as though she read my mind about where we needed to go, and how fast.

We came up to the back of the chapel, which had a swath of green lawn in front of it. There was a small figure pacing back and forth on the grass, radiating distress. Edie.

As I got closer, I saw her face, worried, blue eyes like saucers. Her hand flew to her mouth in alarm as she looked up at me and I couldn't tell whether her look was one of relief, or horror.

"They're—" she broke off, eyes looking up. In the bell tower.

I slid off Rocket and held out the rein of the improvised bridle.

"I can't! I'm afraid of her!" Edie protested, shrinking back.

"Nonsense," I said in my best English governess voice. I took her hand and gently placed the silken cord in it. "She's had her run, and she wouldn't dream of hurting you. Just hold onto this and let her graze."

Rocket reached out her nose and flared her nostrils gently at Edie. Then she sighed, lowered her head and proceeded to sample the grass. I gave the little girl a quick, encouraging grin and ran for the chapel.

I'm too late, I'm too late.

At the front of the chapel, near the front door, I skidded to a halt. Evangeline was sitting there on a bench, sobbing, her slim body bent, and her hands over her face. She looked at me, her eyes going wide with surprise, and then she collapsed in on herself even more.

"I couldn't do it!" she said. "I couldn't kill him. Father's right, I'm no good at anything."

I grabbed her shoulder and shook it. "Where is he?" I demanded. "Where's Raymond?"

Evangeline looked up, indicating the bell tower. "Dead. Most likely. I wanted him to jump."

Christ, I thought—an appropriate enough epithet, I suppose, given the setting.

Inside, I found the stairs that led to the bell tower and took them two at a time. There was no door between the stair and the small room at the top of the bell tower, so when I stopped at the top, breathing hard, I saw the whole tableau.

Raymond stood in front of one of the arched openings, looking a bit rumpled in his pleated trousers and custom-made shirt. On the opposite side of the room stood Charles and Elizabeth Oakes: she, a wraithlike figure in a grayish-pink dress, he looming, the impression of menace amplified by the revolver he held in his right hand.

"Oh, hello darling," said Raymond with impressive *sang-froid* for a man who has a .38 pointed at his midsection from a few feet away. "Mr. Oakes is helping me to remember things."

"Yes, we had just gotten to the part where you caused my daughter's death. Her name was Eleanor, do you even recollect that?"

Raymond spoke, but it was to me. "Darling, you recall I told you just last night that my memories were coming back and that Ellie—Eleanor—was one of them. She was a lovely girl. She was. But that's all. One day she was there and the next ... she wasn't."

My mouth was dry. I stood there catching my breath but otherwise afraid to move lest that cause Oakes to pull the trigger.

"Mrs. Oakes. I'm so very, very sorry about your daughter's death," I said carefully. "I know I can't even imagine how vast your sorrow must be—"

"Shut up!" Oakes snapped, not even looking at me. "Stupid bitch. You can't bring her back."

Then he appeared to think of something. Something that pleased him, in a bitter sort of way. Still looking at Raymond, he said, "You didn't care enough about Eleanor to hear about the fact that she was carrying your child, did you?"

"My God," Raymond said. "I didn't even—"

"But you still care about this one, don't you?" He nodded sharply toward me. "You're still in love with her, it's easy to see."

"No!" I protested.

"Shut up," Oakes snapped again.

"Of course I had you investigated," he said to Raymond. "I know you two were married. It doesn't take much to find that out. Or to learn that you always run crying to her when things don't go your way."

I heard something outside one of the arched windows, like the wind making the workmen's scaffolding creak.

"At least Evangeline brought you to us," Oakes said. "She was never the kind of daughter Eleanor was, the one who made us proud of her every day, right up until—well. But even though she couldn't follow through on getting rid of you, she brought you to us."

He looked down at the gun in his hand.

"It's been a long time since I've had to do anything like this," he said. "But I think it comes back. Like riding a bicycle, eh?"

Oakes stopped and seemed to be considering something. "Since you're too much of a coward to step out the window and end it yourself," he said, "I was just going to end it for you."

He paused. "But I see how you feel about Miss Franklin," he said. "And now I think that maybe it would be better for you to know what it's like to love someone and then have them taken away from you."

He turned, slowly, toward me, his wife shadowing him, wide-eyed, looking eager to see someone's blood spilled.

Well. If I hadn't liked how this was going before, I really did

258

not like it now.

Oakes's eyes were hard, and I thought, fleetingly, that now I was going to find out what it would feel like to be shot. Just like Sam.

But for some reason—maybe he was out of practice at killing people, like he said—Oakes paused before firing, and in that moment, Raymond lunged. He tackled me like I was the opposing team's quarterback, just as the gun went off. We hit the floor with a thud that knocked all the breath out of me, and Oakes's bullet went harmlessly out the window.

The thought flitted crazily through my head that it was good there was no bell in the tower yet—I imagined the noise of a bullet hitting it would have been deafening, not to mention the danger of a ricochet. Then I realized I was pinned under Raymond, closer than I'd felt his body in years, and instinctively, irrationally, tried to squirm free.

But Oakes was still there with the gun, still determined to shoot one or both of us—I don't think it mattered which to him at this point. He pointed the .38 down at both Ray and me.

Another million thoughts went through my head, a million thoughts that were abruptly interrupted by a movement in the window behind Oakes. There was a man in the window, silhouetted against the light, dramatically, looking for all the world like Doug Fairbanks from his *Thief of Bagdad* days.

I blinked. No, not Fairbanks. It was Max, crouched and ready to spring.

Mrs. Oakes screamed, "The Jew!" and scrambled out of the way just as my husband launched himself from the ledge.

Max hit Oakes like a cannonball, and the larger man staggered but didn't fall. With apparently no thought for the fact that his opponent was armed, Max moved, seeking a hold that would take Oakes down. There was a lot of staggering and grunting, and Oakes's hand with the .38 waved wildly as he tried for another shot with Max climbing all over him.

There was another flat *crack!* as the bullet whizzed over Raymond's head and out the window behind us. But Max had found a hold—I don't know if it was a standard, approved wrestling technique at his high school in Indianapolis, but it worked. Oakes overbalanced, toppled, and fell. With Max's legs around his barrel-like torso, and his neck in a choke hold, the old boy's face turned a gratifying shade of red, and the gun fell from his hand and spun on the floor.

Mrs. Oakes had shrunk into the corner, hand to mouth, eyes wide and fixed on Max choking her husband. Finally free of Raymond's desperate grasp, I pounced on the gun, just in case she was thinking of going for it.

Light footsteps came up the stairs right then, and Evangeline, apparently done crying, appeared. We must have presented an odd picture. There was Raymond scrambling to his feet, her mother silent and shocked off to the side, her father on the floor, Max apparently strangling him, and me, holding a gun.

Evangeline must have considered me the biggest threat, but not so big she was afraid of rushing me. She made a move, but Raymond was quicker. He grabbed her in a bear hug from behind, pinning her arms to her sides.

I focused on Max and his captive.

"Let him up, Max," I said.

Max didn't seem to hear me. In fact, he tightened the choke hold. The look on his face was like that of a pirate, but the dangerous kind, not the charming kind.

"Max!" I said softly.

He looked up as though he was just now returning from somewhere primitive and very far away. Then he slowly released his grip on the larger man, stood up, and stepped back. Oakes sat up, rubbing his neck. He put a hand down to lever himself up, but stopped cold when I barked, "Sit!"

Oakes sat, but fixed his daughter with a withering look. "You idiot," he said. "You could've just let them go. I don't know what you were thinking."

As though thinking had anything to do with it, I thought.

"She was snooping around, asking questions," Evangeline said defensively, looking at me. "Mr. Yolanda told me."

I made a mental note to cancel my lingerie order.

Oakes looked at me as though trying to decide something. I

gave him a look and cocked the gun.

"In case you're wondering," I said to Oakes, "I do know how to use one of these. Don't make me prove it."

He seemed to believe me and subsided. Everyone else looked as though they were going to stay where they were for the time being, and I turned to Evangeline.

"So, to continue our conversation from before you were trying to kill us," I said, "you're Annie."

Still in Raymond's grip, she glared at me.

"You're Annie," I said, "and you killed Vernon."

"But—"

"At first," I interrupted, "people thought maybe he drowned trying to save someone, a girl with long, dark hair. The same girl who was living with him and had him wrapped around her little finger."

Evangeline shifted, and I saw her hand twitch. If Raymond hadn't had her arms pinned, she would have reflexively touched her hair, the way women do when it's mentioned, I have no idea why.

"No wonder you returned home from your 'magazine job' with hair cut short as a boy's," I said. "It wasn't for fashion. You'd just grown it out enough so you could cut it. And, just like that, the dark-haired girl was gone."

Oakes made a dismissive sound and Evangeline stuck out her lower lip.

"I didn't know Vernon well, but I thought that maybe it was true that he died trying to save someone," I said. "Although I did consider that he might have been guilt-ridden about the 'accident,' and walked into the ocean to end it all. I thought maybe his girlfriend—this Annie—was trying to talk him out of it, but couldn't keep him from suicide, not even by following him into the ocean."

She shook her head.

"But that wasn't it, was it?" I said. "It was you who switched out the blanks for real bullets in my gun. You showed up on the set and surprised Vernon, but because it meant a tumble on the sofa in his office, he couldn't resist, even though it was

261

something he didn't usually do. But something he did usually do was nearly pass out after making love. You knew he'd be nearly unconscious for a while after, because you'd been having an affair with him and knew that's what happened with Vernon. And that it would give you time to get to the gun."

An indignant cry burst from Mrs. Oakes in the corner. "How dare you!"

"I put the pillow back on the sofa," I said. "I suppose a great detective might have figured out the whole story from that one clue, or the cartridge you dropped on the floor, but I'm new at this."

The Oakeses didn't seem to find this amusing. Tough crowd.

"The only reason you were seeing Vernon at all was that you had found out that he was the head prop man for Fortune Pictures, where Raymond was under contract," I went on. "You were probably looking for any way to get access to something you could use to harm him. And you got lucky: You found out that Raymond would be in a scene with a gun pointed at him. You had hoped that the real bullets would hit Raymond, but you didn't know enough about making pictures to know I wouldn't be aiming right at him. Poor Sam was in the wrong place at the wrong time, and he was hit."

"I didn't mean to—"

"Hurt Sam?" I said. "I'm sure he would find that touching. Anyway, Vernon figured out what had happened, and chased you back to his place. Or drove you there himself. That's something I can picture—he wouldn't have thought the girl he was mad about would do something like this and he probably wanted to talk to you. But you weren't in love with him, you only used him. And you had finally seen your chance. You worked fast. You pretended not to realize what you had done, pretended to be overcome by guilt yourself, and you led him into water over his head, and then drowned him. Or just waited for him to drown. Which was it?"

Evangeline was still as a statue now, silent, and grim.

"I have to give you points for persistence," I said. "I still haven't found out whether you were behind cutting his car's
262

brake lines, even though a fellow confessed to that. But that doesn't matter because some time after that you found out where Raymond went to dry out. And, once you had grown out your hair and could use your own name, you followed him and weaseled your way into his heart. With Longfellow, no less."

Evangeline looked impatient. Maybe she was getting bored.

"But you were only planning to get him here to arrange an accident," I said. "So first you tried to kill him, or at least injure him, by putting that thorn under Rocket's saddle and hoping for a bad fall."

I stopped, thinking for a moment about Rocket now peacefully cropping grass just outside.

"But I scotched your plan by claiming her for myself," I said. "She very likely would have felt the thorn just in time to start bucking at the top of the bluffs … you would even have killed the poor horse."

"I don't care about the damned horse!" Evangeline cried.

"Obviously you didn't," I said. "You sure tried hard. It seems like it would have been easier just to run him over with your car at some point. But you kept trying. And when all else failed, you just decided to hand him over to your father."

"No!" Evangeline cried. "They didn't know! I was going to do it all myself."

"But you screwed it up," Oakes broke in. "Just like you do everything. You took Eleanor to Los Angeles even though you knew she was going there to get into pictures, not go to school. She's dead because of you as much as him. You're just as guilty as he is."

"She kept getting in the way!" Evangeline wailed, pointing her chin at me.

I decided to quote Oakes.

"Shut up," I said. "I'm sick of all of you."

Evangeline was crying now, in the quiet way of someone who knows it's all over.

"You can let her go, Ray," I said. He let her go.

Sirens. Tires crunching on the gravel outside. The Santa Barbara sheriff's department couldn't have had better timing.

"I'll be happy to hand you over to the authorities," I said. "I believe I hear them downstairs now."

I was just settling in to wait when there was a movement and Evangeline crossed the small room, swiftly, going to the window opposite the one Max climbed in—the one with no scaffolding outside. All of us realized at the same time, I think, that she wasn't going over there just to look out.

Mrs. Oakes screamed "No!" The rest of us rushed forward. But Evangeline had climbed, quick and light as a cat, onto the sill and then, without so much as a pause or a look back, jumped.

Later, feeling sick, I imagined I'd heard her body hit the ground, but I couldn't have, not from this far up. No matter what she'd done, her death was just as senseless as Vernon's, and more than I could take in. And as awful as her parents were, I wouldn't have wished this on them. I watched them both stagger toward the door, and let them go. And then another thought hit me.

I said, "Oh, no. Edie!" uncocked the gun and laid it on the floor just as a sheriff's deputy appeared in the doorway.

"That's not mine," I said, and slipped past him.

"Mine, either," I heard Max say behind me.

"Hello, officer," I heard Raymond say, gracious as a host welcoming guests to a cocktail party, as we took to the stairs.

There was a lot going on around the chapel, the Oakeses and the deputies converging on the spot where Evangeline must have landed. I didn't want to look. I only noticed Edie wasn't there, and made for the back of the building, while Max found a deputy to talk to.

Edie and Rocket were still there on the lawn, pretty much where I'd left them, but Edie was holding the makeshift rein as though she had forgotten it was in her hands. She turned huge blue eyes on me, clearly wanting an adult to explain to her all the official cars and men in uniforms who had shown up. I felt my heart breaking for her.

"Thank you for minding Rocket," I said when I was sure I could trust my voice. I took the rein from her. Rocket, who had been grazing as placidly as any old cow, snuffled at me. It made Edie jump.

The little girl looked up, eyes still big and scared, and then flung herself against me, hiding her face in my midsection as my arms went around her. Maybe she did know. I held her tight.

And so people were talked to, an ambulance arrived, and accounts were taken. While Evangeline was being put into the ambulance, I kept Edie occupied by talking about anything I could think of, and spoke to her as though there had just been an accident and we would find out how her sister was later. Cowardly of me, I guess, for wanting to give her just a little more time in a world where her sister still lived.

Eventually Edie's governess came and took her away, and Raymond called me darling and said he was so glad I wasn't hurt. Max nudged him out of the way with a surly look, and took me in his arms.

I hugged him tight, and said, "You came in the window."

"Door was locked," he said into my hair.

Things were a bit of a blur, but as people drifted away from where we were standing, I looked up and saw a familiar bulky form, with a shock of gray hair, wearing a beautifully tailored charcoal-gray suit. I went over to him.

"Mr. Fixx," I said.

"Miss Franklin."

"Somehow your presence here doesn't surprise me."

"I happened to have business in town," he said, and looked around at the grounds of the Oakes place. Like he was thinking of buying it.

"Checking up on me?"

He smiled. "I had business," he said. "Suffice it to say I was speaking with the sheriff at the time the call came in and thought it might be a good idea for me to tag along."

I nodded. Not understanding, not completely, but also not surprised.

Many things had happened this afternoon. Many things I had not ever expected to be involved in, and many things I hoped never to be involved in again.

But thanks to Mr. Fixx, if you were to look it up in every place you could think of—the newspapers, county files—you would find there was no record of Frankie Franklin being anywhere near Santa Barbara that weekend, at all.

Chapter
Thirty-Seven

Martinique's Rose brought Arthur an Academy Award nomination for Best Director, though it was John Ford who won for *The Informer*. I was not even nominated for my turn as the Empress Josephine, though some writers kindly opined that I should have been. A couple added that they never took me seriously until they saw me as a brunette. And we all wished there could have been a category for supporting roles, because Sam had been that good in the picture.

"Maybe they'd get more stars to show up for this if they had more categories for acting," Arthur said.

I was there for Arthur. And Max was there for me, in black tie.

"Glad I already owned these rags," he said as more champagne was poured.

Looking around, I saw a fair number of actors and actresses sitting at the Biltmore Hotel's white-clothed tables, applauding the winners and looking happy for them, whether they felt it or not. That night, in other words, I guess you could have called us the highest-paid extras in town.

Prairie Princess had done so well that a sequel was in the works. Since Sam hadn't been seen in the original, he got to play a different part in *Prairie Lady*: that of my long-lost brother. I was looking forward to that.

I was also looking forward to seeing Sam and Clay the next day, when we were going to have a small party to celebrate Max's and my first anniversary.

Someone had informed me that the traditional gift for a first anniversary was paper. I sure hoped that was right, because, with

Kit's help, I'd tracked down a rare first edition of Scott Joplin's "Maple Leaf Rag" for Max and was ready to surprise him with it.

We begged off nightcaps with Arthur after the awards banquet in favor of an early night. After the excitement in Santa Barbara and winding up one more picture just before the Awards, I just wanted to sleep in.

The excitement in Santa Barbara—as Max and I had come to call the whole experience at the Oakes ranch—had left me with recurring bad dreams. Mr. Fixx had done what he always did, and his efforts combined with the Oakeses' own resources would make sure no one went to prison and as little attention as possible was paid. I didn't mind, though no one asked me. I figured the family had suffered enough, losing a second daughter. I hoped Edie would be all right.

I had tried to buy Rocket, but was told she had been sold already, and had set Kit to the task of finding out who bought her, so I could offer them twice what they had paid.

Raymond's older sister in Connecticut decided, out of the blue, to invite him home, and he had taken the train back there to stay for an indeterminate period of time. I suspected he wouldn't be returning to the pictures.

So the day after the Academy Awards, a bunch of us descended on Clay's place for a first-anniversary luncheon. Mrs. Garcia's best dishes were on the menu and I was going to enjoy myself, I decided. We ate chile rellenos, and avocados, and fresh-squeezed orange juice with champagne in the huge, sunny kitchen with its long table that could seat eighteen.

And then it was time for gifts. I presented Max with the Joplin music, which earned me one of his best devilish-angel smiles.

"And I've got your gift here," Max said, reaching into the breast pocket of his suit. He pulled out an envelope but stopped in the middle of handing it to me. I made a few playful swipes at it and then stopped as Sam spoke.

"Hold on a minute," Sam said, getting up from the table. He went to the window. "Someone's coming up the drive."

Someone was always coming up Clay's drive—friends,

tradespeople, other polo players. But Max looked interested as well. He motioned to me to get up.

Curious, I went to look.

"It's the farm truck and a horse trailer," I said. "Like we see all the time. Hey, wait—"

Now Max tapped me on the shoulder and handed me the envelope. "Happy anniversary," he said. "It was supposed to be paper, right?"

I ripped the envelope open and had a twinge of revulsion seeing the letterhead that said, OAKES RANCH. But then I read the neatly typed note below: "Sold to Pancho Barnes, one eight-year-old chestnut Thoroughbred mare …"

Pancho had crossed out her name and written "Max Gold" above it.

I didn't see the rest, just grabbed Max by the shoulders, while at the same time jumping up and down and saying, "Max! Max! Max!"

And then I planted a big kiss on him and was out the door, jumping off the veranda and running down to the stables just as the truck and trailer reached the end of the tree-lined drive and arrived in the yard.

The driver got out of the truck and tipped his hat to me with a grin. Then, after I hugged him, he went to the back of the trailer and opened the doors. A pair of powerful chestnut hindquarters appeared, backing out carefully, followed by the rest of her. Rocket.

The mare raised her fine head, nostrils flaring delicately, and looked around. Then she saw me and nickered softly. When I went over to her, she pushed her nose gently against me, and I gave her the apple I'd snagged from a bowl on my way out of the kitchen.

"How'd she like the trip down, Doc?" I asked as he handed me the rope to her halter. "I knew Clay had hired a new stable manager, but—"

"She travels well," he said. "And I think she'll like it here as much as I do." He nodded to Clay and the rest of our party, who had joined us.

There was a loud neigh from one of the stalls, and Rocket looked toward it, listening.

"Tornado thinks he has a new girlfriend," Clay said.

"I'm so happy!" I said. "Oh, Max, thank you so much!"

I said that maybe a million times, and then spent half an hour walking Rocket around the place, finally showing her to her new stall and adjoining paddock. The Oakeses' stable had been grand, but Clay's was even nicer, for the horses anyway, with larger stalls and paddocks shaded by trees. Each stall even had an automatic watering mechanism, which a horse could operate by simply pushing down on a lever with its nose.

With Rocket settled in her new home, and Raymond tucked away with his sister on the opposite coast, I felt that this particular adventure had reached its conclusion.

Back home that evening, I snuggled next to Max on one of the big sofas in the library, sipping the perfect bittersweet Negroni he had made me, and watching the flames dance merrily in the fireplace.

"I didn't figure the Oakeses would sell Rocket to me," Max said, "so I called Pancho, and she bought Rocket. And then signed her over to me. High finance with horses."

"You're amazing," I said.

"I'm afraid Kit was in on it, too," Max said, his arm around me. "I asked her to sort of stall for a while—horse pun intended—on finding out who had bought Rocket. I hope you don't mind."

"The surprise was worth it," I said.

We gazed into the fire a bit more, and then I felt Max chuckle. I looked at him.

"You know," he said, "I expected life with you to be exciting. I just didn't expect it to be quite this exciting."

"You and me both, kiddo," I said.

He kissed me on the top of the head.

"I hope the bad dreams stop after a while," he said. "Maybe it would help if you wrote it all down some time."

I sipped my cocktail. "You know," I said, "someday, maybe I will."

Acknowledgments

The author would like to thank the following for: help with research (sharing their own expertise or looking stuff up, whether it made it into the story or not); reading various drafts and making valuable suggestions; encouraging me to write the story; and sometimes just for patiently listening while I went on and on about it while wondering silently to themselves if I ever would finish: my husband, Ralph Douglas "Hawkeye" McCaskey; my children Caroline and William McCaskey; Stephen Kilmer; David Kilmer; Janice Peacock; Karin Stenberg; my parents-in-law Bob and Judy McCaskey; Terri Campbell; John Flores; Julia Sigwart; Nicola Marchi; Linda Good; Morgan and Carolyn Zeitler; Scott Mason, Nadine Doyle Mason and Luke Doylemason; and the guys at the Old West Gun Room in El Cerrito, California.

About the Author

Deb McCaskey is a third-generation native of cool and windy northern California who has always harbored a secret fascination with sunny and apparently carefree southern California. This probably has something to do with Disneyland. A former newspaper editor and writer, she is happy to have the chance now to spend time with the people and movies of Hollywood's Golden Age, imagining new stories featuring America's Kid Sister, Frankie Franklin. Deb lives in the San Francisco Bay Area with her husband and their independent-minded rescue dog Mrs. Hudson.

Connect with
Deb McCaskey

www.debmccaskey.com
www.facebook.com/djmccaskey
www.instagram.com/djmccask

Made in the USA
San Bernardino, CA
12 May 2020